DREW: A NEW YORK PLAYERS NOVEL

LULU MOORE

DREW

A NEW YORK PLAYERS NOVEL: BOOK THREE

By Lulu Moore

To soulmates everywhere
You don't have to believe for them to exist

SOUNDTRACK

FIND DREW'S PLAYLIST ON MY SPOTIFY @LULUMOOREBOOKS

LONDON GRAMMAR - Baby It's You
HOT CHIP - One Night Stand
JESSIE WARE - Save a Kiss
GILL SCOTT HERON, JAMIE XX - I'll Take Care of You
JUNGLE - Heavy, California
BIBIO - You
DAVID BOWIE - Modern Love
CLEAN BANDIT ft. ZARA LARSSON - Symphony
JUSTIN BIEBER - Peaches
WINFIELD PARKER - I Wanna Be With You
JAI WOLF, MR GABRIEL - Starlight
FRANK OCEAN - Nights

PROLOGUE

DREW

Fate and destiny. Different sides of the same coin.

Whatever you want to call it, whatever you want to believe, one of them brought me here.

To where I'm currently standing, dripping in sweat, my heart pounding loudly.

To where I'm waiting for the rest of my life to begin.

Waiting to breathe again.

They say love is a numbers game, so here are some for you.

Last night I lay awake for one hundred and ninety-four minutes, thinking about the girl I haven't seen in three hundred and seventy-two days.

Since then, my heart has beat forty million times. Every single one for her.

Seven billion people in the world.

Three hundred and thirty-one million people in this country.

Nine million people in this city

But only one in my head. Only one my heart.

The probability of seeing her again? Infinitesimal.

And yet there she is. My Lucky Charm.

So I ask you, do you believe in fate? Or do you believe in destiny?

Because either way, I sure as fuck do.

In the way I know fire is hot and ice is cold, I know that we're supposed to be together. Two halves of an indisputable whole.

My soulmate.

And now it all comes down to the next sixty seconds. Standing here. Waiting for her to turn around.

The stakes have been raised. I've thrown my cards on the table.

Because what happened in Vegas, didn't stay there this time.

This time, I'm keeping it.

1

EMERSON

"Emily?" The barista called out, heaving a green juice in the air and waving it around. "Emily?"

I frowned, realizing she meant me having got my name wrong. I knew Emerson wasn't the most common name in the world but wasn't even close to Emily.

Fine. It was a little bit close, but still not the same.

Leaning over the counter, I grabbed my juice from her hands. "Thanks."

I took a long sip as I walked through the door, out of the artificial cool air and right into the fire... and the last person on earth I wanted to see. Nine million people in New York City and for the life of me I couldn't understand how it was impossible to permanently avoid one.

Although I knew this wasn't a coincidence.

My shoulders dropped in frustration, as I backed up far enough away so he couldn't touch me. "What are you doing here? Are you following me now?"

He reached a hand toward me, and I took another step back.

"I'm on my way to work, my shift starts in thirty. And is that any way to greet your boyfriend?"

"Ex-boyfriend." My free hand fisted at my side. "You lost your right to call me that when I caught you fucking another woman in your office."

His face dropped. He did a good job acting remorseful, but I knew from previous experience that it was bullshit.

"She came onto me, I told you. It was a momentary lapse in judgement."

How was I ever in love with this asshole?

"No it wasn't. You did it before. I fell for it the last time you apologized and I'm not falling for it again. We both know you're never going to change."

The mask of repentance dropped, his expression immediately morphing into one of annoyance. I took a twisted pleasure in knowing how much I was pissing him off. Especially as I didn't care.

Dick.

"I would if you married me. I told you, it won't happen again, I promise."

I rolled my eyes. "You have got to be joking. Do I have sucker written on my forehead?"

"Emerson, why won't you marry me?"

"Because you can't keep your dick out of other women." I explained, making sure to speak real slow so he could understand.

The vein on his temple popped as his anger rose. "If you married me, I would. What do you expect me to do when you keep rejecting me?"

My jaw ground hard in frustration and I took a deep breath. "As per usual, this conversation is going nowhere. What part of no do you not understand, because I'm not sure how to make it any clearer. It's been six months Richard, we are done. Please go away and leave me alone. This is really starting to get boring."

He glared at me. "No one walks away from me, Emerson."

I stepped back. "Well, I am. So maybe you need to get used to it."

I walked off, turning the corner of the next block, out of his sight and hopefully out of his mind. I kept going until I reached Chelsea Park, sitting down on the nearest available bench with a sigh, willing my boiling blood to cool down.

My ex-boyfriend was clearly not good at letting go.

I slurped my juice loudly, startling a passer-by.

We'd met at college back in California, where I grew up. He was so charming, vibrant and funny, that I immediately fell head over heels. We'd stayed together almost five years as we moved through school, graduation and beyond.

But it was all a front.

After his first indiscretion, my girlfriends had whisked me away to Vegas.

Oh, Vegas.

The saying was true, because what happened there had stayed there. Because I'd never experienced anything like it since. Or before, actually.

I'd been ruined by Vegas.

Or more specifically, I'd been ruined by a sex god. A god with the face of an angel and a body of well... a god, with heavily sculpted muscles, thick from years of training. He was so perfect he could have come straight from Olympus.

We'd met on the casino floor. I'd refused to tell him my name, trying to hold a semblance of composure, already jolted by the effect he had on me. So he'd called me his Lucky Charm and I was his prize.

For one night he worshipped me, giving me the type of sex you only ever read about in romance novels. Sex I didn't even know existed in real life. Sex I definitely hadn't been experiencing with the guy I was supposed to be in love with.

And then he left my life as quickly as he entered it. Disappearing that morning before we were supposed to meet one last time.

Left me wanting more and consumed with disappointment.

When I got back to California, Richard pleaded with me to come back to him, and I believed his remorse and his promise to change. Three months later, when the opportunity for him to move to New York had come up, we decided to make a fresh start and I'd transferred my job from LA.

But with the fresh start came fresh co-workers and few months of living here later, history repeated itself, with a nurse from his hospital.

And I'd found him balls deep in trouble.

I'd almost been expecting it but was more shocked that I didn't really care, knowing it had everything to do with my Vegas Sex God, who was still in my thoughts way more than a one night stand should be. I'd moved out of our apartment that day and decided I wanted to stay in New York. I could have moved back to California, but this city had grown on me and I wanted to give it a go, to stand on my own two feet. I had a job I loved and good friends, I wasn't going to let my ex-boyfriend dictate my life any longer.

My phone started buzzing in my bag and I stared at the screen as I pulled it out.

Incoming call: *Ashley Work*

She was one of my favorite people, training to be an instructor at the high-end spinning studio I worked at.

"Hey Ash."

"Hi Em, how are you?"

I took one last sip of my juice, drinking it down to the bottom. "Good, how are you?"

"Stuck. I know you already did the early shift but how far away are you from the studio? Can you come back and cover Jace's class? He's sick."

I looked at the time on my phone. "Yes sure, I'm about thirty minutes away. But I need fresh clothes."

"That's fine, there's enough new stuff you can change into here."

"Okay, see you soon."

I stood up, slipping my phone back in my bag before chucking my empty juice container into the nearby trash can, and took off toward the studio.

"Thank you, thank you." Ashley rushed at me and roped me in a hug as I walked in through the main doors.

There was already a small group waiting in the lobby for the next class to begin.

"It's fine, I didn't have any plans."

"I know, but still. I appreciate it. Not everyone would've come back." Her eyes lit up. "The new stock arrived this morning and I picked some out for you, it's really cute."

Every six weeks a new range of branded studio clothing arrived for the staff. I'd had a sneak peak of the latest collection a few weeks ago and was obsessed with the cutest bright purple sports bra and matching pants.

"The purple ones?"

She nodded with a grin, walking back around the counter and handing a small pile over to me.

"Oh, thank you. Okay, we'll call it even." I turned toward the changing rooms and called back over my shoulder. "I'll see you later."

I wasn't surprised to see that the studio was already half full when I walked in. I headed over to the stage, setting up the music and fitting my microphone pack. I noticed a few confused faces as I adjusted the instructor bike.

"Hey guys, I'm covering for Jace today, but don't worry, I'll still be working you just as hard."

It was nearly full when two women entered the room, walking straight toward the bikes directly in front of me. One of them had a rounded belly that made her look at least six months pregnant. Not that I would ask, because there was a lot of potential for that to be awkward as fuck.

I walked over to them. "Hi ladies, I'm Emerson. How are you both?"

They briefly glanced up at me from adjusting their saddles, answering in unison in an accent that definitely wasn't from New York. "Hello. We're good thanks."

"Oh, are you two visiting from England?"

The pregnant one hopped on her bike. "Oh no, we both live here."

I turned to the little brunette to find her staring at me intently, her head tilted. A gaze I was finding slightly odd. And intimidating.

I tried to stop myself from frowning at her penetrating glare, I wasn't sure she'd even blinked. "Have you done this class before?"

"Yes, we normally do Jace's classes." She replied.

"Okay great, well let me know if you need anything." I turned back to the pregnant one. "Please stop if you don't feel well. Go at your own pace, okay?"

She smiled at me. "Yes, we will, thank you."

The brunette was still looking at me. "Sorry, what did you say your name was again?"

"Emerson."

She turned to her blonde friend, her eyebrow raised.

I wasn't sure what her problem was, but I couldn't hold back the frown this time so I walked to my bike on center stage. It was time to kick off. I clipped in and started pedaling, turning up the first track I'd set.

"Okay gang, I hope everyone is doing well today. For those of you who don't know me or have never taken my classes before, I'm Emerson. Jace is sick so I'm filling in. Let's start with a warm up, get those legs moving. Your hearts are going to be pounding today, so I hope you're ready to sweat."

On the screen in front of me, attached to my bike, I could see everyone's speeds and strength metrics and watched them increase as they settled into their rides.

8

"Make sure you stay hydrated throughout and if you need to stop push down hard on the dial in the front. Okay let's go. Turn it up."

Soon everyone was sweating away, pushing hard and pedaling like they were trying to win the Tour de France.

I was keeping an eye on the two women up front, their giant engagement rings catching the light every time they sipped from their water bottles or wiped a towel across their faces. The brunette was surprisingly powerful for someone so short.

Fifty minutes later the class was over and everyone started filing out, spent and sweaty, murmurs of thanks as they passed.

"Well done everyone, great class."

As I turned around, the two at the front were deep in whispered conversation. Something strange was playing out that I couldn't put my finger on, especially given the brunette hadn't stopped staring at me.

"It's her, I'm telling you." She hissed as I walked over to them.

"Fred. Stop. Shush." The blonde whispered back.

Yeah, they were definitely eccentric. Must have been the English thing. With the lights a bit brighter I could see the brunette was also sporting her own little baby bump and her hair was more black than brown.

"How did you like the class ladies?"

She spun around, not realizing I was so close, her eyes flaring momentarily. "Oh, we loved it. We haven't done your classes before. How long have you been here?"

"I've been here around nine months, but I usually teach the six am crew."

"Nine months." The blonde one gasped quietly, before composing herself.

I was starting to think these two might not be entirely sane.

The black haired one carried on as though nothing happened. "No wonder we've not seen you before. Do you do any at a more reasonable hour?"

I laughed. "Yes, I take a Saturday mid-morning class and a couple of the specialist rides, but I'll be doing more."

"We'll definitely be back. I'm Freddie by the way, and this is my sister Wolfie."

"Great, I'd love to see you two again."

They headed toward the door before Freddie turned back to me. "This will sound like a strange question, but have you ever been to Vegas?"

I startled slightly, then nodded.

Wolfie tugged on her sleeve before I could answer out loud. "Francesco we need to go, we're going to be late."

They walked out, leaving me as shivers zipped along my spine. And for the second time that day memories of the best night of my life burned me from the inside and pierced my brain.

2

DREW

Felix walked out of Jasper's pantry, an open bag of chips dangling from his fingers. "How much longer did the girls say they'd be? I'm getting hungry."

"When aren't you?" Huck twisted the cap off a bottle of water and swigged it.

"Hey, I'm a growing boy." He flexed his bicep, one he usually liked to announce was bigger than mine.

It wasn't.

Although, outside of hockey, it would big by anyone else's standards. Felix was a human wall, much like me.

I looked up from the sports section of the newspaper. "They should be here any minute."

Right on cue the elevator doors opened and in walked Wolf and Freddie. Wolfie's stomach seemed to get bigger every time I saw her, although Fred's was starting to catch up.

Cooper's face lit up as he saw her, marching straight over, pulling her into an embrace, his hands circling on her stomach before snaking behind her. Wolfie received a similar greeting from Jasper, who had been sitting quietly at the breakfast bar.

I looked away, the familiar pang of sadness rolling through me like a heavy fog, dulling my senses and I wondered for the thousandth time if I'd ever find what they'd all found. It was the norm for me these days and my mind flashed back to Vegas, to the only woman I'd ever met who'd made me want to have what they had. Someone to wake up to each day, someone to spend time with, someone to be there for.

The only woman I'd lost due to my own stupidity.

Our time together had been so fleeting that I sometimes wondered if I'd dreamt her.

My Lucky Charm.

I peered down at my phone, the photo of us on my lock screen reminding me she had been real.

I'd taken it on our way to my suite after we'd finished gambling in the casino, I'd stared at it so many times that if I had any artistic talent at all, I'd be able to draw her without even looking.

Whatever spell she'd cast, I was still well and truly under it.

I'd tried to get out, but it was proving impossible.

Until Lucky, I hadn't met anyone I'd wanted to spend more than a few nights with.

When we'd first left Vegas and I'd lost her number, I'd attempted to block her out of my head in the only way I knew how. For a month I'd spent all my spare time partying and trying to fuck her out of my system with every woman I met. It got to the point where I could only come when I pictured her face, searching for the high she'd given me when I'd been inside her, next to her, behind her, on top of her.

But where sex had once been my favorite hobby, it had become mundane. I realized I was chasing an elusive dream and knew that only her brand of drug would do it for me now.

So I'd stopped.

Stopped dating, stopped fucking, stopped chasing.

It had been eleven months since I'd been with another woman.

I slipped my phone in my pocket, not wanting to descend into the filthy mood which usually followed when I thought about her too much, and went back to reading the sports pages.

"Hey, Drew?" Freddie moved away from Cooper and walked toward me. "Can I borrow your phone a minute?"

"Er, yeah. Sure." I pulled it out of my pocket and handed it to her.

She glanced at it before looking back up at me with an unreadable expression. I guessed it was probably something to do with the fact Lucky was still on my lock screen. It had been a year and I needed to change the picture but hadn't got around to it.

Okay, didn't want to.

Wasn't ready to.

She passed it over to Wolfie, who also studied it then gasped, her hand flying to her face. Her eyes immediately welled up, tears overspilling as she wiped them with her sleeve, sniffing.

I frowned. That was weird.

The five of us looked at them in confusion. Jasper immediately pulled her into an embrace, kissing her head, before narrowing his eyes at me.

"What did you do to make my wife cry?"

I looked at him and shrugged my shoulders. "Nothing, I've done nothing."

"Dude, she cries at everything at right now." Everyone turned to Felix. "What? She does. No offense, Wolf."

Then Freddie started.

Cooper pulled her onto his lap, looking around at us with a similar expression to the one Jasper held. But Jas shook his head, his hands still full of Wolfie. Everyone turned to look at me.

Wolfie crying was one thing, but Freddie? And fuck me, but women crying were my kryptonite. If this went on any longer, I'd be joining them and I didn't even know why.

I walked over and knelt by her. "Fredster, sweetheart, can I have my phone back, please? And do you think you could tell me why you're crying?"

She looked up at Wolfie, before pulling me into a big hug, her arms wrapping around my neck.

I rubbed her back as she sobbed on my shoulder and coughed away the lump forming in my throat. "Can someone please explain to me what's going on?"

"Baby, let go of Drew before he starts bawling too." Cooper stood up and peeled her away before turning to Wolfie. "Okay, can the pair of you please enlighten us on the tears? We can't fix it if we don't know what's going on."

Freddie sniffed and wiped her arm across her nose, glancing at Wolfie one more time before waving her hand in front of her face.

"Sorry, sorry. These are happy tears." She looked up at me. "Drew, babe, we found her."

I looked around at the boys. All four of them staring back at me, their faces screwed up in confusion.

"Found who?"

She took my phone back, holding it up in front of me and pointed to the screen. "Lucky. We found Lucky."

What?

I blinked several times in fast succession, trying to figure out if I'd heard properly. "I'm sorry. What?"

"We found her." Wolfie repeated.

My brows connected in a deep frown. "I don't understand, what do you mean you found her? Lucky? You know where she is?"

They both nodded.

14

Blood whooshed in my ears, echoing around my brain and pumping to the rhythm of my heart, a beat that was rapidly quickening. It was the only sound I could hear in the silence of the apartment. Everyone else waiting with bated breath for me to react.

Jasper turned to Wolfie, stroking her hair. "Cub, are you sure? This isn't you two trying to be funny?"

Wolfie's eyes filled with indignation, her temper flaring. If you looked up pregnancy mood swings in the dictionary her picture would be next to it.

"No, Jasper. We saw her. We wouldn't make a joke about this, why would we do that? We saw her. Talked to her." She turned back to me, her expression softening again. If I wasn't in a degree of shock, I'd probably be scared. "Freddie asked her if she'd ever been to Vegas and she said yes."

"Tiny, Baby, where did you see her?" Cooper asked before I could, keeping his voice soft and steady, clearly not wanting to make the same mistake as Jasper.

"She was our spinning instructor in the class today. Her name is Emerson Reeves." She rolled her lips nervously, her voice quieting. "She said she's lived here for nine months, but she never normally teaches our class, so we'd never seen her before."

Did I just hear that right? Nine months?

An irrational burst of anger welled up from deep inside exploding like a volcano, turning my blood to lava and swiftly drying the tears I'd built up watching Wolf and Freddie cry.

"Nine months. NINE MONTHS. NINE FUCKING MONTHS IN THIS CITY? RIGHT UNDER MY NOSE?"

I paced back and forth, hands on my head, puffing my cheeks through deep slow breaths of air in case I hyperventilated. My adrenaline spiked and I clenched my fists to stop the shaking, fully aware of everyone staring at me.

"Drew…" Freddie reached out to me tentatively. "Are you okay? This is a good thing, right?"

I looked at her face, worry etched across it, and my heart melted.

In the year she'd been living here with Cooper she'd become one of my best friends. Since the dramatic change in my social life, I'd been pouring all my energy into renovating my house with Freddie's help. We'd worked closely together and she'd become my confidante, listening to me for hours on end while I talked about Lucky. Offering advice, never judging. Although all the boys knew I'd been angry at not finding her, only Freddie and Felix knew the depths of my devastation.

My heartache.

The incessant emptiness I felt like a chill deep in my bones.

"Yes, Fredster, yes it is, thank you for telling me. I'm sorry I shouted." I pulled her into a brief hug, kissing her head, before turning to Jas. "Can I borrow some running shorts? I need to get out of here."

He nodded. "Yeah man, take what you need. There's some clean stuff in the laundry room."

"Thanks." I stormed down the hall, finding a pile of clothes in a basket ready to be put away. Taking a pair off the top, I stripped down and pulled them on.

Felix walked in, picking up a pair for himself.

I frowned. "What are you doing?"

"I'm coming with you." He said in a tone that wasn't worth arguing with.

I gritted my teeth. "Fine, but don't fucking speak to me."

I took off at a punishing pace toward the park, my raging thoughts pushing me forward.

I'd expected my memories to fade over time, but they'd only got stronger and more pronounced, like barrel aged whiskey or a fine wine.

I don't know how I remembered her scent, like rain on a hot summer day or the feel of her soft skin against mine as she fit perfectly into me or the curve of her lower back as I ran my hands over it and down to her round, firm ass. Or the warmth of her exquisite velvety pussy, as she wrang my cock dry with violent convulsions, clenching over and over while I watched her shatter beneath me.

But I did. I remembered it all. And for nine months it had been right here.

In this city.

Under my fucking nose.

I pushed on further, until my lungs were burning, until I couldn't breathe. I pulled up on a quiet spot near the reservoir.

"Fuck. Are you trying to kill me?" Felix bent over, his hands on his knees, before collapsing back on the ground. "It's a good job I've stepped up training before actual pre-season starts."

I walked around him starfished on the ground, a slight smirk curling my lip. "Pussy."

I wanted to be on my own but, as always, I was glad he was here, lifting me out of my morosity, because he knew me better than anyone else in my life.

We'd played together for over a decade, first at college, then the club. It had been so long that we knew what the other was thinking almost before it happened, best friends who could communicate with a single look. We were a pair and everyone knew it and, much to the amusement of our team mates, we regularly appeared in memes which said '*I wish my boyfriend would look at me the way* - insert either one of our names – *looks at...*'. We'd even had it built into our contracts that if one of us was traded, then we both were.

As power forwards we were an indisputable force when it came to the ice and between the pair of us we usually ranked at the top of the annual 'most goals scored' list. With Cooper between us we made up one of the most formidable lines in the NHL, dubbed 'The C Line Express' by our fans, down to the fact that our names – Cooper, Crawley and Cleverly - started with C and that we usually scored within seconds of the puck drop.

He sat up, his arms resting on his knees. "Dude, seriously. Why are you so angry? This is a good thing. Isn't it?"

I linked my fingers behind my neck, pulling on it in frustration. "Because she's been here for nine months. I could have found her already and it's my fault for being a dumbass."

He looked up at me, his eyes sympathetic. "Give yourself a break. You lost her number, people do it all the time. You've definitely done it before."

"Your point?"

He sighed. "My point is, take the pressure off yourself. Remember what Tate said, you might not even like her when you meet her, this might have been a one-time thing that you've built into something more. Don't set yourself up for disappointment."

Tate, Jasper's younger brother, was a sports psychologist and on a couple of occasions when we'd been drinking he'd offered up some unsolicited advice.

I gritted my teeth. It was the same thought that had played like a broken record in my mind over the past year, torturing me, questioning my judgement. But I knew, I felt it like a body blow, hard in my gut. "It isn't. She was different. She was my one."

He curled the stiff rim of his cap as he looked up at me with a questioning gaze. But he knew I wasn't going to budge. "Okay, then what are you going to do if she's with someone else?"

The idea of that was like a bullet to the chest.

Dig a hole for him.

I shrugged.

He pushed off the ground and stood up in front of me. "So, what do you want to do?"

There was no doubt in my mind, I'd lost her once, I wasn't about to do it again. "I want to see her."

"Okay, well let's go back and figure out how to do that without you coming across as a creepy fuckwit." He punched me in the shoulder.

"Yeah, okay."

"Come on, the girls will know what to do."

An hour later we walked into the apartment, complete with a peace offering in the form of a giant box of the cupcakes Wolf and Freddie couldn't seem to get enough of recently. Jas and Coop were in the kitchen and Huck was on the sofa playing Xbox.

Cooper squeezed my shoulder. "How you doin', man?"

"Yeah, okay." I looked around. "Where are the girls?"

"They went for a nap, but will probably be awake soon."

"I'm awake."

I spun around to find Freddie coming toward me. I held the massive box of cupcakes in front of me and her eyes lit up.

"Are those for me?"

I nodded, opening up the lid. "Yes, and Wolf. I'm sorry I shouted."

She peered in, musing, before picking out a red velvet and taking an enormous bite. She looked at me as she chewed, swallowing before she answered.

"You have nothing to be sorry about, you were in shock. We'd have all reacted the same way." She pulled me into a hug. "It'll be okay, we'll make sure of it. This is exciting, it's just the beginning."

I took a deep breath. "I hope so."

Jasper opened the fridge, taking out two sports drinks, handing them to Felix and me. "Do you know what you want to do?"

I downed half the bottle. "I want to see her."

Freddie walked off down the corridor, returning with a sleepy looking Wolf who beelined straight to Jasper. He pulled her into his lap, stroking her belly.

Freddie passed her the cupcake box. "Okay, let's figure out what to do."

Huck joined us from the sofa, taking a seat on one of the bar stools. "What do we know about her?"

Freddie hopped on one of the other stools. "We looked up her classes while you were running. She takes the six am rides on Mondays, Wednesday and Fridays. And she also does a weekend class. They all look really hard, today's was pretty intense. Way harder than the one we usually take."

"Did she look like she had a boyfriend?" Felix bit into a cupcake.

Cooper's eyebrow raised. "What does that look like exactly?"

"I dunno, like these two do I guess." He pointed to Freddie and Wolf. "All dreamy and shit."

Jasper smirked at the girls grimacing.

"No, Clevs. We couldn't tell." Wolfie turned to me. "But we could ask, subtly. If you wanted?"

Freddie's eyes opened wide. "Oooh. Why don't you just go to one of her classes?"

Felix scoffed. "Spinning? Isn't that for girls?"

Freddie and Wolf glared at him. He was walking on very dangerous ground around a pair of slightly volatile, pregnant women.

"No Felix, it is not. It's hard." Wolfie raised her eyebrow. "In fact, I bet you wouldn't be able to handle it."

Jasper dropped his head, hiding his smile. I also had zero sympathy, the dickhead should've known better.

He laughed at her, digging himself a deeper hole. "Course I would. I'm a professional athlete."

She crossed her arms over her belly, staring at him. "Oh yeah? Prove it."

"We could all go." Offered up Huck.

"What?" I coughed out, my inhale catching in my throat.

Freddie clapped her hands. "Oh yes, that's a great idea. Then Drew has our support if he wants it."

I was suddenly swimming in nerves. Seeing her again was becoming real and what if she wasn't how I remembered? Or worse, what if she didn't remember me and our connection had been a figment of my imagination.

"Guys, I don't know about this." I pressed the heel of my palm into my forehead, trying to ease the tension building up.

Jasper looked at me. "Think of it this way, at least you'll know. Plus we have the added benefit of seeing Clevs make a total dick of himself."

"Really?"

He nodded. "Yeah, you're gonna have to rip the Band-Aid with this one. Otherwise, it'll drive you crazy."

I was already going down that highway at full throttle.

I laughed nervously. "Yeah, I guess. Okay, let's go."

Felix leaned back against the counter, crossing his arms. "Just so we're clear, I'm going to support Drew, nothing more."

"Yeah yeah, whatever you say." Wolfie grinned at him. She picked up her laptop. "Right, her next class is tomorrow at eleven. I'm booking us all in."

I looked at my watch.

Twenty hours to go.

3

EMERSON

I scooped a massive spoonful of oatmeal into my mouth, finishing the bowl, while I stood mesmerized by the slow drip drip of the coffee into my mug, which always seemed to take forever.

Saturdays were my favorite day of the week. My class didn't start until eleven, meaning I could enjoy a lie in, a leisurely breakfast and go about my morning routine of stretches, preparing music for my class and wait an eternity for the coffee to fill my mug.

Which it now had. Finally.

I topped it up with Half and Half, blowing into it before taking a sip, too impatient to wait any longer. Looking out of the window, past the fire escape where I liked to sit, I could just make out the bustle of the university streets surrounding Washington Square Park, although seeing the park itself was a stretch when my windows mostly faced the bricks of the buildings opposite.

My apartment was a shoebox at best, although I'd fallen in love with it the second I'd seen it. A tiny one bedroom, the high ceilings in each room made it feel much bigger than it actually was, and although I earned a decent salary it was all I could afford on my own. After I'd moved out of the apartment I'd shared with Richard, I was determined to live alone and stand on my own two feet.

I walked through to my bedroom, placing my coffee on the dresser as I pulled my workout gear from the drawer. I'd taken a few more pieces from the new collection when I'd left the studio yesterday, another matching set and just as cute, this one covered in little green stars with the studio logo and tag line printed along the legs.

Brushing through the knots, I tied my hair back as tightly as I could. Pulling all the loose strands away, I topped it off with a little headband so there wouldn't be any flapping about to annoy me and stick to my face. My classes were always hard, but the Saturday ones were known for being particularly savage – usually used as a way to sweat out the night before or an excuse for a massive brunch afterwards - and I poured with as much sweat as everyone taking it. I'd even known a couple of riders to run out for a mid-class vomit, much to the amusement of everyone else, although it seemed to be viewed as a badge of honor more than anything.

Spying my light hoodie on the sofa in the living room, I threw it over my shoulders, followed by my backpack, and walked out of the door collecting my sunglasses and keys on the way. I lived a thirty-minute walk from the studio and loved taking my time, walking through Greenwich Village up to the north of the Meatpacking District where it was located just off the High Line. Even though I'd grown up in California and spent a lot of my time on the beach or surfing, there was something about the energy of New York City that you couldn't find anywhere else.

It was relatively quiet in the reception when I arrived, while the earlier classes were in progress, I liked to get there in enough time to set up and zone in for the hour ahead. I liked to be there greeting the riders before pushing them to

23

their physical limits and making them as strong as they could be.

I waved to Ashley, who was behind reception talking to two enormous guys with taut, thickly defined muscles. Even from the back I knew they'd definitely never been in my classes before. I didn't often see men who looked as physically fit as they did and for a split-second Vegas Sex God infiltrated my brain again, like a song that was stuck, before I could shake him away.

"Hey Emerson." Ashley pulled shoes out from behind the counter and handed them over.

The guys' heads whipped to face me as she called, both staring at me intently.

Before I had a second to consider their bizarre reaction, I heard my name called again and I spun in the direction it was coming from. The two ladies from yesterday were walking toward me holding almost the entirety of the new season's collection.

"Hi Emerson. How are you? We came back."

"Hey ladies," I looked at the one who'd called me. "Wolfie, right?"

She nodded as she placed everything on the counter for Ashley to ring up.

I turned to the little one. "And Freddie?"

Freddie smiled as she nodded.

"It's great to see you again so soon. You both felt okay yesterday after the class?"

"Yes, we needed a nap, although that's the norm these days." Wolfie ran her hands over her stomach.

"And we've brought some more victims for you." Freddie grabbed one of the two giant men standing behind her. "This is my husband, Cooper, and this is Wolfie's husband, Jasper." She pointed to the other.

"Guys, this is Emerson." She said in a weirdly pointed way that made me feel like she'd been talking about me.

"Hey." They replied in unison, the slightly taller of the two looked like he was trying to hide a smirk.

What was it with this lot?

"Hey guys, hope you're ready for the class."

"Yes, we are and a couple more of our friends are coming too, but we came early so we could shop." Wolfie smiled before a devilish smirk tilted her lip. "By the way, one of them said to us yesterday that spinning was just for girls."

My eyebrows shot up in surprise. "Oh, did he now? Well, it definitely isn't as you both know. So, we'll have to see what we can do about that."

Freddie snorted.

"Cub." Jasper tsked under his breath, wrapping his arm around her and shaking his head.

I laughed at her blatant stirring. "Okay, I need to get ready. See you in there."

I walked off toward the staff locker rooms to put my things away before heading into the studio. The lights were dimmed down so it felt more like a night club than a fitness space, a sweat towel placed on each of the bikes. And they'd need it, especially after that spinning for girls comment.

My classes were hard for everyone.

It was odd too, clearly coming from someone who'd never been to the studios before. The six am classes always had full waiting lists of alpha males and females, all wanting to outcompete each other before heading to their busy jobs in the financial district to do it all over again. It took a special breed of person to get up and exercise at six am on a Monday.

City burnout was real for a reason.

The music started pumping loudly around the room as the first lot of riders began filing in, all familiar faces saying hello, setting up their bikes before jumping on to get their legs moving and warm before we started.

I was greeting everyone when Freddie and Wolfie entered

with their husbands and three more gigantic men. It was hard not to notice them, given their size, but they all seemed to cause an extra stir among the riders already on their bikes. They walked toward a cluster at the back, the girls showing them how to adjust their saddles before getting on.

I looked at the three newcomers, two of whom seemed roughly the same size, and even in their darkened corner of the room I could make out their expansive shoulders and giant chests, straining against the softness of their formfitting tanks cut across thick delts. Sculpted biceps and triceps flexed as they adjusted their bike heights and tightened the screws, and both were wearing knee length skins underneath their looser shorts, hugging massive powerful thighs and heavily defined quads.

I forced myself to blink before I was caught staring.

While all these newcomers were undeniably Grade A male specimens, the one tucked away on the far left was causing nervous knots to sit low in my belly and goosebumps to shoot down my spine. He was wearing a cap, pulled low down his face and I watched as he gave a quiet chuckle to the blonde guy next to him, his pouty lips curling up into a smile showing off straight, white teeth.

Since the girls had turned up yesterday something was happening I couldn't explain, like a memory that I couldn't quite find whispering across my brain.

I turned away to the rest of the class, realizing the room had completely filled in the time I'd been ogling the boys, and tried to convince myself it was merely professional appreciation of finely tuned physiques.

Lies.

I took a deep breath and regained my focus, pushing down on the pedals, moving my legs.

"Welcome all. Welcome to Emerson's Eleven O'clock Show. It's good to see you back and it's good to see new faces. Now, you know I always make you work hard for it, but today it's going to be extra tough because I heard that one of you fine gentlemen out there said spinning was just for girls."

A collective groan went up from the guys in class while the women's faces all dropped in horror, looking round for the one who'd dared to say that. I watched the corner group turn to the blonde one in the middle, outing him as the culprit.

"So let's get going, turn up the resistance high. We're going to be climbing and sprinting today."

I watched everyone reach down and turn their dials, making their bikes heavier as though they were on steep hills.

It wasn't long before they'd started to sweat and we were still in the warm up.

"Come on Coach, stop teasing us." The blonde one called from the corner.

Cheeky fucker.

I raised an eyebrow at him. "I see we have a smart ass in our midst. Okay, we'll turn it up a notch. Everyone reach down, then increase your speed to fifty. This is going to get sticky."

"Fuck's sake Cleverly, shut the fuck up." Cried a man from somewhere on the other side of the room.

Maybe he had been here before if people knew him.

"Hey man, don't hate the player." The blonde one, Cleverly, shouted back clearly enjoying riling everyone up.

A few at the front were puffing away and I kept them all at pace, slowing them down for short breaks before bringing them back up onto harder climbs. I looked around to see if anyone seemed close to throwing up, only to be greeted by red faces and big puddles of sweat forming under each bike.

It was hard work, but they loved it.

Like a moth to a flame, my eyes were drawn to the group in the corner. It had started as a way to keep an eye on Wolfie and Freddie, being pregnant, but as the class went on I barely glanced at them before they landed on the guy in the corner, his cap still low.

My skin prickled with a sixth sense that he was watching me, but every time I looked over, his head was down, his jaw clenched in concentration. I could see from my monitor he was working hard, although from here it appeared as though he was barely sweating. I was becoming hypnotized by the way his muscles relaxed and contracted as he gripped onto the bike every time I asked them to speed up or increase the resistance. And I found myself doing it just so I could watch, one flowing into the other like an infinity loop.

The music changed to a slow, trance beat and I glanced at the clock without thinking, realizing we were at time. I could honestly say I didn't remember a minute of it. For the first time ever I'd taken a class on autopilot, driven to distraction by the mystery guy in the corner.

"Okay, everyone turn it down. Let's flush those legs out. Well done gang, you survived."

I heard a couple of whoops and high fives, as everyone started to jump off their bikes before stretching and leaving to head to their Saturdays for a well-earned brunch.

As the class emptied, I unclipped from my bike, turning to gather my things before the cleaning crew came in.

"Good class, Coach. I concede, spinning isn't just for girls."

I turned to find the man called Cleverly standing in front of me, lifting his shirt to wipe away the sweat which dripped off him, tight abs filling my view.

Up close there was something eerily familiar about him. The nervous knots were seeping back in.

"I told you it wouldn't be easy." Wolfie nudged him in the ribs, making him flinch.

I looked at her, trying to focus on something, anything,

which would rid me of this gnawing. "How are you? Are you feeling okay?"

"Yes, I feel great, I just did what I could. But I come three times a week, so this isn't new to me. Your classes are another level hard though."

I grinned as the rest of them walked over, the hat guy staying at the back, still out of sight.

"Well, I'm glad you enjoyed it, hopefully see you again."

"Oh, you can count on that, Coach." Laughed Cleverly, earning himself a punch on the arm from Jasper.

"Bye Emerson, we'll all see you soon, hopefully." He put his arm around Wolfie before muttering over his shoulder. "We'll wait outside for you, man."

I frowned. Wait outside for who? They all walked out, Freddie shooting me a strange backwards glance with an expression I couldn't read and didn't understand.

And then I realized only six of them had left.

I turned to find him standing behind me, his cap now flipped backwards, his light hazel eyes boring into mine with an intensity that licked fire across my damp skin. And in less than a breath I knew why I'd been so distracted by him during the class. My body clearly remembering before my head caught up.

His face had been etched on my brain for the past twelve months. The face I'd been trying and failing to forget. The face I only allowed to reappear in my fantasies before I fell asleep.

His full cheeks, where a deep dimple materialized when he laughed, but only on the left. The chiseled jaw covered in thick, dark scruff which I knew from experience was soft to the touch. Soft when he kissed me, soft when he lapped between my legs. His perfect lips, full and delicious, that tasted like whiskey and oranges as he pressed them against mine, as our tongues tangled together.

Lips, which were made for kissing.

Sweat was rolling down the thick veins stretching the length of his massive biceps, biceps which had held his body over mine as he fucked me for six straight hours, owning my body with his refusal to let me leave or sleep or do anything that didn't end with the most incredible pleasure of my life. Behind them lay bulging triceps, triceps I'd gripped onto for dear life as another orgasm had been ripped out of me with brute force.

And I knew that under his shirt was the most impressive set of abs I'd ever seen. Abs that rippled when he'd thrust into me, that stayed as defined as carved granite even while our bodies had softened as we'd relaxed in the giant hotel tub, washing our exertions away.

My breathing gave out and I realized I'd been holding it.

"Hi Luck." His deep drawl I'd recognize anywhere, confirming what I already knew.

Vegas Sex God was standing in front of me.

I'd spent a year thinking about what I'd do if I ever saw him again and I could remember none of it. I reached down and pinched myself, hard, frowning at the pain and rubbing my arm where it turned red.

I looked up, he was still there.

I wasn't dreaming.

This was real.

His brow creased. "What did you just do?"

Seven times my heart pounded in my chest before I finally found my voice.

"Pinched myself."

"Why?"

I looked back up at him, nearly drowning in his penetrating gaze. "To see if I'm dreaming."

A slow smile spread across his face, the dimple making an appearance. "You aren't."

"I know, it hurt."

He took my arm and rubbed it gently, his touch creating a

tidal wave of chills even though I was still burning hot from the class. "I was worried you wouldn't remember me."

I took it back. "I remember I waited an hour for you to show up after you begged me to meet you."

His shoulders deflated at my words, sagging low. "I know, I'm so sorry. I fell asleep and the alarm didn't go off. Then when I woke up your number had smudged everywhere. I couldn't read it to text you. But I wanted to, so badly. Please believe me."

I looked at his face, guilt and sadness weighing heavily across it, reminding me of the look Freddie gave me as she walked out.

And I realized this wasn't a coincidence.

"Freddie knew who I was yesterday. How?"

Embarrassment pushed the guilt away, a flush rising up his neck. I watched as he licked his lips nervously, the sight of his tongue doing nothing to quench the inferno blazing through me, because I could remember exactly what that tongue was capable of.

"Do you remember the picture I took before we got in the elevator?"

Barely. I hadn't exactly been sober or concentrating on much but him.

"I still have it and she recognized you from it, I guess." He shrugged.

"And you came here today to what?"

"I wanted to see you." His head tilted, as though there couldn't possibly be any other reason.

"Why?"

"Because I never stopped thinking about you. And I wanted to apologize and see if you'd give me a chance to do what I would have done a year ago."

His honesty was as disarming as his stupid, handsome face.

I rolled my lips, not quite sure I wanted to hear the answer. "And what was that?"

He raised an eyebrow and I was suddenly conscious of how little I was wearing, a droplet of sweat ran between my breasts. I knew he was trying very hard not to look.

"Take you on a proper date, for a start."

I watched in silence as he reached into his pocket, pulling out a Sharpie. He removed the lid with his perfect teeth and, before I could stop him, picked up my arm, writing a number across it just as I had done to him a year ago.

"Why do you have a Sharpie?"

"I always have one."

I scoffed. "You always carry a Sharpie around?"

He looked up at me, his eyes glistening with amusement. "Yes."

He put the lid back on the pen when he'd finished.

"There you go Lucky Charm, call me by tomorrow or I'll be back. I know where you are now, you're not losing me again."

His smiled dropped, his face becoming serious as we stared at each other, both frozen on the spot.

"Fuck, I can't believe you're standing in front of me." He leaned in and kissed my cheek.

His sweaty, musky scent smacked my memory banks hard, sending my senses reeling and stripping me of my words once more.

"I'm going to go before I make a dick out of myself. Please don't make me wait, Luck." He placed my arm gently by my side, running his thumb along my palm, before walking out of the studio. He turned as he reached the door to find me still staring at him. "Oh, Luck. I'm Drew." He winked, then disappeared.

I fell back on to the step of the stage, sucking in deep lungfuls of air as though the oxygen in the room had returned to normal levels and I needed to replenish.

My head was spinning.

I rested my elbows on my knees, leaning forward so my chin fell onto my hands. I sat in silence, trying to replay the last five minutes. It was a lot of information to absorb in a short space of time.

He'd found me.

And he hadn't forgotten me.

And he hadn't stood me up on purpose.

And now he wanted to go on a date.

"Oh, there you are. What are you still doing in here?" Ashley's face peered around the door, snapping me out of my daze.

I stood up, gathering my things and walked over to her. "Just thinking."

The cleaning crew passed me on my way out.

"How was the class?" She was practically bouncing in delight as we walked up the stairs. "Everyone looked wiped as they walked out."

I laughed, the nervous knots in my belly dissolving like an effervescent tablet, leaving bubbles in their wake. "It was good."

"I can't believe some of the Rangers were in there. How were they? Everyone was waiting outside asking for selfies as they left."

"Who?"

"The New York Rangers. Jasper Jacobs and Cooper Marks were at the reception when you walked in earlier. Then Huck Sands, Drew Crawley and Felix Cleverly came after you left."

I flinched as she said his name. Drew Crawley.

I rolled it on my tongue. Drew Crawley.

"They all play ice hockey?" I guess that explained their size and stamina. I was right when I thought they looked like professional athletes.

"Yeah, Jasper Jacobs is Captain." She nodded excitedly

before handing me a folded piece of paper. "One of the girls left you this, by the way."

I took it, opening it up.

Hi Emerson,
Please call us if you want to chat.
917-555-6595
Freddie and Wolf x

So, Vegas Sex God was a professional athlete in New York City. How had I missed that in the nine months I'd been here? I wasn't a massive hockey fan, being from California it was a bit cold for me. And my childhood was mostly spent on the beach or watching my big brother play baseball, but still, it was the type of thing I was usually aware of. And this city worshipped its athletes.

"What's on your arm?"

I looked down, forgetting he'd written on me, and tried to cover it up. "Oh, nothing."

She frowned at me. "Are you okay? You look like you've seen a ghost or something."

Something would be correct.

I tried to shake myself out of my daze. "Yeah. Hey, what time do you finish? Let's see if the girls are around to go dancing tonight."

"Hell yes, way ahead of you. Jessie just left and said to tell you Bar None tonight. I'll message you when I'm done here, and we can meet earlier for some cocktails."

"Sounds good." I turned, opening the front doors. "Okay, see you later."

"Emerson, you don't have your stuff with you."

I turned back, still in my daze. "Whoops."

She looked at me curiously. "Are you sure you're okay?"

I walked back to the locker room, pretending I hadn't heard her. Unsure how to answer that particular question.

4

EMERSON

I'd walked home in a daze, let myself into my apartment, locked the door behind me and positioned myself on the fire escape, where I'd been sitting for the past two hours staring at the number on my arm.

An hour into my staring marathon I broke to look him up on Google, but then stopped myself before I saw anything I didn't like. I was well aware of the reputation sports stars had and, given how I'd met him in the first place decided I wasn't exactly in a position to judge, because I was as bad as the rest of the girls they picked up.

Then I returned to staring.

What did I want to do with this number?

There were infinite possibilities.

Or, well, three that I could think of immediately.

One. Wash it off my arm.

Two. Save it, then wash it off my arm.

Three. Leave it on my arm and decide later on whether to follow options one or two.

I wasn't sure this was a decision I could make entirely on my own. The pressure too much.

I picked up my phone, checking the time. It would be

nine am in Hawaii. She'd definitely be up and done with her first surf of the day.

I dialed through on Facetime, waiting for her to pick up.

My childhood best friend, Mallory, and I had grown up together in California, our mornings spent hitting the beach for a run or a surf, before school. But where I had just enjoyed it for fitness and fun, Mallory had fallen in love with the water and by the time I'd graduated Stanford she was a world champion surfer, travelling the globe. And when she wasn't travelling, she split her time between California and Hawaii where she was right now.

"Hey babe." Her face filled the screen. Her white-blonde hair, lightened from the sun, was wet and from her background I could see she was still on the beach.

"Hey Mal, how was the water?"

"It was okay, pretty calm today. Nothing too major." She winked.

Seeing as I'd seen her surf over fifty-foot waves, major for her meant something different to normal people.

"How was class today? Anyone puke?"

I laughed. "No, no puking." I took a deep breath. "But something else happened."

Her eyes opened wide in anticipation. "Go on."

"Do you remember last year when we were in Vegas?"

She nodded.

"And I hooked up with that guy?"

"Yeah, Vegas Sex God."

I scrunched my face up. "Well, he was in my class today."

Her mouth dropped open. "Get out! No way. Oh my god, what happened? Did he recognize you? Did you speak to him?"

"Yeah, he wasn't there by accident."

She frowned in confusion and I told her the whole story, starting with Freddie's weird stare, realizing it now made sense, so maybe she wasn't as weird and intense as I'd thought.

"I can't believe he kept that photo."

"I know. What do you think I should do? I can't keep this forever." I held my arm up to the screen.

She grinned. "That's pretty funny, you know."

She was right, it was. If I hadn't been in shock at the time, I'd have probably laughed.

"You know, Em, the universe has ways of making things happen when we need them to. It took you ages to stop talking about him, but maybe then wasn't the right time for you. It's been a year since Vegas, and you've had all these months to spend on your own, get yourself away from Richard and gain the confidence to stand on your own two feet. Maybe now is the right time. I say go for it."

"You think?"

"Totally. Don't think about it, just have fun, don't take it too seriously and see where it goes. You said the sex was hot, right?"

I nodded, grinning. "The hottest. Like, once in a lifetime."

"Then make it twice in a lifetime and enjoy it. And if it's not how you remember it, walk away. No biggie."

This is why I loved her, she just made everything so simple. It either worked or it didn't. And from the way my body had lit up in his presence without me even realizing it was him, I had no doubt the sex would still be as hot.

"Yeah, you're right. Okay, I'll text him tomorrow."

"Do it, let me know what happens." She stood up. "Oh, did he tell you what his name was?"

"Oh yes. It's Drew. And get this, he plays for the New York Rangers."

Her eyes widened before she gave a loud snort. "A professional athlete? No wonder he had so much stamina."

"I know, right."

"Yeah, you'll have some fun for sure." She grinned as I grimaced. "What?"

"A professional athlete? Come on, you know what they're like. He's probably just after another hook up."

She looked at me through the screen, contemplating. "You're worried he's going to be like Jupe?"

Jupiter, my big brother, was a baseball player in the major leagues, and not exactly the poster child for professionalism. Since he'd turned pro there was hardly a week when he wasn't out of the gossip pages. He was undoubtedly one of my favorite people, but he was a man whore to put it bluntly. And having been out with him on more than one occasion I was fully aware of the escapades of pro-athletes and their hoards of female fans, even when he tried to shield me from it.

I shrugged. "I dunno, I mean we did meet in Vegas."

"Emerson Reeves." She opened her eyes in horror. "You can't judge him for that when you did the same thing. And if you go off what you've learnt this morning, he seems really cut up about losing your number. I can't imagine Jupe ever giving a shit like that."

She had a point. Jupe had a revolving door of women, he'd just find another one.

"Yeah, maybe."

"I say just go and have fun. You deserve it. Every date you've been on the last few months you've said has been shit, but you already know you have fun with this guy. Enjoy it for what it is and if it becomes more then that's a nice little bonus, right?"

"Yes."

"And don't forget the universe."

I laughed. "No, I won't."

I watched her trying to pick up her board under one arm, wobbling slightly. "Okay, I gotta go. Love you, bye."

"Love you, bye." I hung up the phone.

Using the railing for leverage I pulled myself up and stepped through the open window into my kitchen. Opening my phone, I typed in the numbers, double checking I'd copied it correctly, then saved it. I'd text him tomorrow. He could wait one more day, although I didn't put him past his veiled threat of turning up at the studio again.

I turned the tap on, running my arm under the warm water, lathering it up with soap. The number stayed unchanged, still clear as day. I scrubbed again. And again.

Nothing.

How the fuck was I going to get this off? I couldn't walk around forever with big black numbers scrawled across my arm, like the world's stupidest tattoo. Or even the rest of the day. I was supposed to be going out tonight and it was too warm to wear long sleeves.

I typed *'How to remove Sharpie from skin'* into Google and was provided with the following options - coconut oil, olive oil, toothpaste and make up remover.

I grabbed the coconut oil from the cupboard and slathered it across my arm, rubbing as hard as I could before wiping it with kitchen towel. The only way I knew some had removed was because the kitchen towel had black ink on it, but otherwise it looked no different.

This was ridiculous.

An hour later, I'd given up. My arm almost rubbed raw from oil, toothpaste and make up remover as well as face scrub and a brush. I could still make out a faint trace of his number but hopefully to the untrained eye in a dark bar, no one would notice.

My phone buzzed with a text message.

Ashley: *Meet you in an hour at the bar on the corner in the village?*

I looked down at my arm. It would have to do.

Emerson: *Perfect, see you in an hour.*

Stripping off, I ran to the bathroom and jumped in the shower.

❧

I spotted Ashley, looking her usual perfectly put together self and made my way through the packed crowd to her, pulling out a stool and sitting down. We were in our regular haunt, a cute little bar in Greenwich Village, which never looked that exciting but was always heaving with people due to its excellent and reasonably priced cocktail selection.

She pushed a margarita toward me.

I picked it up, taking a long sip.

"Oh god, thank you." I winced at the tart lime and heavy tequila. "This is good."

"Yeah, they do the best ones in here." She sipped hers. "So, what did you do with the rest of your afternoon? You look gorgeous."

I raised an eyebrow in surprise. Scrubbing my arm had taken so long I'd had very few spare minutes to actually get ready, giving me only enough time to throw on a navy, strapless bandage dress I'd found on my washing pile and some sparkly high tops. My hair still hadn't dried properly, because I'd foregone a full blow out to put on make-up, so was currently curling in a big, bushy wave down my back.

"Thank you. Not much, just walked home and hung out. Spoke to my best friend, Mallory." I jolted forward as someone moved behind me. "Who's coming out later?"

"Jessie, Rose, Finn, Mikey and Jake. I think everyone's had a pretty full-on week and needs to blow off a little steam."

"Yeah, I get that." I could definitely do with blowing off a lot of steam. "Where are we meeting them?"

"Jake's meeting us at the bar, he has a late class, but I think the rest are coming here first." She finished her margarita signaling the waiter for another two, before eyeing me. "But they won't be here for a while, which means there's plenty of time for you to explain your behavior earlier and why your arm is now red from scrubbing off whoever's number that was."

I sighed. "Okay, but can you keep it between us?"

She nodded, her eyes open wide. Clearly expecting a big piece of gossip which, to her, this would be.

"I'm serious, Ash. I don't want anyone knowing about this until I figure it out myself."

Although I felt much better having spoken to Mallory, I was slightly apprehensive of people knowing about Drew when nothing had even happened yet, especially as Ashley had a tendency to get wildly over excited about everything. Her reaction to the boys being in the class this morning was case in point.

"Okay. Jeez." She rolled her eyes at me. "I'm not going to say anything."

I leaned forward, keeping my voice low. "Do you remember I told you that last year my friends and I went to Vegas and I hooked up with that hot guy?"

She nodded. "Yes."

"He'd wanted to see me again and I went to meet him later at the place we'd agreed, but he never showed up. I figured that he must have changed his mind and wanted to keep it as a one night stand or whatever. I'd written my number on his arm, but I never heard from him again."

Her face dropped slightly, before her eyes lit up. "Oh my god, did you see him? Did you bump into him this morning?"

I bit down on the inside of my cheek. "Yeah, kind of."

She looked at me, waiting for me to continue.

"He was in the class."

"Shut. Up." She slammed her hand on the table loudly, and so hard the drinks sloshed in the glasses. "Ohmygod, which one was he? Wait, let me guess." She held her hand up

41

to stop me from interrupting. Not that I had a chance to before she continued on her roll.

I sat back, sipping my margarita as she started listing out guys.

"The tall guy that always buys the new kit when it comes out? He's cute. Oh, the guy that's always early, he comes to your class every weekend. Always first in line."

"No, I've never seen him at the studio before. He's never been."

She drummed her fingers on the table, trying to think, her lips pursed, and face screwed up in concentration.

"Okay, I can't think of anyone new this morning. I was too pre-occupied by the Rangers being in. You need to tell me what they were like by the way. Anyway, who was it?"

She picked up her margarita and I waited until she had some and put it back down, predicting what would happen given her usual dramatic flair.

"Drew Crawley."

She leaned forward across the table until we were almost nose to nose. Her eyes wide, her brows practically in her hairline. "Say again?"

"Drew Crawley."

"Drew Crawley?"

I nodded.

She lowered her voice to a dramatic whisper. "Drew Crawley, right wing for the New York Rangers, is the guy you hooked up with in Vegas and then he was in your class this morning?"

I nodded.

She frowned. "But how did you not know who he was?"

I shrugged. "I'm from California, our family is a baseball family. I don't really follow hockey and I definitely don't know all the players. And I haven't paid much attention to it this past year."

Her mouth dropped open. "Holy fuck. Did he recognize you?"

"Yeah, he knew I was taking the class. Do you remember the two women who arrived early?"

"Yes, Freddie and Wolf. They always take Jace's class. And they always spend a fortune in the shop. I didn't know who they were married to until this morning though."

"Yeah, well, yesterday when I took Jace's class they recognized me from a picture which Drew had taken of us last year. And they brought him this morning. He was there on purpose, they all came in to see me."

"Fucking hell. This is amazing." She smacked the table again, startling the group next to us, then pointed to me. "He wrote his phone number on your arm."

Wow. It was like she was playing the Ashley edition of Crime Scene Investigation.

"Yes." I nodded, trying not to get annoyed at her volume levels.

"Okay, sorry, hang on." She downed her drink in one before taking a deep breath and outwardly composing herself. "Okay, okay. Are you okay? That must have been a shock. No wonder you look like you'd seen a ghost."

I laughed. "Yes, I'm okay, it was a bit of a shock but I'm good now."

"So what are you going to do? Did you call him already? Tell me you saved his number before you washed it off, although you can still see it if you didn't and change your mind."

I looked down, she was right. It was faint, but you could definitely make out the numbers.

"Yes, I saved his number. No, I haven't called him. I will but tomorrow, I needed to get my head together today."

"Yeah that's fair. Oooh, do you think you'll go and watch him this season? Oooh sit with the WAGs."

I rolled my eyes. "Okay Ash, let's take it one date at a time.

And considering we haven't even made plans for the first one, let's wait until that one's done, before we start planning for anything else."

She nodded. "Yep, yep. Good plan, good plan."

Over the top of her head I could see Jessie, Finn, Rose and Mikey walking through the door. I waved at them until they saw me.

I lowered my voice. "Ash, I mean it, please don't say anything."

She zipped her lip. "I won't, I promise."

Mikey got to the table first, kissing the top of my head as he sat down next to me. "Hey ladies, looking fine AF I see."

"Hey Mikey, how are you doing?" Ashley leaned across the table to kiss him as the others sat down. "Hey guys."

Finn picked up my empty glass, sniffing it. "What are you drinking?"

"Margaritas."

"Yeah, I'm going to have a beer. Do you want the same again?" He spun his finger around the table before flagging down the waiter. "Four margaritas and a beer please, man."

He returned a few minutes later with a tray full of cocktails, because we'd forgotten happy hour, and all dived in.

Mikey rubbed his hands together. "Okay ladies, what's the plan for tonight?"

"A few here and then head to the bar, we're meeting the others at nine-ish." Replied Jessie.

He knocked back his drink. "Perfect. I am going to dance my ass off tonight."

"Oh hey, did you guys hear some of the Rangers were in the studio today?" Finn reached for another beer.

I rolled my lips and watched Ashley's eyes flare.

"Oh yeah, their wives are always in. They take Jace's class." She casually sipped her drink.

I smiled a silent thanks for not giving me up.

Several happy hours later and we were all in Bar None on

the depths of the dance floor. Mikey, true to his word, was dancing his ass off to Britney while taking turns to spin Rose, Jessie and Ashley round and round. Finn had gone to the bar with Jake.

"I'm going to find the boys and see where our drinks are." I shouted to them, thumbing to the bar so they could understand me over the thumping bass.

I pushed through the crowd toward where I thought they were but couldn't see them anywhere. And I wasn't going to wait around trying to find them. I walked up the stairs to where I knew a quieter bar was, away from the dancefloor. It was practically empty up there and headed straight over to be served.

The barman tipped his head to me as I leant across the bar.

"Tequila and seltzer water with fresh lime, please."

I watched him free pour a lot of tequila over ice before he put it down on the counter in front of me.

"Let me get that."

I turned and found a man placing a twenty down, which the barman snatched up.

"Oh no, that's okay. Thank you, though."

He smiled at me, he was sort of cute, in a college grad, preppy kind of way.

"Please, I insist." He covered his hand with mine.

I wasn't sober enough to argue with a guy who wanted to buy me a drink.

"Okay, thank you."

He peered at me while he sipped his beer. "Who are you here with? Are you going to tell me your boyfriend? Please say no."

I laughed. "No, I'm with my friends, they're on the dance floor."

"Oh, thank god." He grinned, moving closer to me. "So does that mean I can get your number?"

45

"Well, well, well. Fancy seeing you here." The deep, rich timbre caressed my thighs and sent shivers racing down my spine, riding a Bullet Train with one destination - Vagina Central. "Hey Luck."

He leaned in and kissed my cheek, casually flinging a thickly muscled arm around my shoulder, staking claim and sending my heart soaring until it was jumping around like I'd left it with Mikey on the dancefloor.

Although the guy in front of me didn't seem to notice. He was full on staring open mouthed at Drew.

"Holy shit, you're Drew Crawley. Oh man, I love you."

Drew grinned. "Thanks dude, I appreciate that."

"Fuck, wait 'til the guys hear I saw you." He fumbled around in his pocket for his phone. "Hey, do you think I could get a selfie?"

"Sure, no problem."

The guy thrust his phone at me. "Actually, could you take it?"

And this was another reason why I hated hanging out with my brother and his friends in public.

I scowled at Drew trying to hide his amusement at my annoyance and snatched the phone, snapping a couple of pictures before handing it back.

He flicked through them. "Oh wow, thanks man. You're the best. I can't wait for next season. You and Cleverly are going to smash it."

"Hope so." Drew put his arm back around me. "Hey buddy, do you mind giving us a minute?"

I tried not to be insulted that the guy seemed to care more about his selfie with Drew than he did about being completely cockblocked. Or maybe he hadn't grasped it was actually happening.

Not sure which was worse.

He looked horrified. "Oh sure, sure. I'm sorry. I didn't

realize you were her boyfriend. I would never have asked for her number if I'd known."

Drew placed his hand on the guy's shoulder. "Don't worry, I totally get how smoking hot she is."

He nodded emphatically. "Yeah man, she is. Not sure which one of you is luckier."

What in the actual fuck was happening right now?

Drew laughed out loud. "Oh, that's definitely me."

As he walked off, Drew spun round to face me, leaning against the bar so cocky and casual, a shit eating grin spreading on his gorgeous face, his dimple deepening like a crevasse I could fall into if I wasn't careful. It was as though the air suddenly thinned out whenever he was around, because for the second time that day I found it hard to take a full breath.

Being five feet ten, it wasn't often I had to really look up at a guy but I had to look up at him. And look I did, right into hazel eyes sparkling in amusement and rimmed with long black lashes, lashes that would have taken me several coats of mascara to achieve. He'd had his cap on this morning and I'd forgotten how thick and luscious his hair was, with silky black curls gathered at the base of his neck.

His muscles strained against the soft cotton of his shirt, the buttons undone low enough on his collar that I could see a hint of chest hair peeking out and longed to touch it, run it between my fingers. His sleeves were folded up as far as they would go up on his heavy, roped forearms, an Audemar Piguet on his wrist. He definitely knew how to dress, looking like he'd stepped straight off a magazine cover – slick, classy and expensive.

I crossed my arms in front of me, clenching my fists, so he wouldn't see how much I was shaking with adrenaline. How much he affected me. But if he noticed, I'd just blame the margaritas.

Good plan, Em.

I took a deep breath only for my nostrils to be assaulted by his sexy, earthy man scent, like vetiver and sandalwood, sending my nerves further into overdrive and making me lightheaded. The memory of it tangible and one I'd not smelt since, reminding me of three am kisses and orgasms and laughing so hard my sides hurt. All unique to him.

"You're not my boyfriend."

He took a sip from his glass, his eyes never leaving mine. "Yet."

I frowned. "What?"

"I'm not your boyfriend, yet." He emphasized. "But at this point, it's just a formality."

I blinked at him as I processed what was happening. How did he keep sneaking up on me?

"What are you doing here, are you following me?"

He held his hands up, grinning. "No, I swear it's coincidental. But twice in one day? The universe clearly wants us to be together."

The tension rolled off me and I laughed at him. He sounded just like Mallory, although way sexier and more adorable. And his happiness was infectious.

"Oh yeah?"

"Yeah." His grin got wider.

"Well, I was talking to that guy."

He lifted his eyebrow at me. "Oh, Sweetheart. No, you weren't, he was talking at you. You definitely weren't interested."

I mean, I wasn't. But I also had no plans to make this easy for him either.

I pursed my lips. "You don't know that."

He scoffed. "Luck, have you forgotten? I know what you look like when you're interested."

My breath hitched as he moved closer to me, taking the ends of my hair between his fingers, twisting it around. His eyes slowly trailed the length of my body. And then I watched him lick his lips, my eyes following his pink tongue as it ran along his teeth.

Flashbacks of him naked, standing tall in front of me, flew through my head and a heartbeat awakened between my legs. One that only he'd be able to stir.

Oh god, what did I look like right now? Because I was seconds away from throwing myself at him.

His expression softened as he cupped my face in one of his huge hands, rubbing his thumb along my cheek. I could feel the scratch of his callouses against my skin.

"You are so fucking beautiful. I've thought about this every day for a year, thought about what I would do if I ever found you again."

I couldn't breathe. My heart was pounding everywhere, I could feel it from the tips of my toes to the top of my head.

"And what did you decide?" My voice was barely a whisper, heavy with anticipation.

He pulled me away from the bar, to a quieter corner, pushing me up against the wall. His eyes locked into mine, the hazel blazing with fiery lust, shooting flames which climbed the length of my body. His hands moved to the back of my head, fingers scraping up through my hair and he pulled me as close as he could get me without actually touching, breathing in the air I expelled, taking his time, until my body was shaking, almost delirious with need.

"That I've waited so fucking long and I can't wait any longer."

The air shifted and like the snap of a magnet his mouth bolted onto mine, taking me hostage. His tongue ran along the seam of my lips until I opened up and we collided together, reacquainting after a year apart.

The flavor of oranges and whiskey danced on my tongue as he stroked against me, his hunger deepening, matching mine, want coursing through us as though it was the last kiss there would ever be. Hot and heavy, dripping in desperation, we completely lost ourselves in each other. The loud, thumping music drowned out by the beating of our hearts.

My fingers ran the length of his hair, gripping onto the silky curls at the base of his neck. He let out a deep groan and the ripple effect sent fire curling around my spine like a corkscrew. He surrounded me further, pushing me into the wall with his body, creating a vacuum between us and the outside world. Because that's what it was. Us and everyone else.

His cock was rock hard, pressing into my groin and with every slow, rhythmic movement of his tongue my hunger increased to combustible levels, gasoline replacing the blood in my veins, ready to go up in flames at the drop of a match. The friction was shooting sparks to my clit and sending deep pulses through my pussy, but it wasn't enough. It wouldn't be enough unless I could push him down and straddle him, ride him for hours until our bodies were spent and sweaty.

One hand still firmly on the back of my head, the other moved down until it rested on the top of my ass, his fingers kneading into my flesh, before his whole hand scooped a cheek squeezing it hard as he groaned deeper. He gently fisted my hair, pulling my head back, taking my lower lip with him as he moved, making me moan in protest as he let go.

His eyes were still blazing and trained on my mouth. "Fuck. That was better than I could have ever imagined."

I didn't disagree. I was having a hard time staying upright, my legs had practically given way. He brushed my hair away from my face as I tried to catch my breath.

"Luck, we need to get out of here. I want to talk to you in private. Where are your friends? Do you need to stay, because I'll wait? But otherwise please can we leave? Can you come with me? Please?"

I could barely form a coherent thought, let alone remember

who I'd arrived here with. But I couldn't have refused him anything, even if his nervousness and pleading wasn't pulling at my heartstrings. I walked to the balcony which overlooked the dance floor. I had no idea how long I'd been up here, but time seemed to stand still when I was with him. I searched around until I saw what I was looking for, Jake and Finn were back with the rest of the group, still jumping away.

They wouldn't miss me.

I took my phone and shot them a group text to let them know I was tired and heading home. Then a separate one to Ashley.

I looked up at him, his expression serious and guarded, watching for my decision.

"Okay, we can go."

He moved his hands around the back of my head, pressing his lips to mine once more, mumbling against them. "Thank you."

He took his phone out and dialed a number. "We're coming out in two minutes."

I didn't have time to think about it as he wrapped my hand in his and lead me off, but instead of going toward the front where I'd walked in, he guided me down a set of back stairs pushing open a fire door at the bottom.

A black SUV was waiting as we stepped outside into an alley. He opened the back door for me and I jumped in before he closed it behind me and ran around to get in the other side.

"Okay Luck, what's your address?"

"Greene Street, by NYU."

He leant forward to the driver. "Ralphie, you got that?"

"Yes, sir." He nodded and drove to the end of the alley, pulling out into the road.

Drew turned his massive body toward mine, holding my hand, his eyes tracing every inch of my face, memorizing it.

He lifted my hand and kissed the palm, holding it against his cheek.

"Lucky Charm, you know I told you that for the past year I'd thought about what I'd do if I ever saw you again?"

I bit my bottom lip, nervously. "Yes."

He pulled it free with his thumb, running the pad along it. "I meant what I said earlier. I want to do it properly. I want to take you on a date."

I looked at him, his face earnest, waiting for my reaction. The confidence that exuded from his every pore became more of an undertone and I wondered if this was as nerve wracking for him as it was to me.

"Okay. What does that mean?"

He rubbed my arm where he'd written his number. "It means I'm going to drop you at yours and then go back to mine."

I blinked, more than once, shifting back a little. I absolutely was not expecting him to say that. I was so desperate to feel him inside me again, experience the level of euphoria only he'd been able to provide right up to this second in my life. Disappointment collided with the nerves in my belly, swirling around in a vortex, making me feel much more sober than I had any right to considering how much I'd been drinking.

I'd always been shit at hiding my emotions and this time was no different, because he cupped my cheek leaning in, brushing my lips with utmost tenderness before letting out a deep sigh.

"Luck, please give me a chance to take you on a proper date. Will you do that?"

His hazel eyes searched mine, imploring me.

It was hard to think with him so close, let alone deny him. But who was I kidding? I wanted to see him again as badly as I needed to breathe.

"Yes."

"Did you save my number before you rubbed it off?" He lifted my arm to me.

I raised my eyebrow. "It's not rubbed off, it won't come out. It took me an hour just to get it like this."

He smirked. "Yeah, Sharpies don't smudge."

"I'll remember that next time I'm hooking up with a random man in Vegas and can only find a regular pen." I shot back.

His eyes narrowed with an ill-concealed jealousy that made my heart flutter. "Show me where you saved my number."

I frowned. "No."

His face fell, his features painted in a vulnerability I'd never have expected from him, a professional athlete and sex god. "Please Luck, show me. I need to know you didn't just try and wipe it off."

I reached into my purse, unlocking my phone before handing it to him. "Here."

He took it and dialed his number, bringing up where I'd saved him in my contacts. His phone buzzed in his hand, my number flashing across the screen, which he saved. I could see him fiddling around with the messages as I held my hand out for him to give my phone back to me.

He placed it in my palm before snatching it back. "What's VSG?"

Fuck.

I'd forgotten that's what I'd saved him under.

My eyes flared, a flush scorching across my cheeks, I didn't need a mirror to know I was bright pink. Thank god the car was dark so he couldn't see the extent.

"What is it? Tell me."

With anyone else I might have put up more of a fight, but he seemed to have stripped me of any inhibitions, just like he did a year ago. I closed my eyes taking a deep breath, preparing myself for the mortification I was about to subject myself to, partially re-opening one to find him looking at me, expectantly.

"Luck?"

"Vegas Sex God." I mumbled as an ambulance passed, sirens blaring.

His face scrunched up as he tried to figure out what I'd said. "What?"

"Vegas Sex God." I enunciated loudly.

For a split second his eyes sparkled in amusement, then in a blink filled with so much heat they lasered straight into mine, pooling molten lava deep in the pits of my belly. The throb intensified between my legs and a fresh flood of wetness soaked my panties.

How was it possible to have this much chemistry with one person? Especially when you were only seeing them for the second time in a year.

He groaned loudly, shifting his crotch. At least I wasn't the only one uncomfortable.

"Oh fuck, you're going to be the death of me, but we're doing this properly. I want to date." He sounded like he was trying to convince himself, as if he said it out loud then it would become true.

"Drew, we're on Greene Street." Called his driver.

I looked out of the window. "It's just up here on the left."

The car pulled over.

"Come on, I'm walking you to the door."

I put my hand on his thigh. "You don't have to."

The look he gave me told me I'd have an easier time convincing him to take me back to the club, so I could continue my conversation with the college boy.

"Are you kidding? And miss out on the opportunity for a goodbye kiss? No dice, Luck."

He jumped out and rounded the back, opening the passenger door for me, taking my hand so I could hop out.

He leaned back into the car. "Ralph, just give me five."

Lacing our fingers together, we walked to the door. I turned to face him as we reached the top step.

His eyebrow raised as he waited. "Put the key in the lock, Luck. I'm taking you to your apartment door."

I did, and we walked through in silence, broken only by the sound of our heavy breathing. We got into the elevator standing on opposite sides, the air thick and heavy like the calm before a lightning storm. His eyes never left mine. Railings ran around the edges and his hands were gripping them so tightly his knuckles had turned white.

As the bell pinged, he dragged me out. "Which door?"

I pointed to the end of the hall. "6B"

He pushed me against the wall right as we reached it, his massive body pressing into me once more and I could feel every thick, solid inch of him. His mouth crashed down, his perfect pillowy lips engulfing me. His tongue, hot and soft and wet, stroked against mine while his hand found the back of my head. He pushed himself further into my mouth with unbridled need, greedy and desperate, like he was swallowing me whole and couldn't get close enough.

My entire body was shaking, burst of pure lust shooting out of my throbbing clit and he swallowed a low moan which had barreled up from the depths of my throat. I started rocking against him, desperate for the friction.

He tilted my head, moving his lips along my jaw without ever breaking contact. Nibbling at the pulse point under my ear, shockwaves reverberated around my body. His tongue moved along my collarbone, soaking my panties further and tightening my nipples, before he licked long and flat along the column of my neck, moving back up to quickly press his lips to mine a final time.

My skin was blazing so hot from his touch I could set the fire alarms off.

"I need to go." His already deep voice was thick and sticky like molasses, coating my skin.

He leant in and kissed me on the cheek then turned and walked away, giving me a backward glance, winking as he stepped on the elevator.

My hands were shaking as I reached for the lock, taking four tries before I managed to slot the key in. My phone buzzed as I shut the door behind me.

VSG: *I'm so happy I found you. Sleep tight, Lucky Charm. I'll call you tomorrow X*

I walked through and flopped onto my bed, my heart still pounding in my chest and nothing could hold back my smile as I thought about everything that had happened that day.

Glancing at his message again, I realized my screen looked different.

Opening it up, I now knew what he'd been doing when I'd watched him fiddling with my phone. Staring back at me was the photo he'd taken in Vegas, the memory of us waiting for the elevator smacking me hard. He'd practically dragged me away with him back to his suite, making me laugh until I cried and I was looking up at his impossibly beautiful face with a level of happiness I hadn't seen in myself for a really long time.

I ran my finger across his dimple.

That dimple was going to get me in trouble.

No doubt about it.

5

DREW

What the fuck was that noise?

I was in the country, right? I definitely didn't stay in the city?

I felt around the bed to see if I could tell, not wanting to open my eyes to figure it out. It was too early.

The beeping got louder and I threw a pillow over my ears trying to block it. Which didn't work.

I opened my eyes. Yep, I was in the country.

And it was seven fucking am.

On a Monday.

This should be illegal.

I groaned, flinging back the covers, and followed the noise to the windows which overlooked the driveway and the front of my house, where I found Freddie directing a dozen workmen and two massive flatbed trucks filled with trees, reversing toward the front door. I wish I could say this was the weirdest thing I'd ever seen her doing, but that would be a lie.

I quickly brushed my teeth and took a piss before grabbing some shorts and a hoodie, and ran downstairs.

"Fred?" I was still rubbing my eyes when I opened the door.

She turned around, confused. "Hey, what are you doing here? I thought you were in the city." She took in my face. "Sorry, did I wake you up?"

I nodded. "Yeah, but it's okay." I looked around, knowing it was better to not ask. "How long are you going to be?"

"Give me five minutes and I'll be there, let me sort these guys out."

"Okay." I walked back in, straight into the kitchen.

The sun was shining through the glass paneling which stretched across the back of the kitchen and I flipped the switch making them glide open on their tracks, letting the outdoors in.

I scratched my beard, breathing in the fresh air, walking out to the backyard across the patio and onto the paving stones which ran down the length of the garden. The sky was cloudless, the early morning sun drying the final drops of dew off the newly laid grass. In the distance I could see the water in the pool sparkling blue. It was going to be a beautiful day and I suddenly had a new appreciation of the space Freddie helped me create.

I'd bought this house before I'd met Lucky, but renovated it after. I remember turning up every day, trying to push away the loneliness that would creep in if I let it, wondering if this would ever be a house I'd share with someone, build a life with, grow a family with, occasionally daring to imagine I'd share it with her.

If I'd ever see her again.

Since Freddie had found her three days ago, the ache had disappeared in my chest. Since I'd kissed her two nights ago, I'd struggled to contain the overwhelming excitement which consumed me every time I thought about her.

Something I'd tried to limit to once every two minutes.

The crippling nerves I'd had about seeing her again,

worrying whether she'd remember me, worrying whether she wouldn't be how I'd remembered her, had been eviscerated to fuck the second she'd looked at me. Her big turquoise eyes shining, the golden flecks flashing with fire, flaming arrows shooting straight to my heart.

I was having to consciously stop myself from calling her just to hear her voice. Trying to hold onto a shred on self-control.

But I wanted her here. I wanted her with me.

More than I'd ever wanted anything else.

After I'd left her outside her apartment I'd gone home and straight into a freezing cold shower where I'd stayed for nearly an hour. The ache which had made camp in my chest was now firmly in my balls and I was surprised my dick wasn't severely chafed from the amount I'd jerked off in the last thirty-six hours.

But now I'd tasted her again I knew without a doubt I was never going to taste anything better.

Just like I knew I wanted to do this properly.

I hadn't had sex for eleven months, the longest I'd gone since I'd lost my virginity. Fuck, it was the longest I'd gone after a week. So, I could wait a bit longer if Lucky was my prize at the end of it, because I was going to win her.

I was going to make her mine.

I looked at the time on my phone. Seven twenty. She would have just finished her first class. Before I could stop myself, I typed a message and hit send.

Drew: *Good morning, Lucky Charm. How was class today? X*

I put it in my pocket so I didn't stare at the screen like a loser waiting for her reply. It was bad enough I wanted to.

Because that's who I was now.

I spun as I heard a noise, to see Freddie carrying a large box through the archway into the kitchen and sprinted back inside to take it from her, placing it on the kitchen table.

"Shit, don't tell Coop I let you carry this." Although it was much lighter than it looked, it was still big enough to topple her very small stature.

She rolled her eyes. "Cooper Marks needs to chill the fuck out. Or I will end up committing murder before this baby arrives."

I rubbed her slightly swollen belly, bending down to her height, whispering. "I'd stay in there for as long as you can, baby. It's safer."

"Yeah, yeah." She walked around the counter and pulled out the griddle. "Can you grab the buttermilk and flour?"

"Yeah."

I walked into the pantry, taking the flour off the shelf and buttermilk from the fridge, as well as juice and almond milk because I'd only have to make another trip when she remembered she wanted it. Since I'd moved in I kept this place well stocked, because Freddie was always hungry. Ordering grown workmen around built quite the appetite.

I placed it all on the counter and she started mixing up the best pancakes in existence. A recipe from Cooper's grandfather that had slowly been passed around our group.

I flipped the coffee machine on. "Are you having a coffee today?"

"Yes please, although you'd better make it a decaf or I won't hear the end of it." She grumbled, but only because she missed caffeine more than was normal for a person and Cooper had rationed her.

"So, what's going on outside?"

"They're the trees which are going to line the top of the driveway and then two giant bays for the front door."

I wasn't entirely sure what a giant bay was.

"Oh."

"Don't worry, it'll look good."

I believed her. Most of the time I just went along with whatever she said, trusting her to know what was best. I put the coffees on the counter, taking a seat on a stool to watch her cook. I'd learnt at the beginning of this renovation process that it was pointless putting up a fight because she just did what she wanted, including breakfast.

She ladled the batter onto the griddle, hissing as it hit. I watched them bubble up before she flipped them. "Anyway, how are you? Did you hear from Emerson?"

I'd forgotten no one knew I'd seen her except Felix, and that was because he'd been with me at the club.

After seeing her, I'd left the studio and walked into a wall of Rangers' fans who'd been waiting outside. The boys were already signing autographs and the requests for selfies kept us there for longer after I'd arrived. I'd done everything on autopilot – smile, sign, smile, sign – before the boys pulled me away. The rest of the day was spent in a manic swirl of anxiety, my heart barely able to take the pressure. One minute I was riding on the crest of the wave, high off seeing her, the next I'd crashed into the depths of the ocean, my phone screen still blank.

For hours I teetered of the edge of puking.

No one told me this is what it would feel like to put your heart on the line.

After I'd checked my phone for the seventeen thousandth time, Felix had dragged me to a new club he'd been banging on about since it opened at the beginning of the summer. It was the first time I'd properly been out in months.

I was about to go home then there she was.

And my heart fucking stopped.

She was walking up the stairs, like a heavenly mirage of golden legs, fiery hair and eyes so blue I wanted to dive right in. She'd been wearing a dress that looked like it had been made for her body. Hugging every mouth-watering inch of her, it left little to the imagination, accentuating every curve, and pushing up her tits in a way that caused my dick to pay immediate attention.

I'd been so desperate to see her, I'd rubbed my eyes, convinced I was dreaming.

I froze on the spot, watching her, until that fucking frat boy thought he was worthy enough to be in her presence, which he wasn't, and then I'd taken off quicker than Coop at the puck drop.

"Yeah. I saw her on Saturday night. I went out and she was in the club I was in."

Her eyebrows shot up in surprise. "No way, seriously? She's been here nine months and then twice in one day?"

I took a deep breath. "Don't. It still makes me rage. But I'm choosing to believe the universe is now ready for us to be together."

I repeated back the words she'd drilled into me for the past year, the only thing that provided me with a shred of hope. And it looked like she was right.

She grinned at me in an *'I told you so'* way, while opening the cupboard to remove plates, laying them on the counter. "So, what happened?"

I sipped my coffee, flashbacks of being pressed against her smoking body flickering through my brain. "We made out like horny teenagers. Then I took her home and walked her to the door. And spent the rest of the night in a cold shower."

"Oh babe." She cackled, stacking the pancakes. "How was the making out? God, there's nothing better than good snog."

I realized we were missing vital ingredients and ran to the pantry to get the maple syrup, as well as berries and yoghurt, lining it along the counter for her to take while I grabbed the cutlery from the drawer. I sat back down, pulling my plate over and spooned everything on top of my pancakes before drowning them in syrup.

I fucking loved breakfast.

As I forked a massive mouthful, I looked up to find Freddie staring. "What?"

62

"How was it?"

I grinned. "Amazing. Off the charts hot."

Her grin mirrored mine. "Bet it was hard to leave her at the end of the night."

I picked up my coffee. "Hardest thing I've ever done."

I wasn't kidding.

"She's the one, Fred. She's it."

Saying it out loud made it sound so right.

Her eyes filled with tears. Fuck, I wasn't emotionally prepared to see her crying again this early in the day. I always forgot how quickly they started.

"Fredster?"

"No, no. It's fine." She sniffed, pushing back on the stool and rubbed her belly. "When are you going to see her again then?"

We'd spent most of yesterday texting. Even though it was mostly light-hearted nonsense between stupid memes, funny gifs and her grumbling that my number was still on her arm, it confirmed what I already knew.

That she was special.

And I didn't want to wait. I couldn't wait.

I needed to get to know her properly. We needed to get to know each other.

Starting ASAP.

"Tomorrow."

"What are you going to do?"

I poured out two glasses of fresh orange juice, passing one to her. "I've not decided yet."

"What about your list?" She raised her eyebrow, her lip quivering slightly in amusement.

I groaned.

My list.

When I first began to realize that Lucky was different to anyone else I'd met, I'd started thinking about all the things I'd like to do if we were together and mentally stored them up. Jasper and Wolfie hadn't long been married, Cooper and Freddie were glued together, and all their love had started infiltrating our bachelor ways. In the misery I'd felt, I'd watched how happy they were.

I'd told Freddie about it one night when we'd all been out drinking, we were both wasted but she'd conveniently remembered and hadn't let me forget. If that wasn't bad enough, she also renamed it 'Drew and Lucky's list of Perfect Dates'. It wasn't all big hearts and flowers, it was smaller things that I'd never done with a woman before, like brunch or reading the papers in bed together or taking her to my favorite places.

And I'd made her promise not to breathe a word of it because even saying it in my head sounded lame as fuck.

"Yeah, I still have it. But I don't know if I need to do something better." I wasn't sure my list was going to win me any points. "Fred, how many dates do I need to take her on until we can have sex?"

She snorted loudly, shaking her head.

I threw my hands in the air, frustrated. "What? I've never dated before and I don't want to fuck it up."

She got up to make another coffee. "I'm not the best person to ask. Coop and I weren't exactly dating but you know Jas and Wolf didn't have sex for three and half months. Actually, they didn't even kiss."

I'd forgotten that. Forgotten what a grumpy fuck Jasper had been.

"Fuck that, I'm not waiting that long. That's insane. My balls will fall off."

After Saturday I wasn't sure I'd make it to the end of the week.

"Yeah, but it worked for them. They got to know each other properly and fell in love. If they'd had sex sooner, they'd have both freaked out." She tilted her head, her expression softening. "Just do what feels right. There's no rule. But I will say something, I know people think sex is easy, and it is. But off the charts, amazing hot sex with someone you love, that shit only comes along once."

"Yeah." I nodded.

"And you've already had that, you know you have the chemistry, right?"

"Yeah."

"And she feels the same?"

A flashback of her shaking in my arms two nights ago as I sucked on her bottom lip, was branded on my brain for life.

"Yeah, I'm pretty sure she feels the same."

"Then you have nothing to lose." Her little hand covered mine. "Drew, you're the sweetest guy I know. Don't worry about fucking up. You've got this."

There was something to be said for girl talk.

"Thanks Fredster, I hope so. Thank you for helping me so much. And for listening to me."

"I just want to see you happy again." She handed me a fresh coffee. "Come on, let me show you the trees, before you head to practice."

I threw the empty plates into the sink and followed her outside.

❉

I tightened my laces, stood up and grabbed my pads, sliding them over my head and walked out of the locker room, pulling on my jersey. The corridor was as empty as the lockers had been. As I'd woken up way earlier than I generally liked to during the off season, I'd arrived at the rink way earlier than I generally needed to and the usual noise levels of the teams, coaching and management staff milling around were eerily low.

The door to the Strength and Conditioning suites opened and out walked Felix.

"Hey man, what're you doing here so early?"

"Physio. My hamstring has been tight and I don't want to fuck it up before the season starts." He scanned me up and down. "What are you doing here?"

"Freddie woke me up with a delivery."

His t-shirt lifted up as he scratched his stomach. "Have you eaten?"

"Yeah."

"Give me ten and I'll meet you on the ice."

"Cool."

He jogged off to the locker room and I headed to the arena, the smell of ice getting stronger with every step. I grabbed a bag of pucks, stepping out onto the rink. I loved being here, especially when I was the first out, first one to experience the virgin ice of the day after it had been cleaned the night before, first one to take solace in the calm before the storm.

I skated a couple of laps to warm up, then opened up the bag, dumping the pucks out, kicking them like soccer balls so they spread about. I chased them, sprinting around each one before knocking them into goal. By the time Felix turned up I'd scored with nearly all of them.

He didn't say anything as he skated down to gather some pucks from where they'd landed in the crease. He flicked one up, catching it with the end of his stick and started bouncing it on the blade. I began skating slowly down one side, waiting for what I knew was about to happen. It was a game we liked to play, we'd see how far we could throw the puck and catch it, all while speeding up. First one to drop had to do a hundred push-ups on the ice.

He tossed the puck into the air, hurtling across the rink. It was going way wide and I sped forward, just catching it with the end of my stick. I heard Felix chuckle from his side of the rink.

"Dick."

"Sure you're head's in it, Crawley?"

"My head's fine." I flung it back at him as he hit the corner and we crossed each other at the crease, skating down the opposite side.

We were getting faster, the puck still moving back and forth between us. Felix barely catching the last one I flung his way.

"Come on, you gotta do better than that." He tossed it back over, flinging it up so high that there was no way I was going to get it. It caught the end of my blade and bounced onto the ice. "That'll be a benny, I do believe."

I shook my head, laughing and started my push-ups, Felix skating over to make sure I did them all. I was so pumped up from the past thirty-six hours that I finished them in record time.

I sat back on my haunches, grinning up at him.

"Take it you didn't get laid then." His head fell back as he laughed at his own joke.

I jumped up on my skates. "Fuck off. I've not got laid in eleven months, I can wait a bit longer."

He rubbed his head, hard. "Shit, I think my balls would fall off if I went without for that long. I don't know how you've done it." He looked at me intently. "Seriously, I admire you, Dude. I know the last year hasn't been easy."

"Thanks. But it's not that admirable, I just couldn't picture anyone else but her, I didn't want to be with anyone else but her."

We skated over to the pucks and started gathering them up before the morning drills. Coach would be taking the rookies through their paces.

"Good job you found her then, isn't it?"

Truer words had never been spoken.

"Yeah." I couldn't keep the smile from sneaking up.

"When are we going back to spinning? Don't tell Wolf,

67

but it was fucking hard. I'm sure that's why my hamstrings were sore."

I knew I'd seen him hobbling. Served him right.

My head fell back, laughing hard. "You're such a pussy. You're not wrong though."

He knocked the pucks over to where the bag was still on the boards. "So, what's the plan? And when am I going to meet her properly?"

"I'm going to see her tomorrow, I'm not waiting around for this. Been waiting too fucking long as it is." I repeated what I'd told Freddie.

"What are you two ladies gassing about?

We turned to see Huck standing by the boards.

Felix slapped me on the back. "Drew's recently unbroken heart."

"Yeah? How does that feel?"

"Fucking fantastic." I sent some pucks to his feet. "Make yourself useful and put these in the bag."

"I would, but I'm telling you, my fucking hamstrings after that spinning class. They're on fire. I could not fucking move yesterday without them burning."

"Man, I feel you. I just came from physio."

I looked between the two of them, whining like little kids. "Not just for girls then?"

"Fuck no, I take that back."

"Good, because we'll be returning."

6

DREW

F *uck me.*

　　She picked up on the third ring, her face filling the screen. Even though it had barely been a day since I'd seen her, I was still momentarily stunned that she was really real.

Everything I'd been dreaming about finally within my grasp.

"Hey." She smiled at me, a scattering of freckles spreading wide across her face. She was like a rainbow after a storm, warmth radiating out of her, hitting me square in the chest.

"Hey yourself."

"What's up?"

I sat back on my sofa, propping my phone up and settling in so I could stare at her face as long as possible. "Nothing, just wanted to see how your class went, how your day was, see your face and hear your voice. In no particular order."

She laughed. "Oh, is that all?"

"Yep, that's all."

Her smile grew, making her eyes sparkle. "Class was good."

"Even at six am on a Monday? Sounds like punishment to me."

Her eyebrows raised up. "You say that but there's always a wait list. People love a bit of competition. And don't try to tell me you're not familiar with the early morning workout."

"Yeah, but that's my job, which I get paid for. I don't voluntarily get up to exercise before the sun is up if I don't have to."

"You should try it one day."

I snorted. "Sweetheart, the only way I'm exercising voluntarily with you at that time is if you're next to me and naked."

Her cheeks turned pink, but not before she licked her lips. Fuck, she was so fucking sexy. At this rate, I was definitely not going to last a week.

I wanted her too badly.

"Okay, Luck. Are you working tomorrow?"

She shook her head. "No, I have tomorrow off."

My eyes widened. "You're free all day? I can have the whole day with you?"

I don't think it would have been possible for me to sound any more excited.

She tapped her fingers to her lower lip as she thought. "How about the afternoon? I've got a couple of things to do in the morning and I'm going to go for a run."

"Just as long as we're clear the afternoon starts at twelve, Luck."

"Is that about the time you get out of bed?" Her eyes flashed in amusement.

I clasped my hands to my heart. "Oooh, you wound me."

"Maybe you should get an early night, just so you're ready for the morning."

I grinned wide, excitement going apeshit deep in my belly. "Don't you worry about me, Lucky Charm. I'll be ready."

"Ralphie, can you just pull up outside her apartment?"

It was eight am and I'd taken a leaf out of Jasper's stalking book. I hoped I hadn't already missed her going out, but I figured that given she usually had to wake up at the crack of dawn she'd probably sleep a bit later on her days off.

I hoped anyway.

Prayed even.

I got out of the car and waited, leaning against the door, watching. Last night, I'd decided that I was going running with her and our date was starting early. And it had nothing to do with wanting to see her in skin-tight lycra, especially after the little number she had on in her class the other day, hugging her body to perfection, showing off her delicious curves and round, peachy ass.

Nothing at all.

I was just drifting off into another fantasy about her spectacular tits, when the door opened and out she walked. My mouth dried up, I was not going to be able to run comfortably with my dick in the state it was right now.

Rock hard.

Thank fuck I had skins on under my shorts.

She was wearing dark red pants which made her legs look seven feet long, and were cut across her belly, showing off toned abs I wanted to run my tongue along. A matching sports bra was both squashing her breasts down and pushing them up all at the same time, in way that made me desperate to free them and kiss them until they were better.

Her long, fiery auburn hair was scraped back from her face, her eyes shielded from the glare of the sun by aviators, headphones in, and she was fiddling with her phone as she moved down the steps.

She was heartstopping.

I stood there waiting for her to look up at me, a slow grin spreading across her face as she did, and I gave myself a

71

secret high five knowing I'd done a good thing and not scared her off too early in our relationship.

Because that's what this was.

She removed one of her headphones, walked over and stopped in front of me, pulling her glasses down with her finger, the golden flecks making her eyes twinkle.

"This isn't twelve."

I twisted my cap backwards. "No, I changed the plans up. I wanted to prove to you I could get up and exercise voluntarily."

"It's not six am though."

"It's eight thirty. I'll work up to six."

She looked me up and down, taking in my attire, her eyebrow raised.

"Does this mean you're coming for a run with me? I know you're a professional athlete and all, but I'm not slowing down for you. You need to keep pace."

My dick twitched at her confidence.

I pushed off the car. "Don't worry about me Sweetheart, I'll keep pace. But I'll warn you now, when I drop back it's only so I can stare at your ass."

She burst out laughing in a way so perfect I couldn't resist pulling her into me, wrapping my arms around her waist, running my hands up her back to cup her neck. Our lips touched and I tasted berries as my tongue slid against hers, caressing her mouth, pulling her in tighter.

This was already the best run I'd ever been on.

She took her lips back. "Okay Romeo, let's go."

I stole one more kiss before I released my grip. "Okay, now as you have your headphones in does that mean we're listening to music?"

"I'm going to be listening to music. You can do what you want."

Such a fucking wise ass.

I turned to Ralph so she wouldn't see me grinning. "Hey man, you can take off. I'll call you when I need you later."

"Okay Drew, I'll wait to hear from you." He drove off.

I put my phone in my pocket, taking out my own pair of aviators, sliding them on. "Right, Emerson Reeves, lead the way."

She set off at a pace that made me thankful I'd kept up my training regime during the off season. I was at peak physical fitness but being two hundred and thirty pounds, I wasn't exactly built to run high speeds for long distances. It was a good job I warned her I'd be falling behind to look at her ass, because that's exactly where I was.

Not that I minded in any way, it was a fucking fine ass and was helping me concentrate on not falling behind further, which was a challenge in itself. Her long legs were powering her forward, eating up the sidewalk with ease as her ponytail swished like a metronome with each stride.

We reached the Financial District heading toward Battery Park before she slowed down, turning around to see where I was, running backwards.

She took her headphones out. "You okay back there?"

"I'm good thanks, I have a great view."

She laughed, moving forwards again, running a little further before stopping at the spot overlooking Governor's Island and the Statue of Liberty. The boats had already started ferrying tourists over for the day. I watched as she started stretching out of habit to stop her limbs from seizing, lifting her leg against the railings to keep her hamstrings loose.

I groaned internally. "Luck, you can't stretch like that in front of me in public. You'll get us arrested."

She turned, confused. "What? How?"

"Because I won't be able to control myself."

She slowly placed her leg back down, then propped herself against the rails, leaning back. "Better?"

I walked over to her. "Much."

I removed my sunglasses, sweat was running down my face and I lifted my shirt to wipe it off. As I dropped it, I could see her gaze through her aviators locked on my abs.

Fuck me.

"Eyes up here, Sweetheart." They shot up and I moved closer pinning her into the railings. "You keep looking at me like that and we won't make it through this date."

Her eyes creased in amusement. "This is a date?"

"Sure is. Our first one. The second starts this afternoon. Twelve on the dot."

As I grinned at her she reached out and pushed her finger into my cheek.

"What are you doing?"

"I just wanted to poke your dimple." She giggled.

My dick jerked in the confines of my shorts.

I leaned in, dropping my voice. "I'll poke your dimple."

Her breath hitched.

I pulled her glasses off her nose and put them next to mine on the collar of my shirt. Her skin was flushed pink from the run, sweat was dripping down the sides of her face to the column of her neck, rolling between her breasts which were still heaving slightly. Although I had an inkling it was more to do with our proximity to each other than the run we'd been on.

Because I was the same.

Her eyes dropped to my lips. Her pupils dilated turning the turquoise to darker blue, the flecks sparkling gold with lust.

I was not against making out in public.

I dipped down slowly, catching her mouth with mine and ran my tongue along the soft outline of her full, pouty lips. She moaned under me, opening up wide and I stroked against her. She returned it ten-fold as we savored the flavor of each other in a way that was bordering on indecent for nine thirty on a Tuesday morning. I cupped her face, not wanting it to ever end but pulling back before I got carried away. A pink flush crept up her cheeks, making her freckles stand out even more and I wondered how long it would take me to count them all.

Her lips were swollen and I'd never seen anyone so fucking beautiful. I ran my thumb back and forth along her jaw line. I groaned, feeling it deep in my ever-tightening balls, so tight they were aching.

"I know I said I wanted to do this properly but I'm not sure I'll make it past date two at this rate."

She put her arms around my neck, her elbows resting on my shoulders. "You really want to date properly?"

I leant back, looking at her face, at her expression filled with apprehension. I brushed my fingers over her cheek. "Yes. I do. I told you I did."

She sighed. "I know, but we were pretty drunk the other night."

"I wasn't."

She frowned.

"I wasn't." I protested. "The only drink I had was the one you saw me with at the bar when that douche frat boy was trying to hit on you."

Her eyes widened. "So, you really meant it?"

The confidence I'd only ever seen her wearing, slipped slightly.

"Luck, what's this about?"

She shook her head, dropping it. "Nothing."

I gently tipped her chin back up. I wanted her to look in my eyes and see the sincerity. To believe every word I was saying to her. Because if she looked hard enough, she'd see her name carved into my soul.

"Emerson, tell me. We need to be honest with each other."

She sighed. "It's just that over this last year, you were this enigma to me. I never thought or expected to see you again.

75

And now you're here and it's still hard to believe that it's real." A soft smile curled on her lip. "But we have this insane chemistry and ever since Saturday all I want to do is jump you, like I have no self-control whatsoever. And it's over-whelming."

I smirked. "I'm still not sure what the problem is."

She tried to look away but I wouldn't let her, tipping her eyes back up to meet mine. "Did you really think of me a lot? This isn't just another hook up? You're a professional athlete, I know how that works."

I stared at her, blinking, unsure what to say. I reached out and began twisting the end of her ponytail in my fingers, choosing my words carefully, not wanting to scare her away, but needing her to understand.

"Sweetheart, I thought about you every day."

I studied her reaction, her pupils flaring in surprise, her lips parting slightly for a sharp inhale.

"Really?"

"I haven't even looked at another woman in eleven months. I've been slowly going crazy."

"What about the first month?"

I winced. But now was not the time for lying. If this was going anywhere it had to be truth or nothing.

"I'll be honest, I did briefly try and fuck you out of my head." Her face dropped slightly, making my heart beat faster. "But it didn't work. You're right, we have this insane chemistry. I've never felt it before or since. Finding you again has been all I've wished for, so yes I want to date you, I defi-nitely want to jump you, but I also want to do all the bits in between. I want to know everything about you."

Her freckles danced across her nose and cheeks from her smile as she leaned in to kiss me, but I pulled back before she could. I needed to know this wasn't one sided.

"What about you?"

"What about me?"

"Is this just a hook up for you?"

Like me, she waited to answer, gathering her thoughts. "I've thought about you so much over the past year and if the last two days is anything to go by I don't think I'll get you out of my head any time soon." She stared up at me through thick, black lashes. "No, it's not just a hook up. I want to try for the bits in between too."

I put my arms around her, enveloping her in a crushing hug, surrounding her mouth with mine again. Her hands cupped the back of my head, pulling me in even closer, wanting me as much as I wanted her.

"Get a room." A distant shout rudely jolted us out of our teenage make out session and I pulled back, laughing.

"I will get a fucking room." I muttered, moving my lips to her cheek. "Come on. Let's walk back and get some breakfast. Probably not the best idea to be going at it in public."

A look I couldn't decipher flashed across her face.

I took her sunglasses off my collar and carefully placed them back onto her head, kissing her nose, before putting mine on.

I held my hand out. "I'll put your headphones in my pocket."

She uncurled her fingers, opening her palm. I took them, keeping hold of her hand and wrapping it in mine. Then I subtly shifted my dick to a more comfortable position, something I knew I'd be doing a lot of around her.

❦

The waitress placed our order down. Big fluffy omelets, toast, granola, juice and coffee.

We were in one of my favorite brunch spots in Tribeca, a place I came to a lot because they looked after me and I could sit mostly unbothered. She picked up her juice, drinking it, it was a shade so green it could have been radioactive. Even looking at it made me feel healthier.

"You want some?" She offered me her straw.

I pulled a face of disgust. "No thanks. I'll pass."

She snorted.

"Okay, so let's start small." I sipped my much more palatable coffee. "I grew up in Massachusetts. I have one sister, Phoebe, who's studying for an MBA. My parents are divorced, but actually they get on better now than they did when they were married. They come to a lot of my home games together. I've been playing hockey since I was four and have been with the Rangers my whole professional career. Now your turn."

I picked up a piece of toast, biting into it, and looked at her wide eyed while I waited for her to begin.

She laughed loudly, putting down her nuclear waste juice. "Okay, I grew up in California. I have one older brother and one older sister."

I grinned at her. "You're the baby?"

"Yeah."

"And how did you get into fitness?"

"I studied sports science and performance at Stanford, then when I graduated I was working as a personal trainer and muscle specialist, then moved to the LA branch of the studio I'm at now."

Smart and sexy. Ding, ding, ding. We have a winner.

"Personal trainer, huh? Wanna be mine?" I winked, flashing her my best cheeky grin. The one that usually worked to my advantage and got me anything I wanted, something about the dimple which I already knew she had a weakness for.

She laughed. "I'm not sure you need my help in that department."

An irrational thought suddenly crossed my mind.

"You're not anyone's trainer right now, are you?"

78

I tried to keep the growl out of my voice, because I was not sure I wanted her getting that close to any man who wasn't me.

Actually, I definitely didn't.

"No, but one day I'd like my own gym and training facility."

"That's a great plan, you'd be really good at it." I swallowed the mouthful of granola I had. "And what about your brother and sister, what do they do?"

"My sister, Piper, has two kids, she stays at home to look after them." She dropped her eyes, looking away from me. "And my brother, Jupiter, plays baseball."

"Oh yeah, he any good?" But a lightbulb went off because that was not a common name, and I continued before she could answer. "Wait, your surname is Reeves. Is Jupiter Reeves your brother? Jupiter Reeves, third baseman for the Dodgers?"

She nodded slowly, her shoulders tensing up. "Yeah, you know him?"

Woah. Holy shit.

Jupiter Reeves, the bad boy of baseball. He was worse than Felix, or at least less discreet. I vaguely remembered a night at the ESPN Awards a few years ago where they'd had a competition of who could fuck the newest Victoria's Secret model first. The only reason I hadn't joined that bet was because I'd already had my hands full. No wonder she was wary of hook ups. And pro athletes.

I had some serious work to do.

"We've met a few times at award shows but not really, we'd know each other to say hi to."

"Oh, okay."

"I've never been out partying with him." I answered the question she didn't want to ask.

She visibly relaxed in a way I wasn't sure I was comfortable with.

"Your comment earlier about pro-athletes? Was that because of Jupiter?"

She sighed and nodded. "I love him, he's one of my favorite people. But I also know what he's like, even on the nights I've been out with him and his teammates and he's toned it down or tried to shield me from it. I'm not judging him, I see what happens, but that's not me. Contrary to what happened in Vegas."

I frowned at her, not liking what I was hearing. "Hey, we were both in Vegas. Don't do that. Vegas was amazing. The best night of my life so far and we're here now because of it."

"I know. You're right." She gave weak smile.

I put my coffee down and took her hands in mine.

"Without wanting to dig myself into a hole, Jupiter is a single guy. Could he be a little more discreet? Probably. But until you meet the one, then that's the single life for a pro-athlete." I took a deep breath. "And you should know, the reason I've never been in a relationship is because I knew I could never stay faithful. Never met anyone I wanted to spend time with, never met anyone I wanted to commit to until you. Before you my life wasn't much different to Jupiter's. But I told you earlier, I haven't even looked at another woman in nearly a year and that's the truth. I promise I will never give you a reason to doubt me."

She reached over and brushed my cheek, her touch electric, the imprint of her fingertips still warming my skin after she dropped her hand back.

"Thank you."

"You're welcome." I started on the omelets. "Now tell me why you left California."

It was her turn to wince. "My ex-boyfriend and I came here, he was relocated to a new job in the city."

My fork stopped mid-air as I quickly did the math. Ex-boyfriend. She'd been here nine months, three months after Vegas.

What the actual fuck.

I narrowed my eyes. "Emerson, were you in a relationship when we met?"

She shook her head violently. "No. My girlfriends took me to Vegas because I'd broken up with my boyfriend. I broke up with him. But after I got back to California he spent a month begging me to get back together, so I did. And when he was offered a new job here, we saw it as a fresh start. But three months in I caught him with one of the nurses at his hospital and I moved out that same day."

"He's a doctor?"

She nodded. "A surgeon at Mercy on the Upper West Side."

"Why did you break up in the first place."

She laughed, although it wasn't filled with any humor. "Because I caught him with one of his nurses."

I frowned. "Why did you get back together with him then?"

Her face dropped again.

"Luck?"

She took a beat before answering and I watched in silence. "Because I was sad. Because I gave you my number and you didn't call me. You didn't come and meet me after you begged me to wait for you. Because I was embarrassed that I wanted you to come, I wanted to see you again so badly. And I thought maybe I'd imagined our connection and the chemistry hadn't been real. That it was just my one chance at glimpsing what incredible sex could be like."

My heart was torn, cracking a little at the pain she'd suffered and the pain I'd inadvertently caused, but skipping a beat at hearing how upset she'd been that we hadn't got our second chance. That she felt how I felt. And my dick stirred again as I thought about our first night together.

"Oh Sweetheart, I'm so sorry."

"It's okay." She looked up at me, with a shrug of one

shoulder before her face split into a toothy smile. "I guess it's what the universe wanted, right. I'd never be in New York and we wouldn't be here if I hadn't got back together with him."

"That is very true." I laughed. "Do you still see him if he's in New York?"

"Not on purpose, but he has an annoying habit of turning up where I am, I'm sure he follows me sometimes. He wants me to give him another chance."

Rage struck like lightning.

"That's not fucking happening." I practically shouted.

"No, it's not." She said calmly. "I don't even know why he wants to, or why we stayed together so long because we were badly matched. But I thought about it a lot and I'm sure it's only because of Jupe."

"What do you mean?"

"He used to drop Jupiter's name all the time. I'm sure he tried to get known as a big shot surgeon who had ties to professional athletes. Especially whenever he got injured."

If I didn't hate this guy already for hurting her, I probably would now. What a cock. I'd definitely come across a few of those in my time.

"Well Luck, at least with me you know I'll never do that. I'm already a big shot pro-athlete." I waggled my brows, making her laugh again and it was quickly becoming my new favorite sound.

I looked down at the table, all the food gone, she'd almost put away as much as me, which was impressive.

"Do you want anything else?"

"No, thank you."

I threw some cash down and stood up, glancing at my watch, it was twelve on the dot. I held it out to show her.

"Would you look at that. Our second date has officially started."

We walked back outside into the sunshine, my arm

draped over her shoulder. She fitted into me like the missing piece of a jigsaw.

She put her sunglasses back on. "What's next then?"

I looked down at her. "Now you have a choice, so use it wisely."

She smirked. "Okay."

"One. We go back to yours, you have a shower and change. Then we go to mine, so I can change. And we stay in the city for the day, maybe hit up the park."

She tapped her finger to her lip. "What's two?"

"Two is we go back to yours, we grab your tiniest bikini then head back to the country and spend the day lounging by the pool."

"Wait, you have two places?"

I nodded.

"Yep, I actually live in that building there." I pointed to the tall red brick building at the end of the street. "But I'm selling it."

"Why?"

"Because I don't want that life anymore." I shrugged, casually. "So come on, which is it going to be?"

"Pool."

"Correct answer."

I pulled out my phone and dialed my driver. He picked up immediately. "Hey Ralph, please can you meet us at Emerson's place in thirty minutes, then we'll head out to the country."

"Sure thing. See you there." He hung up.

Two hours later we pulled up at my gates, waiting for them to open.

I turned to her. "Just to warn you, it's only just been finished, so might still be a bit of a mess."

As we drove down the driveway, the trees that Freddie had delivered were all planted. And what I now knew as giant bays were flanking my front door and I had to admit, it looked good.

The car pulled to a stop and I jumped out, running around to open the door for Emerson. "Welcome to my house, Luck." I tapped on the roof as she got out. "Thanks Ralph, you're good to take off. I'll call you tomorrow if I need you."

She looked up at me, her eyebrow raised in question.

"I'll be driving you home later." The car pulled away and I held my hand out to her. "Let me give you the tour."

As much as I hated the impression her brother had left on her, the fact that he was also a pro-athlete played in my favor. I was one of the top earners in the league, with my endorsements I took home close to sixteen million dollars a year, but compared to Jupiter Reeves it was fuck all and I knew she didn't see me as a paycheck.

Or really seem to care. That's if she was even aware.

The house was so newly completed that apart from the core group of boys, plus Fred and Wolfie, no one had been here or seen it. I hadn't even had a housewarming. The thought that she would be the first outsider, made me feel... well...

Before I finished that sentence, I counted out the slaps Felix would have given me if he'd been privy to my internal narrative today. It was easily topping fifty.

Get a fucking grip.

I looked down at her, so tiny next to the giant double doors as I opened them up, holding them so she could walk through.

Art, still yet to be hung, was propped up against the walls. The furniture for the hallway was still to be delivered so it was currently a huge empty space, bar the large set of stairs which ran down the middle.

I guided her along a corridor and through the big arch to the kitchen, the only room I'd been using properly since I'd

84

still only partially moved in. Grey slate floors travelled through the kitchen and out into the garden, so that when the backdoors were fully open it was one continuous space to the outside. Or so Freddie had told me. I could see she'd also left some of her trees on the patio area out where the barbecue was.

If I wasn't careful, she was gonna turn this place into a jungle.

Emerson walked through to the glass back.

"Luck." She turned and I pointed to the button on the wall. "Press that switch."

She did and the doors started rolling.

"Wow, that's so cool." She looked over to me. "It's really beautiful here."

My cheeks started to get hot at her compliment.

Who the fuck was I turning into? It was like I was fucking fifteen again.

"Thank you."

"Did you do it yourself?"

"No." I scoffed. "God no. Freddie did it all. All I had to do was choose between the options she'd give me. But I think I did a pretty good job there, don't you?"

She laughed out loud, walking back toward me, her hips swaying as she moved. We were still in our workout gear, she'd not bothered to change when we got to hers and I was desperate to peel it off her.

I wrapped my hands around her when she reached me, gently pulling on the end of her ponytail, tipping her head back for a kiss. Her soft, delicious mouth and berry pink lips opening under mine just enough for me to slip my tongue inside, sliding against hers one more time.

I would never get enough of kissing her. My dick twitched in agreement.

"Let me show you where you can change." I took her hand and led her down to the pool house at the bottom of the garden. "Everything you need is here, I'm going to run inside and get my trunks."

I took the stairs two at a time, sprinting into my closet, stripping off and grabbing the first pair of shorts I could find. My dick had been existing in a state of permanent half chub and I debated on whether to quickly jerk off before it got too uncomfortable, but decided against it.

I ran back outside and down to the pool, stopping dead.

I'd made a huge mistake.

I shouldn't have changed my mind.

A low rumble rolled up my throat, my mouth drying immediately.

She was a walking wet dream.

Yep, it was decided. Two dates was an acceptable amount of time before having sex. Acceptable because that's all I was going to last. Or one and half. Still, definitely something to be proud of.

I should award myself a medal.

This medal is awarded to Drew Alexander Crawley for holding out a record five hours and forty-three minutes (plus the two days since the club, which totally counts) against Emerson Reeves, the most tempting vixen in the world.

Why, thank you very much. I accept this award.

You know sometimes when almost naked is more naked than actual naked? Because that's exactly what she was, almost naked, standing in front of me, in her bikini.

Although I'm not even sure you could call what she was wearing a bikini. It was more like three miniature triangles.

Miniature.

And so fucking sexy.

I gave a silent prayer that she'd never ever worn in it public.

Even though it was eighty nine degrees, her nipples were

rock hard. Literally pointing right at me, desperate for my attention, like they'd missed me as much as I'd missed them.

My mouth started watering.

Here's the thing about me, on any given day if I was asked which part of a woman's body was my favorite, it would be tits. No question. I wouldn't even have to think about it. I loved them.

Loved them.

Nuzzling them, sucking them, squeezing them, fucking them.

And there, right in front of me, was the most remarkable pair I'd ever had the privilege to lay eyes on, let alone touch, in my entire life, all full and bouncy and pert.

And one hundred per cent natural.

Tits that had been the star of nearly all my fantasies for the past year. And even then, I hadn't done them justice. But there they were, barely contained in two flimsy isosceles triangles.

I had no doubt, Mr Pennies, my sixth-grade math teacher would be proud of me for remembering that little nugget of geometry and applying it to a real-life situation.

Because I was no longer dreaming, and this was definitely a real-life situation.

As she looked up, her incredible breasts wriggled like excitable puppies, susceptible to the slightest movement, ecstatic at being let loose from that hideous sports bra jail she'd kept them locked up in all morning.

Her gaze travelled along my body, soaking me in, making my dick swell to painful proportions. Licking her lips like I was her next meal, a dark smile curved along her mouth, telling me she knew exactly what she was doing to me.

This woman was danger and magic and fire all rolled into one.

And she fucking owned me.

I'm not sure why I'd been so determined to hold out sex,

because in that precise moment I couldn't even remember my own name.

I walked over to her, running my nose along her jaw, inhaling her warm intoxicating scent of sweat and sunshine. I took her earlobe between my teeth and felt her body shiver in reaction.

"You're determined to make me break, aren't you?"

She moved back, looking at me with wide doe eyes, glistening in desire. Her voice dropped to a whisper. "I'm just not sure why we need to wait when it's something we're both desperate for."

"Because I wanted to make you understand that you are more important to me than sex."

She responded by tilting her neck to give me better access and my lips found her pulse point hammering against her soft skin. I ran my hand around her back, trailing my fingers down her spine until they rested at the top of her crack.

She let out a whimper.

"If my fingers go lower, how wet will they find you?"

"Very." Her voice broke with need.

I slipped further down her ass, gently kneading it. Her legs moved apart a fraction to allow me through and my fingers became instantly drenched.

I breathed in against her quivering lips. "Fuuuck. You are. So slick and needy for me."

She whimpered again, her body softening in my arms as my fingers continued their journey caressing her skin, running a slippery path between her slit and her ass. I licked along her jawline, my other hand stroking across her stomach until it reached her heavy breast. Cupping it so it fitted perfectly into my hand, I barely had to move my fingers before it escaped from the fabric, her nipples rock hard under my thumb circling around the nub.

I groaned into her neck before moving back up, my hunger for her crashing though me like a tsunami. Taking her mouth with mine in a vicious assault, suctioning on and stabbing her frantically with my tongue, she gripped my head, hard, needing it as much as I did.

Without breaking contact I scooped her ass into my hands, carrying her over to one of the big loungers surrounding the pool, laying her down. I pulled out her hair tie, raking through the strands as I stood up, staring at her.

The sun was shining on her heavenly body, skin golden from the summer with her dark, auburn hair tumbling around her. She looked like fire. Gazing up at me, her turquoise eyes were glazed and heavy with lust, her lips parted. I'd never seen anything more perfect and beautiful.

My heart may have stopped.

I dropped to my knees, pulling her long legs toward the end of the bed and over my shoulder. Untying the bows at the sides of her bottoms, the fabric fell away and I was greeted with the most incredible sight. Even in my dreams I'd done a poor job of remembering how beautiful her pussy was, the tiny white stretch of skin contrasting with her tan lines, making her appear all the more delicate. Pink and glistening, swollen with arousal and dripping all for me.

I ran my thumb along her slit, spreading her juices everywhere, trembling under my touch.

She tried to push my head away as I got closer. "No, Drew, we haven't showered."

I couldn't have given less of a fuck. Nothing was keeping me away from her.

"Shut up and enjoy it." I grabbed her hands in mine, holding them tight, pinning them against her thighs which I held wide open before taking a long, hard lap.

She was the best thing I'd ever tasted.

Her head fell back in a loud groan which only got louder as I slid a finger inside her, curling up against her G-spot, adding another to loosen up her tight, silky soft muscles.

My tongue flicked at her clit as I pumped my fingers,

switching up to slow, undemanding long laps and gentle nibbles, not giving her the exact pressure she needed. Every so often attacking her clit, sucking hard, before caressing her back down and edging her closer to detonation, making her so fucking wet I thought I might come in my trunks before my dick had even been let out to play.

I built up the pace again and her trembling turned to violent shakes, her mewing growing louder as the scruff of my beard tickled against her thighs. She started grinding her hips into my mouth for more friction, lifting them into me before her back arched high out of the lounger as an orgasm ripped through her, nearly pulling me along with it.

I watched her pulse in front of me while I stroked and licked her down until she couldn't take it anymore and pushed me away.

I stood up, wiping my forearm across my mouth removing the excess of her honeyed cum and shed my shorts. My dick throbbed in unbridled excitement at being allowed out and near this heavenly creature as if he remembered her as clearly as I did. She watched me through hooded eyes as I stroked myself, willing my heart rate to steady. My dick was so hard it was painful and my balls were seconds away from exploding.

And then I realized I'd forgotten any protection.

"Fuck." I turned to run back. "I need to get condoms."

"No, Drew stop."

I froze, looking at her. Had she changed her mind? I hoped not, but I'd give her anything she wanted.

"I'm on birth control, you don't need to go."

My heart filled to the brim from the level of trust she had in me. I knelt by her and stroked her cheek. "Sweetheart, are you sure? Are you positive? Because I can run inside, it'll only take a second."

She nodded. "I'm sure."

Fuck. I wasn't. Even without my nearly year long abstinence I would be lasting less than a minute.

"I promise I'm clean. And I've never been bare before, with anyone." My voice was low and quivering, and I didn't recognize it.

"I trust you." She brushed her lips to mine. "Please just fuck me."

She didn't need to ask twice.

I hovered over her, pushing her thighs apart until my dick nudged between her dripping wet folds. She was leaning against the back of the lounger, her body slightly lifted so she could watch me.

"Is this okay here? Are you comfortable?"

She nodded, frantic for another release, her chest heaving as she waited for me, her nipples so hard they could cut glass.

"Wrap your legs around me."

Even from just wetting the tip of my dick in her, I knew without doubt I'd never experienced a feeling like this. Of being skin to skin. Every sensation magnified to nearly overwhelming proportions. The year of not having her in my arms almost worth it for how incredible this moment was.

This was where I was supposed to be.

I inched forward slowly trying to hold my composure with every move I made, which was hard with the amount she was clenching around me, each one sending a jolt down my spine hitting me like a red hot poker straight in the balls. I closed my eyes, my jaw clenching, breathing through the adrenalin which was surging through my body until I fit snug against her, right up to the hilt.

Then she started pushing herself onto me.

My vision became blurry with need as I tried to control the pressure building inside me, using every weapon in my arsenal to stop myself from coming within seconds.

Who first signed the Declaration of Independence? Hancock
Who was our first President? Washington.

What was the score of the Yankees game last night? Who fucking cares.

I gripped onto her hips, stilling them. "Fuck, Sweetheart, hang on. Please. I'm not going to last, I can feel every single muscle of yours clench against me."

Her eyes were almost rolling back in her head. "No, Drew, I can't, I need more. You feel too good. I need it."

Fuck. I had to change this up.

She cried out as I scooped her up and spun around, pushing to the hilt in one long thrust, pulling her up so she balanced on my legs. "You control it, baby."

She looked down at me, her eyes so full with lust and desire that I nearly lost it. I lifted my chin up and she dropped her lips to mine brushing against them softly, tasting like summer.

Wrapping her arms around my shoulders, she arched her back and slowly began rocking gently against me. I gripped onto her hips, burying my face in her bouncing tits before looking down to watch as she rode me, watch the impeccable sight of her sliding onto my thick cock while she whimpered softly into the air around us. Each excruciating movement making him swell to explosive proportions.

Stroking her clit, I was rewarded with a spasm of walls clamping down like velvety jaws, sending another spiral of pressure straight to the balls. My groan arrived deep and dripping in desperation.

"Fucking hell, you are amazing."

Everything was pooling at the base of my spine.

Wrapping a fistful of hair into my hands, I pulled her back so her tits arched into my mouth, I sucked in a nipple and bit down, my ears filling with her loud ecstatic cries.

"Drew, holy shit, this is too good. You feel so good. I can't get enough."

"I know, Luck. Christ I'm not going to last much longer."

Her legs started shaking and she increased her pace,

building up to punishing levels, the strength of her orgasm about to crash through her like a seismic wave. I gripped her hips harder, forcing her down onto me, her luscious breasts bouncing firm in my face. Her walls clenched around me, squeezing the life from my dick and I finally lost control, my orgasm shooting through me like an eighteen-wheeler powering down the interstate, the air around us sucked into the vortex of our creation.

She collapsed against me as her pussy continued throbbing, milking me for every drop I could give her. Hot and slick with sweat, we stayed together as our hearts pounded against our ribcages, our chests heaving from exertion.

As our breathing levelled out she lifted her head to look at me. Her cheeks were flushed pink, her freckles dancing across her face, lips swollen from our kisses. My heart was freefalling with such an overwhelming sense of completeness it made me dizzy.

I was home.

I swallowed hard as my throat thickened, my eyes prickling hot with emotion, from the relief of having her in my arms again, of everything being as I'd dreamed it would be and I don't know how I'd managed a year without her.

She was the most incredible woman I'd ever met.

She was my soulmate.

And I was never letting her go again.

7

EMERSON

I tipped the blender upside down banging the end, trying to get the remains of my workout shake into the cup underneath. I'd just finished my second class of the morning, hunger creeping up on me quicker than usual. My stomach feeling like it was eating itself.

I blamed the sex.

The hot as fuck, raw, animalistic, life changing sex I'd been having for the past few weeks, every spare moment of every day. I was slightly concerned I'd become a sex addict, because I couldn't get enough. Drew worked my body harder than any class I took, causing it to ache in places I never knew existed. I don't even know how he wasn't more exhausted, when most of his days were now taken up with punishing practice schedules. But however tired he was, it was like he came alive again the second he saw me, making up for the time we'd been apart. Whether that was the year since Vegas or the hours since we'd been together.

I'd never experienced anything like it.

When Richard and I had first met it had been good, but I'd always felt too clunky, too tall, too big for him. And he'd hated when I initiated.

So I stopped.

But Drew matched me in every way, worshipped me, encouraged me to tell him what I wanted, what I liked, and reignited the fire he'd lit in me a year ago.

And when we weren't having sex, we were cuddling, his massive body holding me close in some way, because he always had to be touching me. Touching my skin. Touching my boobs, a hand cupping one whenever we were watching television, like they were his personal stress relievers. He'd even go to sleep holding them as he spooned me.

I'd thought about him so much over the past year that for a terrifying second every morning before I opened my eyes, I'd have to convince myself he was real and would still be there next to me.

That I wasn't living in an alternate dream state.

But the reality exceeded the dream.

He was so easy and sweet and funny, making me laugh until I cried, opening my eyes to how it should be between two people. My heart was growing bigger every day and it was all for him, because of him.

My world had finally been turned the right way up.

Like we were meant to be.

Our connection in Vegas only the tip of the iceberg.

I walked over to the reception desk where Mikey and some of the girls were huddled around, Ashley behind the counter.

"Hey guys, how are you?"

Mikey wrapped his arm around my waist and hugged me to his side, sucking on the straw in my smoothie. "Good, how was your class?"

"It was fun, the riders last week picked the music for today, so they were all pumped for it. But it was better than I expected it to be."

"Em, have you had any more Rangers in?" Rose looked

around the group. "Has anyone seen them again? The wait lists have all shot up since they were in."

I choked on my drink, hiding it in a cough.

"Fuck they're so hot. I wish I'd been here when they came in. I try not to perv on the hot guys in my class, but I'd definitely struggle with them." Mikey whined. "Have you seen their muscles, they're practically obscene."

Jessie snorted. "Totally. Hey Ash, check the classes for this week, have any of them booked?"

I stood there, trying to act as normal as possible and hold it the fuck together. I looked at Ashley who was glowing bright red, staring hard at her screen. I was shit at lying but she was worse.

"I can't see any."

"Maybe they booked under an alias. See what comes up for that class they were in and cross check." Suggested Rose.

Seriously? Did they all side-hustle as PIs or something?

She nudged me. "Em, it was your class wasn't it? What were they like?"

I sucked up the bottom of my shake, trying to pay attention to what was left instead of their eyes, all trained on me. "Oh, I didn't know who they were until Ash mentioned. I don't follow hockey."

That wasn't a lie.

Mikey held his finger up. "Oh honey, you'd definitely know if you saw them, they're so effing hot."

Rose sniggered. "Fuck yes. Drew Crawley is in my dreams on a regular basis."

I realized my teeth had started grinding. I didn't know where to look.

Please stop talking.

Jessie high-fived her. "Oh yeah. He's such a playboy though, my friend fucked him last year and she said it was the hottest sex she'd ever had."

My stomach dropped, jealousy winding me hard. The

96

thought of him being anywhere near anyone else made my skin crawl with the intensity of a thousand spiders. I was going to be sick.

I picked up my bag from the floor. "Shit, I just remembered I have to be home for a delivery. See you guys later."

I stormed out of the front doors, not waiting for them to answer. Not wanting to be part of their conversation for a second longer.

I couldn't hold back the tears from falling as I walked down the block.

I wasn't an idiot. I knew he'd had sex with other women, because he'd told me. I knew he'd behaved like my stupid man-whore brother because he'd told me. He'd done nothing but tell me the truth.

But hearing it from him and hearing it from a random who'd said it was the hottest sex they'd ever had, was not the same thing.

It was the hottest sex *I'd* ever had.

But maybe that was just the reaction from every woman he'd ever had sex with. Because that's just what he did. Give people hot sex.

And I'd had sex with a total of five people. Including him. None of which had given me hot sex. Except him.

I didn't want him to give it to anyone else. I didn't want anyone else to have experienced what I'd experienced. Share with him what we'd shared.

The green-eyed monster flared up again to almost suffocating proportions, crushing my chest until I was gasping for air. It was a sensation I didn't like or ever remembered feeling so intensely. Even with Richard, and he'd *actually* cheated.

I'd been firmly served an eviction notice from Cloud Number Nine, the one I'd been living on since he'd walked into my class. Hot shame flushed my cheeks and I brushed away another angry tear.

"Emerson?"

I turned back in the direction of the voice as I passed it, remembering too late I was an irate, ugly crying mess.

Freddie and Wolfie were standing on the street, staring at me.

"Emerson, are you okay? What's wrong?" Wolfie pulled me into a hug, although it was more of a one-armed pat given her massive belly was blocking the way.

I sniffed, wiping my face again. "Yes. I'm fine."

I watched in confusion as their eyes became watery and overspilled.

"Why are you two crying?"

Freddie rubbed her nose on her sleeve. "It's the hormones, whenever we see someone crying, we start. And it's not limited to crying either. Cute stuff, tiny stuff, my favorite cupcake. It's really fucking annoying. Sorry."

I laughed. "That's okay."

"Emerson, what's wrong? Why were you crying?" Wolfie asked again. "Is it Drew?"

I nodded, the tears starting up again.

"Come on, let's go and get a coffee, then you can tell us about it."

I looked at them, both dressed in workout gear. "Were you headed to a class?"

"Yes, but this is more important." Freddie linked her arm in mine marching me down the street and into the nearest coffee shop.

Considering I was nearly a foot taller than her she could move me with surprising strength.

We walked past the counter and sat down at a table.

"What did he do?"

The waitress walked over and took our order. Freddie rolled her eyes dramatically when Wolfie asked for theirs to both be decaf, then turned back to me, staring and waiting for my response.

"He didn't do anything." I sighed. "Not directly, anyway."

The coffees were placed in front of us, I took mine, stirring it while they sat there in silence as I told them what happened. Repeating it only exacerbated the nausea bubbling up in my belly.

I could see them holding back their tears as they listened.

Wolfie reached over and stroked my arm. "Emerson we're so sorry you heard that, we honestly know how you feel. Neither of us came from a hockey background, or even an American sports background, so it was a real wake up call for us too."

I shrugged.

"I get it. I do. My brother plays baseball and I've seen what happens when they're out and partying, especially after a game. It's just that I never expected to hear it like that. I haven't told anyone at work yet because I wanted to keep it to myself for a while, but now I've heard them all talking about him like a piece of meat I'm embarrassed to tell anyone."

I dropped my head.

"We've practically spent every night together for the last few weeks and," I rolled my eyes, "it sounds so dumb, but I just wanted to be special."

"It's not dumb Emerson, you are special. The hockey girls that hang out are... well..."

"Disgusting." Freddie interrupted.

Wolfie pursed her lips at her.

"Yes, in a word. And they're easy for the boys, but they aren't who they want to go home with at the end of the day. Look, you really need to talk to Drew about how you feel, because only he can help with this. But what we will say is that since we found you in class a few weeks ago it's like we've got the old Drew back."

My brows knotted together. "What do you mean?"

"Drew is one of the best guys we know, he's sweet and

funny and kind. He has a heart of gold. But since you guys met in Vegas and he lost your number, for a while he was super angry but then he stopped with that and for the last, I don't know how long, he's just been sad and empty. It was like his heart had broken."

I looked at them, hope blooming, pushing the jealousy away slightly. I wanted to believe everything they said.

Freddie put her coffee down. "Yeah, but the past few weeks he's been so happy. Even Coop mentioned it when he came back from practice the other day."

"Yeah, Jas did too." Wolfie pulled a face, wincing as she rubbed her belly. "Sorry, this baby is kicking me a lot today."

"The skanky girls will never go away, so you need to decide whether you trust Drew enough to make peace with it."

They were right, I did need to trust him and really, he'd never given me any reason not to.

"Thank you for being so kind. I'm glad I bumped into you, I really needed to hear that. I'm sorry I never called you, I meant to, I just got caught up in everything the past few weeks."

Freddie cackled. "We thought we might have heard from you, but I guess we now know why we haven't. You've had no spare time."

Wolfie sipped on her coffee. "Why don't you come over soon and watch an away game with us? Or we can go shopping or to lunch. But either way, we're always here if you need to talk, because we understand what you're going through. Plus we'd love to spend time with you, we don't have a ton of girlfriends in the city."

"Yes, I'd really like that. Thank you."

"Good." Freddie looked around for the waitress. "And now we're not torturing ourselves in a class I'm making the most of this morning and ordering cake for my second breakfast."

I stepped out of the shower, exhausted, ready for bed. I knew Drew had been at practice with the boys and they'd spent the afternoon together, so I hadn't heard much from him except a few texts.

After more coffee and cake, Wolfie and Freddie had headed home for a nap and I'd walked back to my apartment. My tears had dried up, the pressure in my chest eased. I'd thought about what the girls had said and they were right, I needed to trust him.

And I knew deep down I did.

It was just all so new and the last few weeks had been a lot, even if it did feel so normal and right and easy. Like we'd known each other for a lifetime.

I would talk to Drew properly when I saw him, but I'd decided tonight I was going to be on my own.

By myself.

I was going to stand strong against his charms and my weakness, because I already knew he'd try and see me, and I would cave without question. Because I wanted to see him too. Because I had absolutely no self-control when it came to Drew Crawley.

I walked into the kitchen, picking up my phone from the table.

Dickhead: 5 x missed calls

Dickhead: *Emerson stop this childish behavior. Pick up the phone when I ring you*

Jesus, Richard, will you fucking fuck off. Take the fucking hint.

It buzzed in my hand and I jumped out of my skin, causing it to fly into the air. I reached out for it, barely catching it before it could smash on the floor but managed to answer before it stopped buzzing. I sat back against the wall, catching my breath from the unexpected exertion.

Drew's face flashed across the screen.

"There she is, there's my beautiful girl."

He was so gorgeous, the edges of his hazel eyes creasing as he grinned at me. His happiness was infectious as always, spreading through my veins and rooting in my heart, taking hold until it bloomed.

My smile was permanent when he was around.

"Hi babe."

"How was your day?"

I tried to keep my face as neutral as possible, I didn't want to do this over the phone. "Not bad. How was yours?"

He frowned. "Sweetheart, what's wrong?"

"Nothing, I'm just tired."

I really needed to get better at lying.

"Luck…" He stared at me. "You're sitting on the floor in a towel."

Stupid FaceTime. I stood up, pushing away from the wall and gripping my towel so it didn't fall. "I dropped my phone as I answered."

"And...?"

"And what?"

"Are you going to tell me what's wrong?"

I sighed. "Nothing babe, honestly. I'm just super tired and I'm going to go to bed."

His eyes narrowed. "Luck, I'll call you back in twenty."

He hung up.

Well, that was weird. My chest sunk like a lead weight, the happiness I'd felt at seeing his face, vanished. My head fell back against the wall, where I was still standing. Today had been a rollercoaster ride and I was currently in the front carriage, stuck in the Tunnel of Doom and Gloom.

Which wasn't even a thing.

Urgh.

I'd been so wrapped up in his bubble, cocooned in the

massive arms he'd surrounded me with every night, that now I wasn't going to bed without them I felt empty.

What was happening to me?

I was probably getting my period.

With a grumble, I walked into my bedroom, dressing in sweatpants and a hoodie. I was only going to solve this with a Netflix marathon but before I could flop on the sofa, a pounding at my door had me jumping out of my skin for the second time.

Double urgh.

But then my stomach performed a triple somersault, leaving me breathless, because the most beautiful man I'd ever seen in my life was standing in the doorway when I opened it, his huge body taking up the entire door frame.

His warm, delicious scent overpowered my senses and hot tears started working their way back up my thickening throat.

"What are you doing here?" I asked, my voice breaking.

He walked inside, kicking the door shut with his foot and pulled me into his arms, holding me tight, kissing my head. "Two reasons. First, because something's wrong and I want to know what."

I sunk into his massive chest, absorbing his strength, allowing myself to feel protected. He was so big, he made me feel tiny and delicate. Something I'd never had before and now relished to the point of addiction.

He moved us over to the sofa, sitting me on his lap, stroking my hair and holding me tight.

"What's the other reason?"

"Because waking up next to you is something I thought about every day for a year and I'm going to do it every opportunity I can, including tomorrow. The season starts in a few days and I'm going to be away for the first two games, so I'm getting it in. I want to hold on to all the days I can between away stretches."

Was this guy for real?

This giant wall of muscle was made of nothing but marshmallow and he was so insanely sweet I was going to need a trip to the dentist. I turned round in his lap so I could see him properly.

His eyes bore into mine, brimming with warmth and concern. He leant down and brushed my lips with his.

"Tell me, Luck."

I bit my cheek nervously, taking a deep breath.

"Today when I came out of the class, Mikey and some of the girls were hanging around the desk. And they were talking about you and the boys coming into the class."

I dropped my head, only for Drew to lift my chin up. "Em, what were they saying?"

"Jessie said her friend had sex with you last year."

I didn't want to repeat the rest. Even thinking it still made me nauseous.

He closed his eyes briefly, his expression twisting in shame and frustration. Cupping my face, he rubbed his thumb against my cheek.

"I'm so sorry. I'm so sorry you heard that."

I shifted in his lap again. "You don't have to say sorry, it's not your fault. It was just a shock. I mean, I know you've had sex with women, I just didn't expect to be confronted with it so soon, especially when we haven't had a conversation about us really. But we've spent every night together and I was raging with jealously that someone got to share with you what we share and I didn't like it."

I dropped my head again, I was rambling.

He brought my eyes back to his, filled with guilt. "Okay, first off. I am sorry and I'm so sorry you were put in that position because of me and I wish I could protect you from it. I can't hide my past, but Lucky, that's all it is. Past. And I want to make something very clear." He picked my hand up and placed it on his heart. "What we have, what I share with you, I have never shared with anyone. No one has had with me what we have together. No one. And after the last few weeks, this, between us, I'm never letting go. I knew it a year ago and I know it now. I've never been more certain of anything. Whatever you hear otherwise is bullshit."

He brought his lips to mine again. "And as far as a conversation goes, where I'm concerned, you're my girlfriend. No question about it."

My eyes widened to cartoon proportions, I didn't expect him to say girlfriend.

"Does that make you my boyfriend?"

"Yes I fucking am." He growled, before a shadow of vulnerability crossed his face. "If you want me to be."

And I did.

Almost as if it was the easiest decision in the world.

I nodded, a smile splitting my face. His relief was palpable, his eyes returned to their usual sparkly happiness.

"Good." He brushed his lips to mine while his hands started burrowing under my hoodie, trying to find skin. The warmth of his fingers shot goosebumps across my body. "But I have to say that right now you're wearing far too many clothes for my liking."

The familiar thump started up between my legs, growing heavier as his lips moved to my neck, nipping a wet trail of kisses along my jaw. I let out a soft moan.

He stood up with me in his arms, walking us through to my bedroom, his mouth never veering off the path it was travelling against my skin. He put me down by the edge of the bed and moved back, he was so large in my tiny bedroom. I'd been waking up in a bed so big I didn't even know if it had an official name, his feet would definitely be hanging off the end of my queen.

I looked around and frowned. "Maybe we should stay at yours."

"Oh no, we're staying here. The smaller the bed, the more we get to cuddle. This bed was made for spooning."

His hands slid back under my hoodie, bringing it up over my head. His eyes darkened, feasting on my naked breasts and I lost my train of thought as his thumbs brushed over my nipples, hardening them further. His head dipped down, taking one slowly in his mouth, a low growl escaping before he moved across my chest, his lips pressing into me while he squeezed them together against his face.

"Fucking incredible." He murmured against me, flooding my panties.

His hands moved around my body, sliding under the waistband of my sweatpants, pushing them down, taking my underwear with them. He dropped to his knees, helping me step out of them, running his hands along the backs of my trembling legs, kissing along my stomach before he stood up again.

He reached out, taking the tie from my hair, raking it through his fingers until it tumbled down my back. He lifted up the strands, bringing them to his nose and inhaled deeply.

"I fucking love your hair."

Dropping his head, he captured my mouth in his, gently brushing against me, his tongue teasing along my lips asking for permission. I couldn't have denied him anything, my body coursing with a deep longing to feel him inside me, frantically searching for any release he could provide.

I opened up and his lips surrounded mine. His massive hands cupped my face as his fingers wrapped around the back of my head, scraping through my scalp. He roamed through my mouth, torturously slow and rhythmic, his tongue stroking against mine on and on until I was so heady with lust I could barely stand, my body molding like warm putty to his touch.

This was a kiss I'd need a map to get out of.

I groaned loudly, desperation wracking my body, and

pushed myself against his hard cock straining in his jeans. I badly needed the friction he could provide but wasn't, I wanted more. More of him.

He pulled my head back, sensing my need. "No, we're not fucking tonight, Emerson. Tonight, I'm making love to my girlfriend."

He dipped us down, laying me on the bed, spreading my legs before standing back over me. His eyes were glowing, the hazel burning bright as autumn leaves in the sunshine. Reaching behind him, he pulled his shirt off, before shucking his jeans and briefs.

My breath caught.

I would never get over seeing him naked for the first time, every time. He was a sight to behold, power and strength personified. Absolutely beautiful. His broad chest was covered in fine, dark hair that did nothing to hide the dense, sculpted muscles underneath. A hard plane of abs sat between sharp, strongly corded ribs and the most defined obliques I'd ever seen, emphasizing his narrow hips.

He was the embodiment of male perfection. My very own Vitruvian Man.

I watched his bicep flex as he took hold of his cock. Thick and heavy and hard, pre-cum dripping out as he tugged on it long and slow, making my pussy convulse in expectation.

I wanted him in my mouth, wanted to taste him at the back of my throat.

He scanned the length of my body.

"Do you have any idea how beautiful you are, all laid out in front of me and glistening with need just for me?" His eyes glazed over and his voice dropped an octave. "This is going to last all night long, Luck. I hope you're ready."

I swallowed the saliva which suddenly filled my mouth.

He ran his hands along my calves, moving up my thighs, widening them further as he hovered over me. My body quivered violently.

His lips touched mine. "You blow my fucking mind."

Holding himself up with one arm, he stroked my cheek with the back of his fingers before they trailed down my body, starting at my neck slowly travelling over every inch of my burning skin. His gaze held mine, his eyes flashing with the same need he could see in me as his hand moved down. He cupped my breast, his thumb running underneath, brushing my nipples, hardening them to painful proportions.

"God, Drew…" I groaned.

My stomach convulsed as his hand moved lower, his rock-hard cock brushing against my leg. My chest was heaving in rapid bursts, my breath shallow from the anticipation of an impending orgasm I knew would rip me in half. I didn't need him to touch me to know I was soaking wet.

His fingers slipped through my slick folds opening me up, my eyelids rolling closed, as he slid two fingers inside.

"Eyes open." He growled, his fingers curling up. "Oh fucking hell, always so ready for me. You're perfect, Luck. You always feel so good."

My legs started shaking violently as his thumb brushed my clit. His body moved down mine, until his head rested between my legs, his beard scratching softly against the inside of my thighs.

I began to whimper.

"Shhhhh, not yet, Sweetheart, hold it for me. The first time you come will be on my dick, with me, after I've buried myself so fucking deep inside you. But I need a taste before that happens."

His tongue took a long, flat lick, flicking my clit at the end and sending my synapses furiously shooting across my entire body, making me moan so loudly it would put any porn star to shame. Except this was one hundred percent real as he edged me closer and closer to explosion.

There was no fucking way I was going to be able to hold this.

He pulled away groaning, rising up he started sliding the tip of his cock back and forth across my clit, his breathing more and more erratic, before positioning it against my entrance. He closed his eyes, stilling himself. A fresh flood of wetness poured out of me, I was so turned on from seeing him this amped up, from seeing how much I affected him.

"Drew, please... I need you..."

His eyes shot open, blazing fire. "I'm here, baby."

He sunk down, moving my legs wider still with his massive thighs, pushing my knees up, holding onto my hips, controlling the movement. A deep rumble travelled up his throat as he started sliding inside me, his dick stretching me out to the max, slow and deliberate until I was so full of him I could hardly breathe, the sensation overwhelming.

"Oh fuck, you feel incredible. How is it like this every time?" He rested his weight on his elbows, pushing to the hilt, his balls snuggling up against me. "Kiss me."

I ran my fingers through his hair, lifting my head up to meet his. My juices still glistening on his lips, tasting myself as I ran my tongue along them. He swept round my mouth, unhurried and delicious, moving in rhythm with his hips as he pulled all the way out before torturously plunging back in. His massive cock thickened more with each stroke, frying every single one of my nerve endings in white hot torture.

As if it had a mind of its own, my back arched and his lips moved down, tracing the column of my neck and searing my skin, the imprint of his kisses leaving a watermark along the way, his mouth never breaking contact. I could feel him everywhere, his massive body owning mine, beads of sweat erupting from the sensory overload.

He took both my hands in one of his, pinning them above my head, the other running down the length of my body, curling around my calf and positioning it on his hip. The movement jarred his thick cock against my G-spot, shooting spasms through my pussy.

"Oh Jesus, Em… fuck… this is so good. Fuck, you feel incredible. Every muscle of yours is gripping my cock. You make me so fucking hard." He growled into my neck, the vibrations hitting me right in the clit, the pressure of my orgasm building to nuclear levels.

"Babe, I can't hold this much longer. I need it."

"Wrap your legs around me."

I did and he rose up on his hands, his hips moving in deep, forceful strokes, pushing himself further inside every time. He hit my G-spot over and over until my entire body was shuddering so ferociously from the eruption looming and growing inside me, I was almost scared of the force which was about to hit.

"Now, Luck."

His words unleashed an atomic crescendo and I finally let go of the pressure I'd been gripping onto for dear life, allowing the power of it take hold. My bones melted, wave after wave crashing through me as he kept thrusting into me, not letting me come down until it claimed him too.

His mouth engulfed mine again, swallowing my cries, his cock swelling a final time before rupturing in his own explosion with a loud groan. He collapsed to the side, shuddering through the aftershocks, his dick still pumping inside me.

We lay there, tangled together, our chests heaving until our breathing returned to normal and he began trailing his fingertips across my skin, calming my racing heart. Turning his body toward mine he pulled me close, his eyes soft, contentment spread across his face and my chest tightened, heavy with the emotions still flowing through me.

Brushing away hair that had stuck to my forehead, he kissed me on and on with unrelenting tenderness.

"You are so perfect. I can't believe I have to leave for the new season already, when I only just found you again." He rubbed his nose against mine and the unwelcome scratch of tears formed in my throat.

There was nothing for me to say, because it was true. I knew full well how punishing the sports season could be and I didn't want to add to the burden of that.

He got up and walked silently out of the room, I could hear him rummaging around in the kitchen before he returned carrying two bottles of blue electrolytes. I looked at him, questioningly as he handed one to me.

"You need to stay hydrated, we're about to go in for round two. And this time I'm not planning to be gentle, I'm gonna be so deep inside you tonight you'll be feeling me until I get back."

I stared at him, unblinking as he twisted the cap off the bottle, a dark grin snaking his lips before he downed the contents.

The pulse between my legs started up again.

It was official.

He had completely ruined me.

DREW

I exhaled loudly through my teeth as I pushed the hundred pound dumbbells out and over my chest. It was the end of my third set of reps and my pecs were on fire, lactic acid burning me from the inside.

I grunted and dropped them on the floor by my side.

We were flying out tomorrow for our first game of the season, an away against Philly then Carolina. And for the first time ever I wasn't as pumped as I normally would have been, knowing it had everything to do with the beautiful, freckle faced, auburn haired wonder I'd left in bed this morning.

I'd woken up long before her, a rarity over the past few weeks, and had taken the opportunity to soak her in as much as possible, committing her to memory before I left, and use it to keep my anxiety at bay. Long, thick lashes had fluttered gently against her cheeks as she quietly dreamed, her face peaceful, her pink lips soft and still slightly swollen from where I'd kissed her all night long. I counted her freckles, she had seventy three dotted across her sunkissed skin - nineteen on her nose, thirty one on the right cheek and twenty three on the left.

I didn't know if it was the happiness of finally getting her back or the freshness she brought to my life, but I knew that the time I'd spent with her had been the best I'd ever had.

She'd anchored me.

I watched her sleep, my heart filling up with her, filling up with the love I had for her. Filled to bursting. I loved her.

I was so fucking in love with her.

And now I had to leave for five days.

I looked around, some of this season's rookies were over on the mats in the far corner of the gym, rolling and stretching out.

I could hear Carter Rice grunting nearby in the squat rack. Huck and Brogan Bartlett were spotting each other on a chest press. Dante Manners was doing pull-ups on the overhead bars, racing against one of the new guys.

Everyone behaving like normal.

I reached for the dumbbells again.

"Bro, you're gonna wear those out if you're not careful."

I looked up to see Felix and Cooper standing behind me in the mirror. I grunted through another eight reps while they watched, unimpressed. Although they should have been, I knew for a fact Coop couldn't lift as much as me.

"Are things not going well with Lucky?"

I rubbed the ache in my pecs, loosening the muscles. "Yeah, they're great."

"Then what's with the face? You look like a sad bastard."

I shrugged.

Cooper sat down on the bench opposite, regarding me with his eyebrows raised. "You don't want to leave her."

It wasn't a question.

At that moment Jasper stormed into the gym, nearly taking the door off its hinges. He thrust a piece of paper at Cooper.

He took it, studying it, then glanced back up at Jasper. "Dude, I'm sorry."

"Yeah. Fuck." He ran his hands down his face, his shoulders dropping.

Felix looked between the pair of them. "Do you two want to explain what's going on?"

Jasper turned, frustration and worry etched on his face. "We're on an away stretch on Wolfie's due date."

Fuck. That was bad.

"Shit, Jas. I'm sorry." I reached out and squeezed his shoulder. "I'm sure it'll be fine though, Freddie keeps telling me they never come on time."

They all stared at me.

"What? She talks a lot."

Cooper shook his head with a chuckle. "Yeah, our kid is definitely going to be late."

Jasper gave a deep sigh. "Yeah, I hope ours is too. Or early. Whatever, I just don't want to miss it."

There wasn't much we could say, it fucking sucked to travel so much, and getting Lucky back made me realize just how badly it did. I didn't want to leave her and I hadn't even told her I loved her yet. This was Jasper's first kid.

The NHL was an asshole sometimes.

"Anyway, what are you all doing?" He looked around.

"We're trying to cheer Drew up. Or at least stop him crying."

Jasper snorted.

I rolled my eyes. "Fuck's sake. I wasn't fucking crying."

"You were about to." Felix raised his eyebrow.

"No. I fucking wasn't."

Jasper nudged me. "Drew, spill it. What's going on?"

God, they were like a fucking bunch of nosy old ladies.

"Nothing, it's stupid."

"He doesn't want to leave Lucky." Cooper answered for me.

Jasper's expression filled with empathy. "Buddy, that's normal."

"Yeah, but it's not like I'm leaving my heavily pregnant wife." I ran my hands through my hair, looking at them all. My shoulders dropped in a big sigh. "I've just got her back and it's great. No, it's fucking amazing. But last night she was really upset because she'd overheard some girl saying I'd had sex with one of her friends or something."

Cooper and Jasper tried and failed to hide their amusement. I glared at them.

"When?"

I shrugged. "Last year I think, I dunno. I've only had sex with Emerson this year."

Felix snorted. "Dude, that's fucking funny."

"No it isn't. She already has a dislike of pro-athletes because of her brother and I don't want to jeopardize anything. I've always loved away games and now I don't want to go."

Coop looked at me in confusion. "What's her brother got to do with anything?"

"Oh fuck, I forgot to tell you. Her brother is Jupiter Reeves."

Jasper gave a low whistle.

Felix's mouth dropped open in surprise. "No way? Ask her to find out if he's still pissed I got the girl."

"Yeah, I'm not going to do that. Dickhead."

"Look, Man." Cooper stopped Felix from continuing. "Yeah, it's hard, not gonna lie. But getting home is amazing."

I looked up at him. "Yeah?"

"Yeah, it's better than make up sex."

"Plus, phone sex." Jasper added helpfully.

I thought about it, maybe it wouldn't be so bad.

"I guess, but it's not even about the sex, I just don't want to be away from her."

"You'll be fine, Dude. Give it a year and you'll be in the same position as Jas and me."

I stopped and thought. A future with Emerson. A tiny little baby Lucky Charm.

Yeah, I could go for that.

Dante kicked open the doors to the locker room and we followed him in.

"Fuck's sake." He held a towel over his eye to stem the bleeding from the cut underneath, before one of the team physicians walked over to patch him up.

I ripped off my sweaty jersey and pads, rolling my shoulders back, easing them up a little from the weight and the battering we'd just taken. Exhibition games were supposed to be for testing out new plays and lines, new transfers and the rookies who'd moved up.

Which is what happened in the first period.

The second, however, had just ended and been brutal as fuck, starting with a nasty hit on Carter Rice that escalated into an all-out brawl which didn't seem to finish. Along with more than a few black eyes, including Dante's, a total of twelve players had been sent off, eight of ours and four of theirs and the score which was three nil to us at the end of the first, was now standing at three all.

The third period would be all to play for.

Jasper stood in the middle of the room. "Listen up, Coach is on the way and about to tear us a new one. So lock it the fuck down and keep your mouths shut."

He walked over to Carter Rice whose head was hanging low, a big purple bruise forming on his cheek, and squeezed his shoulder.

"You okay, Rook?"

He looked up. "Yeah Cap, I'm good."

The door flew open and everyone turned, then groaned

as Felix walked in with a massive grin on face, also sporting a black eye.

"That was fucking epic. But heads up, Coach is coming."

A few of the guys visibly winced as Coach stormed into the room, followed by his assistants.

"WOULD SOMEONE LIKE TO EXPLAIN TO ME WHAT THE FUCK PERIOD I JUST WATCHED?"

No one answered, only a few dared to breathe. Coach was formidable at the best of times, but when he was in a rage he was the scariest fucking guy I'd ever met and I couldn't recall a time I'd seen him angrier. I looked around the room, none of the guys meeting Coach's eye.

I nudged Jasper, who'd taken a seat next to me, lowering my voice to a whisper.

"Devon Walls is a piece of shit. He deserved a misconduct for that."

He nodded. "He's a sneaky fuck, he should have had a fucking suspension. I'm surprised Rook didn't get knocked out."

"Clevs and I will deal with it."

"ANYONE?"

There were some mumbles of "No Coach" but for the most part the guys stayed wisely silent.

"WELL LET ME TELL YOU, THAT WAS THE MOST FUCKING AMATEUR DISPLAY I'VE EVER SEEN. YOU'RE BEHAVING LIKE A BUNCH OF KINDER-GARTENERS. YOU SHOULD ALL BE FUCKING EMBAR-RASSED. IT WAS A CLEAN HIT. DO YOU NEED ME TO EXPLAIN THE RULES OF HOCKEY TO YOU?"

He glared around the room.

"I ASKED YOU A FUCKING QUESTION. DO YOU NEED ME TO EXPLAIN THE RULES OF HOCKEY TO YOU?"

"No Coach."

He narrowed his eyes, until you could barely see the

anger piercing through, and dropped his voice to a menacingly quiet level.

"If this continues in the final period and we have to go to extra time, you're all benched for the rest of the season and I'll bring a new team up."

And with that, he turned and stormed out, his assistants following. The locker room staff started handing round electrolytes, water and snacks to refuel us before the next period. A couple of the team physicians and therapists were checking over the guys who'd been hit.

"Rook, you okay?" Felix shouted across the locker room as he stuffed a cereal bar into his mouth.

"Yeah, Clevs. I'm good thanks."

"Good boy." He turned to me. "Drew? We're on this right?"

"Yeah man."

Huck looked up from taping his stick, a gumshield hanging out of his mouth. "Count me in, too."

Jasper stood up, his back to the room, his head moving between us. "Get the puck first, then sort it. This is my last year, I don't want to spend it on the bench."

I pulled a clean jersey over my head. "Don't worry Cap, we got it."

Time was called and we made our way back out to the benches, Brogan heading out to the crease.

Coach was waiting with his hands on his hips. "Cleverly, Crawley, Marks, Sands, Jacobs. You're up."

"Fuck yes." Cooper muttered under his breath. "They're not fucking get through us. Boys, no brakes tonight. Balls to the fucking wall."

Cooper was one of the fastest skaters in the NHL and the speed he hit the puck was no different, one of the reasons he scored so many goals was because the goalie could never see it coming.

We took our positions on the ice, Cooper in center, Felix

and I flanking him on the wing while Jasper and Huck were behind in defense. The Philly team got in their places opposite us, Devon Walls included.

The puck dropped and Cooper snatched it away with lightning speed, passing it over to Felix who was sprinting up the ice, me closely following. I could see Devon Walls reaching out for the puck as Felix passed it back to Cooper across the ice, but he was too late. Huck dropped his shoulder and took him out in an open ice hit, knocking him hard on his ass and out of the way.

"Clean hit, motherfucker." Huck called, skating off.

I gained control of the puck from Cooper, rounding the goal before shooting off my backhand and hitting the far corner of the net, taking us four - three up. The crowd roared, the ones near the board banging on the plexiglass and I skated over, the boys all jumping on me.

"You fucking beauty." Jasper smacked his helmet against mine. "A couple more and we're golden."

With seconds left, we'd scored twice more not letting Philly near the puck. The tension between the teams was high and it was clear we were heading for another brawl, especially as Felix had been baiting Devon Walls for the entire period.

The final buzzer went while Huck chased down Billy McKenzie, right wing for Philly, but before he could reach him he went flying into the boards, smashed at full speed by Walls. His head smacked against the plexiglass and he slid to the floor, his helmet falling off.

The green light for battle had been switched on.

Felix immediately pounced on Walls, gloves flying before they started punching each other, Walls tried to get loose, but Felix was holding him with an iron tight grip on his jersey. I jumped in, Cooper and Jas swarming with the rest of the Philly team, smaller fights breaking out around us.

Cooper was going at it with Jack Howards, their left

wing, while Jasper was holding the Philly goalie when another of their team collided into them, knocking them all into the net, sending it skidding across the ice. The noise levels from the crowds increased, echoing off the arena walls and made louder by the rest of the teams still on the benches banging their sticks against the boards.

The refs quickly followed, whistles blowing like crazy, trying to pull us all apart unsuccessfully.

I tried to grab Walls who was on top of Felix, the pair of them sliding on the ice as they each attempted to land a punch, neither of them willing or able to get up.

"Go fuck yourself, Walls." Felix caught him with a decent left hook.

He retaliated with a cross, that missed. "I'm good, thanks."

"Really, you sure? Because no one else is going to do it. You irrelevant piece of shit."

I lurched backwards as a fist hit me square on my left cheekbone, which stung like fuck. Righting myself I saw Cooper with his arms around Billy McKenzie, holding him from punching me again.

"Fuck off, McKenzie." I caught him with a swift jab before Brogan took over, having skated up from his goal, wanting a piece of the action.

I moved to where Huck was sitting against the boards, the team physicians checking him over.

"Dude, you okay?"

He looked up at me, his eyes not totally focused. "Yeah."

The refs were still tearing the different fights apart, Jasper had succeeded in pulling Walls off Felix and was holding him in a headlock, pulling him back with the help of one linesman. Another one had taken position in between the two of them, trying to stop their fists from connecting with each other.

I helped the officials get Huck to his feet and moved off the ice, away from the continuing fracas. The rink was littered with discarded gloves and sticks, along with most of our helmets. As we neared the benches, Huck went off with the doctors to get fully checked out and I headed down the tunnel to the locker room.

I could hear the showers running in the distance, most of the guys were already stripped down, when I walked in. The attendant handed me an ice pack and I held it over my cheek, which was fucking throbbing. Taking a seat on the benches, I leaned back puffing out my cheeks, watching the rest of the guys slowly wander in.

"What a fucking game." Cooper opened his locker, taking out his phone and letting out a loud groan. "Well, Freddie was watching."

"Yeah?" I glanced up at him for an explanation.

"Fucking hormones, man." He shook his head.

"She not happy about the game?"

"Not exactly."

Yeah, I can't imagine that fight looked pretty from the comfort of home. Hopefully they'd cut to commercials before we'd really started laying into each other, it always looked worse than it really was. Although this one had been bad.

"To be fair, we've not fought like that in a long time and that fucktard's had it coming for ages."

"Yeah, she'll be fine, I didn't get hit at least. How's your face?"

"Bit sore, but no big deal. Come on let's hit the showers and get a drink. We fucking need one."

He started to remove his pads. "You're not heading back to speak to Emerson?"

"Nah, she's in bed already, she has her early class tomorrow. I spoke to her before we went on."

I realized I hadn't actually checked my phone because I assumed she wouldn't be watching and I kind of hoped she hadn't been after Freddie's reaction. I'd never given a shit about getting into fights before because, aside from my parents, there wasn't anyone watching who would have really cared about me being punched, without understanding it wasn't part of the game. The thought of Emerson watching that fight gripped my insides slightly.

As I stood up to reach into my locker, Coach Campbell walked in and the room fell silent. He stood there waiting, his arms crossed until everyone turned to face him, those standing taking a seat on the benches.

"Well, that was a complete shit show. A disgraceful display of sportsmanship. You are an elite team of players and I expect you to conduct yourself as such. I don't give a fuck what the other teams do or how they behave. You don't behave like that." He aggressively pointed his fingers at us. "You're lucky you pulled it back for a win or you can bet your asses you'd be getting benched. Get dressed and be on the bus in fifteen, anyone late can make their own way back. And if you think you're all going partying tonight, you can think the fuck again."

He didn't wait for a reaction before marching out.

Everyone started stripping out of their gear, rushing to get in the showers, no one wanting to piss Coach off further.

"Looks like we'll be drinking in our rooms then." Felix muttered dryly.

The tough love worked. We won the next game three – nil, with no fighting and after four nights away from Emerson, I'd never been more desperate to get back home.

She picked up her phone on the third ring.

"Hi baby."

Even though I'd spoken to her several times every day her voice was still like a warm balm the first time I heard it, soothing away my aches and pains, easing my heart. And I fucking lived for the times she called me baby.

"Hey Sweetheart, how's your day been?"

"Not bad, how's yours? How's your face?"

"It's been okay, but it'll get better the second this plane takes off and lands in New York and I'm with you. I'll be back in three hours, where are you going to be waiting? At mine or yours?"

She laughed. "I'll be at mine."

"Okay, Luck. I can't fucking wait to see you. I'll be there soon." I dropped my voice in case anyone could hear me. "And you better be naked, because there won't be time to remove your clothes before I rip them off."

Her responding groan made my pants very tight. Fuck, four nights away from her was definitely too long.

"Okay babe, see you soon."

Three hours later my car pulled up outside her apartment, I hopped out and buzzed her door.

"Thanks Ralph, I'll call you in the morning." I tapped on the roof and he drove off.

After the world's slowest elevator journey, I reached her floor and I legged it down the hallway to hers, the door ajar. I walked in, dumping my bag on the floor, my mouth drying up at the sight in front of me.

I kicked it shut behind me without breaking my gaze on her. My hand was already on my tie, loosening it, then undoing the top button of my shirt.

"Holy fuck. That's better than naked."

She was standing in nothing but my jersey and even though she was drowning in it, the length of her bare, golden legs meant it only just covered her ass and the tops of her thighs.

She was a sight to behold and the ache I'd had in my balls the past four days dialed up to DEFCON one levels.

"Turn around." I was so amped up, my voice was more of a growl.

I watched her slowly spin, my name appearing on her back as she did. My dick hardened with every second she stood in front of me, constricting itself in my pants until it was almost unbearably painful.

"Lift it up."

And she did. The little vixen was bare underneath, just like I'd ordered, and I could see her pussy glistening, ready and desperate for my touch.

I started to undo my flies as I stalked toward her like she was my prey, because I was definitely about to devour her. Her breath hitched as she took in my predatory expression and started moving backwards across the room, but her eyes only flashed with deep seated lust, the golden flecks burning bright with the same need that lit my veins.

She hit the kitchen table and I closed in, trailing my fingers up the soft expanse of her legs.

"Emerson, this is the sexiest fucking thing I've ever seen."

Her lips parted as my fingers moved higher, until they reached a trickle of stickiness near her apex. Continuing their journey, a monumental groan escaped me, one I could feel in my ever tightening balls, because they'd reached Nirvana and it soaked the palm of my hands.

I plunged three fingers deep inside and it was her turn to groan, feral and raw. She was so turned on I was getting high from the scent of it.

"I don't have any patience to wait right now, Luck. I'm about to bust." I pulled my dick out of my pants, hard as a steel rod.

Lifting her onto the edge of the table I pushed her back to lie down and spread her legs wide in front of me, lining myself up to her dripping wet, swollen pussy. She let out a loud cry as I thrust inside her in one swift motion, straight to the hilt, stretching her tight, silky slick muscles as they rippled against my cock.

"Fucking hell, this is going to be quick." I gritted my teeth, looking down at her still in my jersey and watched her take me, watched her pussy suction onto me and watched my dick disappear inside her again and again as I thrust my hips.

This was another level.

I was so close to coming, my balls had turned into a grenade. "Fuck, you're amazing."

The table started banging against the wall.

I was like a frenzied animal, fucking her into oblivion and she tried to grip onto something for leverage, but came up short on the flat surface, sending things flying as she searched around. I could already feel her legs quivering against me, hardening my cock more than I thought was possible. Her clit was slick with her juices and I started rubbing my thumb against it, bringing her closer to the brink, her throaty mewing getting louder.

Her legs wrapped round me, her heels locking onto my ass as I pulled her further off the edge of the table. Digging my fingers into her hips, I tilted her, gripping her harder while I drove my dick deeper and deeper inside her. I bore down on her clit and she crashed around me with a scream, her pulses firing surges of electricity down my spine, increasing the pressure in my balls until my own release punched me so fucking hard I toppled forward, exploding inside her.

"Jesus Fucking Christ."

I lifted her shuddering body up from the table, my dick still throbbing violently trapped in her tight, satiny vise and sunk my lips into hers, sweeping my tongue around her mouth kissing her on and on, claiming her as mine.

I pulled back, our chests still heaving from exertion, sweat beading our foreheads, but even from the force of both our orgasms I knew we weren't anywhere near being satiated. And I had plans to fuck her for hours.

I wouldn't ever get enough.

"Oh Sweetheart, I'm sorry. That was so fucking selfish of me. You're just too fucking sexy for your own good in my jersey and I couldn't wait. But I promise I'll make it up to you for the rest of the night."

I touched my lips to hers once more and she wrapped her arms around my neck, so soft and supple, her eyes still glazed.

"I'm not going to stop you and I'm definitely not complaining if that's what I'm getting every time you come home."

I gave a dark chuckle, taking her bottom lip between my teeth. "Be careful what you wish for."

I was still inside her when my dick started hardening again. I picked her up and moved us through to her bedroom, kicking off my shoes and shucking my pants as I walked.

Because I always made good on my promises.

9

EMERSON

I put my toothbrush back in the holder and walked through the closet to Drew's bedroom, grabbing a t-shirt from the drawer. We were in his big country house with a rare Saturday off. He'd had a home game last night, with another tomorrow night, and as soon as I'd found out, I called in the favor with Jace to cover my Saturday class, seeing as he still owed me. Which meant we almost had a whole weekend together.

And I was so excited I thought I might burst.

In the time since he'd been back in my life, the only nights we spent apart were the ones when he was travelling. And even with the breakneck speed at which it had all happened, it still felt so normal, like it had been years not months of being together.

Because he got me in a way no one else ever had.

He knew what it took to keep my body in the shape I needed it to be. He understood the drive which woke me up every other day for my six am classes, even if he did want me to stay in bed longer. And he understood my ambition to be the very best I could be, pushing my limits and toward my goal of one day owning my own studio.

All the things that Richard used to fight me on, that he used to try and control me on, Drew encouraged. He was the anti-Richard, filling my life with sweetness and fun.

And it was the same for me.

I loved that our need for fitness united us instead divided. I loved watching him work out in his home gym. In fact, watching his massive muscles flex and contract under the strain of heavy weights was like having my own personal porn channel. And when I could, I'd join him, although that was always cut short when one of us inevitably got distracted by the other.

Usually me. Because he drove me to distraction every single day.

And I never begrudged him travelling, even though I was missing him more every time he left, it was absolutely worth it when he got back and spent an entire night worshiping me. That I also knew he was finding it hard to be apart, made it easier.

Walking into the bedroom I discovered him sitting on the bed in his boxers, staring down at his phone with a frown on his face. But as I got closer I realized it wasn't his phone he was holding, it was mine.

"Babe, what's up?"

He looked at me, his brows knitted together. "Your phone was ringing."

"Okay..."

"Luck, there are seventeen missed calls from 'dickhead'." He airquoted, raising his eyebrow at me. "I take it this is your ex-boyfriend."

I nodded, pulling the t-shirt over my head.

"How often does this happen?"

I shrugged. "I dunno. Once a week, maybe."

His eyes bugged in horror. "Once a week?"

"I think, I don't know."

His frown reappeared, deeper and mixed with an expression of worry. "Emerson, this isn't normal. This guy is clearly tapped."

I'd never really thought about it because the second it stopped ringing I'd forget about him. And I'd been ignoring him for so long now that I realized it never actually occurred to me how weird it was, beyond it being super annoying. I just figured he'd stop eventually.

"I never answer."

He pulled me in to stand between his legs, his hands running up and down the backs of my thighs, making me lose my train of thought. "I know, Sweetheart, but it doesn't matter, this is fucked behavior. He knows you don't want anything to do with him, right?"

"Yes, I've told him several times. We broke up nine months ago, I haven't spoken to him in ages."

He nodded, as though confirming he was right in his assessment of Richard's craziness. He lifted my phone up, holding it to my face to unlock it. I watched him go through the contacts to find Richard's details.

"What are you doing?"

"Blocking him." He looked up, daring me to challenge him, but I didn't because I wasn't sure why I hadn't done it already.

I shrugged again. "Okay."

He threw the phone on the bed once he was done, pulling me down to straddle him. His hands moved across my legs and up around my back, nudging under the fabric of my tee. I could feel the calluses on his palms scratch along my skin, although it only served to comfort me. He leaned in, his nose against my chest and breathed deeply before letting out a contented sigh.

"So, are you excited about your first live game tomorrow? Because I, for one, cannot fucking wait to see you cheering me on from the stands wearing my jersey. Even thinking about it is making me hard."

And if I needed proof, his dick twitched underneath me.

I leaned down to kiss him, lightly pressing my lips to his. "I am, very much so."

I hadn't been to watch him live yet, which was mostly down to a combination of our schedules not matching up, but a small part was also because I knew that it would change our relationship slightly, propelling it forward. All the time we'd spent together had been just us, keeping to ourselves, growing closer day by day. We'd been learning about each other at our own pace, without thinking about when we'd fully acknowledge ourselves as a couple to the outside world.

I didn't want to admit it, but I was also slightly reticent about being outed, besides Mallory and my mom no one knew.

After that conversation where Jessie had been bragging about her friend, I still hadn't told anyone at work except Ashley. Although it wouldn't be long before they figured it out, especially as he'd turned up to more than one of my classes with a protesting Felix in tow, each time causing a small scene with both the riders and the rest of staff team. Mikey and Jessie had even started turning up on their days off, in case the boys made an appearance. And I just wanted keep him to myself for a little longer without hearing another story about someone who'd fucked him once.

His hands moved into my hair, pushing up from the base of my neck, running his fingers through the long strands, bringing a halt to my spiraling thoughts.

"Good. And you've made plans for coming with Wolfie and Fred? You're all going to arrive together? Because I'll already be there, remember?"

I kissed him again, pushing away his worry that I might be on my own. "Yes, Baby, I'm going to go over to Freddie's first and then we'll all leave together."

He looked up at me through his thick boy lashes, happiness spread through his beautiful smile, making his dimple pop. He was literally the antithesis of resting bitch face, joy constantly radiating out of him like a sunbeam. His inherent sweetness always wrapping around me like a warm hug.

But his excitement of having me come to a game was another level entirely, giving me the good type of butterflies deep inside my chest.

"Okay Luck, we have a whole day of uninterrupted togetherness ahead." He lifted me off his lap and smacked my ass hard, making me squeal. "I'll kiss that better later, but first I think we need to start our date."

"Our date?"

He stood up. "Yeah, we've not had a whole day together since our first day when we went for a run and I want to show you one of my favorite places."

"And where's that?"

"It's a surprise." He took my hand and pulled us back into his closet. "Come on, we need to get dressed. Wrap up, because it's not that warm today."

Fifteen minutes later we were in his dark green, custom Ferrari, the seats tailored to fit snug around his huge shoulders, speeding out of the gates and onto the road. Drew's fingers were entwined with mine, resting on his lap. Every few minutes he'd lift my hand up and kiss it, before placing it back where it was.

We started driving along I95, Long Island Sound visible in the distance, reminding me of California and the Pacific. A place I suddenly longed to share with Drew.

"Are you going to tell me where we're going?"

"We're going out to the coast, where the little fishing villages are. I'm going to show you my favorite."

"Oh yeah?"

"Yeah. When I was a kid, before my parents divorced, my dad was always really good at making sure I got time away from the rink, making sure that I wasn't totally consumed by hockey and that we spent time together as a family. He'd bundle Phoebe and me up super early, put us in the car and we'd drive down the coast. Every time we'd go to a new village, my dad would park the car and find somewhere to eat pizza or waffles or pancakes, then we'd go for a long walk along the beaches before heading home." He turned to me, grinning. "It was epic."

I could imagine him as a little boy, all dimples and curls and so much cheekiness it was making my ovaries ache. If cherubs were real, they'd look like Drew.

"You're pretty cute, you know."

"I know. Don't tell anyone. But you can definitely give me a kiss for that." He hooked his finger at me, making me laugh.

I leaned over and kissed him quickly.

"So why's this one your favorite?"

"This is going to sound weird, but it's the one my parents brought us to, to tell us they were divorcing."

"What, really?"

He looked out of the rear-view mirror before answering, slipping out from between two cars and surging forward on the empty lane. All while still holding my hand, his other on the steering wheel, forearm flexing as he barely nudged it.

So fucking sexy. I had to actively stop myself from zoning out and staring as he started talking again.

"I was just about to head to college and my parents wanted us together. We drove down here and they sat us down to say that they loved us and each other, but they were better as friends. And to be fair to them, they stayed friends, it's never been weird for us. Maybe because we were older, but they're both really happy. And then when I got drafted to New York, I kept coming here when the chaos of the city got too much or I needed to think."

"Do you come a lot?"

"I haven't been since I found you again." He lifted my palm to his lips, kissing it. "But when I thought I'd lost you, I was here nearly every week."

My heart clenched tight at the memory of how that had felt. How I'd felt the past year. There but not quite there, wondering if I'd ever see him again.

My Vegas Sex God.

I'd been forced to acknowledge how fleeting chance was, knowing you had to grasp it when you could, and in the end I'd convinced myself the chemistry had been in my head, that you couldn't have a lasting connection with a one night stand.

How wrong I was.

I took my hand back, stroking his face, running my fingers through his hair. "I'm here now, we're together."

"Yes, we are. And I'm not letting you go again."

Another flutter of the good butterflies filled my chest.

I stared out of the window marveling at the scenery, the car eating up the road. I'd never experienced a New England fall and the pictures I'd seen had got nowhere near doing it justice.

Tall trees on either side of us were glowing in the sunshine, their leaves a blanket made from a hundred different shades of orange, red, pink and yellow, burning bright like flames. In between, periodic glimpses of the coast emerged alongside the occasional lighthouse. Soon, boats started to appear, scattering the water, bobbing about on the waves. He turned off the interstate, slowing the car as we passed the picturesque, chocolate box houses so typical of the east coast region, before crossing a welcome bridge signaling our entrance into the village.

It was like a real-life Nancy Meyer's movie.

The main street was filled with people. It seemed we weren't the only ones who'd decided to come for a walk in the October sunshine and we drove along until we found a space, parking up. He cut the engine and turned to me, his hands cupping the back of my head, pulling me into him. As soon as his lips touched mine, I opened up for him without a second thought allowing him access, wanting him so badly, wanting his sweetness to consume me.

I sighed.

My boyfriend is so fucking dreamy.

His tongue stroked round my mouth, his grip at the base of my neck tightening, deepening our kiss. A low moan rumbled through him, hitting me straight between my thighs and I fought the urge to dry hump him until I came.

Which wouldn't take long.

He pulled back, his eyes flashing in amusement at my desperation.

"More of that later." He straightened the collar of my hoodie, pulling it up at the back so it rested against my neck. "Come on, I'm hungry."

He reached into the backseat, retrieving a ball cap and pulled it down low on his face. We both jumped out, meeting at the front of the car. He slung his arm over my shoulder, kissing my head, and for the millionth time I reveled in his height and size.

I stopped as we turned the corner. Okay, this was seriously cute.

The place was already decorated up for Halloween even though it was a still few weeks away. Pumpkins were on every shop stoop, the windows covered in decals of ghosts and witches. Festive bunting lights were strung up across the street.

Drew looked down at me, questioning. "Luck, why have we stopped walking?"

"Because I was just taking in how cute this place is."

"Not as cute as me though, right?" He laughed, kissing me quickly.

I rolled my eyes. "No, not as cute as you."

"Good, good." He pulled me along and into a busy diner.

The scent of maple syrup, sugar and coffee hit me hard, saliva rapidly filled my mouth and my stomach rumbled loudly, desperate for food. Drew looked down at me, his eyebrow raised, he'd clearly heard it.

I shrugged. "I'm hungry."

The waitress guided us to a booth by the window and we slid in, Drew's massive body filling the space and making me laugh.

"What?"

"Nothing, you're just so big."

His eyebrow raised again.

"You know what I mean."

He glanced down at the menu hiding a grin just as the waitress approached.

"What can I get you kids? You want coffee to start?"

Drew looked up at her. "Yes please, plus a large stack and eggs and two juices."

"Okay, that everything?"

"Yeah, we're gonna share."

"Great." She took off, returning a minute later with two steaming mugs of coffee.

I grabbed it from her before she had a chance to place it on the table, blowing on it and taking a big gulp. Drew's eyes were on me as I put it down.

"What?"

One shoulder lifted in a lopsided shrug. "Nothing, I just like seeing you here is all."

He held my gaze as I smiled at him.

"I like being here. This place is seriously cute, it's so unlike California. It's like a movie set."

He nodded as he sipped his coffee. "They're all like this, but this one is the best for sure. They always go all out for decorations too."

I glanced out of the window. "I can see that."

"Do you like Halloween?"

"Yeah, it's fun. The parties are always good. What about you?"

"I love it, usually the club has a big charity Halloween party, but we can't this year because of an away stretch, so we're doing it for New Year instead." He laughed. "Every year Felix and I dress in the most ridiculous costumes."

"Like what?"

He lifted his cap up and rubbed his head. "We've been as so much, he really gets into it and starts planning our costumes months in advance. One year we went as two guys from the Blackhawks that we have a stupid rivalry with, that was fucking funny. The press had a field day with it." His laugh got louder as he remembered more. "A couple of years ago we went as giant pumpkins. Giant. They were so big we kept knocking everything over, people were getting really pissed, especially Coop. It was fucking hilarious."

"You'll still get dressed for New Year?"

"Yeah, I don't know what the theme is yet but we will." He smirked. "You wanna match with me?"

"Maybe." I grinned at him.

Our food arrived, the biggest stack of pancakes I'd ever seen was placed on the table. Drew forked a couple off and put them on my plate.

"Thank you." I picked up the syrup and poured it over.

Drew held his pancakes out for me do to the same, his mouth already full and we ate in silence, both too hungry to speak.

"I fucking love breakfast."

Soon, our bellies were full, pancakes and eggs washed down with juice and coffee. I was glad I'd worn yoga pants instead of jeans because I was sure I was about to burst.

Drew peeled some notes off a wad of cash he pulled from his pocket and placed them on the table.

"Come on, I want to show you the rest."

He stood up, holding his hand out and I took it, his fingers threaded through mine as we said goodbye to the waitress and walked out onto the street again. The Saturday bustle seemed to have increased as the brunch crowd started to emerge. We walked along the sidewalk, taking in the stores and decorations deciding which ones were our favorite.

"Excuse me."

We stopped and turned. Two boys aged around nine years old, both wearing Rangers hoodies, were looking up at Drew in wide eyed awe.

He towered over them. "Hi bud. You okay there?"

Their mouths dropped in surprise that he was actually talking to them. They stood there staring before one of them plucked up the courage to speak, his voice shaky. "Are you Drew Crawley?"

Drew smiled. "I sure am. And who might you be?"

"I'm Sam and this is Bennett." Sam replied, pointing to Bennett.

"Hi Sam and Bennett. I like your hoodies, I have one just like that. You guys Rangers fans?"

The boys nodded vigorously in delight at seeing Drew, who was very clearly one of their heroes.

Their nerves seemed to vanish as they answered in unison. "Yes, you and Felix Cleverley are our favorites. We practice hard so we can be like you when we're older."

Drew chuckled. "Oh yeah, well keep practicing hard and make sure you eat properly and I bet I get to play with you one day."

My head passed back and forth between the three of them, watching this interaction with fascination. Drew, an immense giant, easily double their height, was talking to these two boys with inherent gentleness. And he almost seemed more excited at meeting two genuine fans than they did at meeting him.

"We will." Bennett replied, bobbing about from one foot to the other. "Um, also, do you think we could have a picture with you?"

"Yeah sure, buddy. I can sign your hoodie too if you'd like me to?"

"Yes, that would be awesome." Exclaimed Sam, his eyes big and wide.

Drew pulled a Sharpie from his pocket, throwing a wink at me as he did. The boys pointed to where they wanted it and he scrawled his name.

I held my hand out. "Would you like me to take the picture?"

As though they'd only just noticed I was standing next to Drew, their nerves reappeared as they took me in, silently handing me their phone. Drew bent down and put one arm around each of them. I took a couple of shots before handing it back.

"Thank you, Mr Crawley."

"Hey, it's Drew." He reached into his pocket again, pulling out two business cards. "Are you coming to the game tomorrow night?"

They shook their heads, each taking a card. "No, sir. Not this time."

"Well if you want to, or want to come to another game, you email this address." He tapped the card. "Put your details in the email and in the subject line you need to write Lucky Charm tickets and my team will get them sorted for you. You got that?"

I jumped slightly at the mention of my name.

They looked at it with reverence. "Yes, sir. Thank you."

"Good. Lucky Charm tickets, don't forget. I hope to see you there. It was great meeting you both." He reached down and took my hand back in his. "See you around soon."

They turned and walked away, their heads together whispering.

I ran my hand around the back of his neck, stretched up and kissed him on the cheek. "That was amazing."

He smiled, wrapping his arms around me.

"I like to give back to genuine fans." He shrugged like it was nothing, but I noticed the edges of his neck flush. "Your brother must do the same."

"I've never seen kids come up to my brother. I think they're scared of the tattoos."

Drew threw his head back laughing, maneuvering us to start walking again. "Yeah, I can see why."

True story. Jupiter was covered in tattoos, usually wearing a scowl, intimidating to anyone who didn't know him, and to most people who did. But what was never publicized was the amount of time he spent in the local communities, helping children find sports through grass roots. He made sure everything was kept private and low key, so that his tabloid life never overshadowed it.

I'd begged him to change his mind, but it was an argument I never won.

We turned left at the end of the street, away from where the car was parked, heading toward the beach. The salty sea air hit us with a gust of wind, blowing away the sluggishness from our massive pancake feast.

It was still warm enough for kids to be running along the water's edge without their shoes on, while more built sandcastles nearby. Seagulls were diving onto the water, carrying lone fish away in their beaks, taking what was left from the hauls brought in on the fishing boats anchored offshore.

We stepped onto the sand, it was wet and compacted enough that it didn't kick up our heels with every step. Drew flung his arm back around me, his biceps resting on the back of my neck, his hand dangling off my shoulder. I reached up, linking our fingers back together, my arm crossing my chest. Happiness washed over me, I could stay like this forever.

"Have you told him about me?" He asked quietly.

"Told who?"

"Jupiter, does he know about me?"

I shook my head. "No. I haven't, not yet. I haven't spoken

to him for a few weeks actually. He's getting ready for the World Series."

We carried on walking in contented silence.

"Does anyone know about me?"

"What do you mean?"

"Emerson, stop being obtuse. You know what I mean. Have you told anyone that we're in a relationship?" He snapped.

I jolted at his tone and stopped us walking, he'd never spoken to me like that before and I couldn't read his expression as I studied his face.

"Babe? Where's this coming from?"

"I was just thinking about the conversation we'd had about your brother and professional athletes. And with what happened at work. I just…" He trailed off.

"Just what?"

He dropped his head. "Are you ashamed of me?"

If I couldn't hear the vulnerability weighing heavy in his voice I'd have laughed, because at the very least I'd have thought he was joking. But I'd been slowly learning the impact our year apart had on him, and as our feelings deepened every so often insecurity flared, because there was more at stake now.

I dipped down below the rim of his ballcap, so I could look into his eyes. "No, of course I'm not. Why would you even think that?"

He lifted his head back up. I ran my thumb through the soft scruff on his cheek, looking at him while I waited for an answer.

"I want to be someone you deserve and are proud of. I've never been in a relationship before. And you have."

Doubt flashed through his eyes and it made my heart ache.

I took my hand and placed it on his chest. "This is nothing like what I've been in before."

He let out a deep sigh, trying to expel his fears. "I've never cared before what people think of me, I've always just done what I want. But now I have you I don't want my past actions to impact us."

I ran my arms up around his neck, cupping the back of his head so he was forced to look at me. "I don't care what people think either. I've already experienced enough gossip when Richard and I were together and turned out he was sleeping with half the nursing staff, everyone talked behind my back. But I haven't not told anyone because I'm ashamed of you."

His eyebrows shot up, hopeful. "Really?"

I nodded. "Yes really. And people do know. I've told Mallory, my best friend in the world, I've told my mom and I've told Ashley from work. I haven't told my brother because he's busy and I haven't told anyone else at work because I just wanted to keep you to myself a bit longer before I became the center of their gossip, but I don't care that I will. Baby, I think you're incredible and I am proud of you. You're part of my life now."

And that was the absolute truth, he'd been seeping so deep into my bones I couldn't imagine being without him.

There was a nanosecond where I saw his face light up before his mouth slanted onto mine, his lips enveloping me in warmth and happiness. His palms, cool from the sea air, held my cheeks, his long fingers wrapping around the back of my neck. One hand left my face for a second while he spun his cap around needing more access, then came back, pulling me in closer to a kiss so brimming with emotion I could almost cry.

His tongue swept through my mouth, gentle but needy and with a soft moan he deepened further, tangling us together hot and wanting. I ran my hands up to hold the back of his head, standing on the very tips of my toes for leverage, sinking into him, desperate for more. My entire

body was heating up and the ache that seemed to permanently reside in the pit of my belly grew heavier. I could feel
his cock, hard against my groin, and I tried to rub against it,
desperate for friction without a single care for the fact that
we were on a public beach.

He slowed down and pulled away, taking my lower lip
with him until he let it go with a pop, looking at me.

"You make me happy, Emerson. A level of happiness I
didn't even know existed and I want to give it back to you."
He kissed my nose. "Come on, let's go home. I've had enough
of being outside where I can't get you naked."

10
——————
EMERSON

Mallory: *How are thing with VSG?*
         Emerson: *Good, dreamy, perfect*
Mallory: *How's the sex?*
Emerson: *World rocking*
Mallory: *That's what I like to hear. Are you excited for your first live game?*
Emerson: *Haha. Yes, I am. Nervous excited.*
Mallory: *I gotta say Em, I tried to watch a game and had zero fucking clue what was going on. I practically went cross eyed trying to find the puck*

Sounds about right.

I laughed and flopped back on the bed, throwing my phone to the side, wanting to concentrate on my current view rather than my phone. I was heading over to meet Freddie and Wolfie in a few hours, but for the moment I was content in watching Drew get ready to head out, fascinated by his routine.

We'd woken up early and, when normally I was the one leaving, he shot up and instead of having sex with me, started rushing around. So naturally I'd tried to have sex with him

143

only to get rejected, because *'gotta keep the boys in check before the game'.*

Whatever the fuck that meant.

I'd tried getting in the shower with him, but found myself banned, so instead I went downstairs and made him a coffee, like a good girlfriend, and he'd taken it with him to practice.

While he was gone I'd used his gym, which was easily four times the size of my apartment.

I'd never been in there alone, all other times with Drew, where I always tried to contain my excitement at how seriously impressive it was even for a professional athlete. Filled with top of the range equipment, it was sectioned up into areas for working each muscle group, plus a space for plyometrics and stretching. He also had a massage room, steam and sauna.

It was exactly how I'd imagined my dream gym to look if the day ever came when I opened my own.

He'd got back at lunchtime for a two-hour nap which he insisted on taking with me, fully clothed, moving me into the little spoon and snuggling me tightly. And even though I hadn't felt remotely tired, his soft breathing had lulled me into such a state of relaxation that I'd fallen into my own deep sleep, content and deliriously happy.

And now here I was, still in bed, watching him in his dressing room, tying his tie in the mirror.

I didn't think it was possible for him to look more beautiful, but in an impeccably fitted, custom suit he was another level. His pants hung perfectly off his hips, accentuating his incredible ass and the way the shirt hugged his muscles was almost obscene. Memories of the night I'd met him in Vegas, when he'd been dressed in a similar fashion, came hurtling back into focus.

It was no wonder I'd never been able to get over him, I'd fallen under his spell then and I was under it now.

I was practically drooling.

He snapped me out of my daydream, looking at me in the reflection.

"Luck, don't look at me like that. I told you, no sex before the game. But I promise you, when we get home later, I'll fuck you so hard you won't ever question my no sex rule again."

He went back to getting dressed, so nonchalant, like he hadn't just made my panties flood in anticipation because my vagina would never get enough of him.

When the show was over, he walked toward me and tipped my chin up. "Now come downstairs please and give me a kiss."

He pulled me to standing and walked us out of his bedroom, down the stairs to the front door where his hockey bag was on the floor. Wrapping his arms around my waist he pressed his lips to mine, more chastely than he'd ever done before. Instead of granting me access to his mouth, his lips travelled along the edge of my jaw, taking a deep inhale at the pulse point below my ear. It was a stark reminder to my body that we hadn't had sex today, subconsciously pushing itself further into him.

"Emerson." He growled in a warning tone against my neck, the goosebumps already pebbling my skin increased tenfold.

He stepped back.

"Sweetheart, I have to go. Don't forget, Ralph will be here to collect you in two hours, then take you to Freddie's and bring you to the Garden. I've sent his number to you so you have it, but call me if there are any problems." He picked up an envelope from the console table, tipping out the contents. "Here are your passes. You need to keep them with you at all times, they'll get you everywhere you need to be. Okay?"

I opened the door for him. "I'm good. I'll be fine, I'll be with Wolfie and Freddie too. I'll see you in a few hours."

"Yes, good. Okay." He visibly relaxed, his hands moving to

the back of my head. "I'm so fucking excited to see you in my jersey."

I grinned at him. "Me too, Baby. I'm so fucking excited to watch."

He smacked his lips to mine once more, then picked up his bag and walked out. I watched him drive off, waiting until he was out of sight before heading back to the bedroom to find my phone. There was a message from Freddie.

Freddie: *Hey, looking forward to seeing you later. Ready for your first live game?*

Emerson: *Can't wait. See you soon, pick you guys up in a few hours.*

Freddie: *Perfect.*

I walked into Drew's closet where he'd hung some of my things, alongside the jersey he wanted me to wear. His jersey. I removed it from the rail, along with a pair of skinny jeans and laid it out on the bed, contemplating my next move.

I wasn't normally the type of girl who spent hours getting ready, but I also wasn't an idiot. If I'd learnt anything from spending any time with my brother, I knew full well there was a chance I'd end up in a photo somewhere and didn't relish being ripped apart by the gossip columns. Drew liked me fresh faced and in sweats, but I'd be damned if I looked anything less than hot as fuck, and it always took longer to appear like you hadn't spent any effort at all. Which is what I'd decided I was going for.

I turned the shower up hot and stepped in.

Ralph pulled up in front of Cooper and Freddie's gigantic house and the front doors opened as we pulled to a stop, Wolfie's enormous bump leading the way. She'd recently stopped coming to the studio, so I hadn't seen her for a few weeks. I jumped out and gave her a hug, helping her down the steps.

She was so big I wasn't sure how she'd get in the car.

"Do you want to sit in the front?"

Ralph was holding the door open for her.

"Yes I think so, I'm finding it hard to maneuver much at all these days with this bloody baby."

"Not long now though, right?"

She climbed into the front seat of the SUV and rubbed her belly, groaning. "I feel ready to burst, but still ten days until my due date. I'm sure the doctors got it wrong. This is my last home game for a bit though, I had to sleep all day just to get the energy for this."

I laughed, getting into the back seat. I saw Freddie walk out of the house, shutting the door behind her before she got in the car next to me. With the three of us in matching jerseys we looked like some kind of girl band.

"Hi ladies, ready to go?"

"You bet."

Ralph drove off and we were soon on the interstate heading into the city.

Freddie's hand patted my knee. "First live game! You look good in Drew's jersey."

Even though I was only in jeans and biker boots, it was a nice change to move out of my usual yoga pants. It had taken me an hour to get my thick hair under control, but I'd blown it out into big waves and it currently rested down my shoulders.

I smiled. "Thank you. He was pretty excited about this. And yes, I am, but I've watched most of them on tv already."

"Just wait until you see it live, it's so different being there."

"The atmosphere?"

"Yes. It's just raw and packed with testosterone. It's like foreplay." She cackled. "Watching Coop has always turned me on, but right now with these baby hormones I can barely make it home without jumping him. Plus he won't have sex with me before a game, which makes it ten times worse. I'm lucky he's an athlete with a lot of stamina. Because if I'm not crying, I'm horny. Thankfully I've not cried during sex yet."

I threw my head back, laughing. Over the last few months, I'd spent a lot of time with Wolfie and Freddie, they'd taken it upon themselves to befriend me and show me the ropes of dating a Ranger, and I was incredibly grateful. They were funny and sweet, and I'd just about got used to their slightly strange English ways and Freddie's unfiltered, forthright way of speaking.

We hit Midtown, I could see the iconic Madison Square Garden in the distance, lit up in red, white and blue. I'd never been here before and nervous excitement started to flutter in my belly. We turned into the players' entrance through big security gates, flashing our passes, and driving down the ramp underneath the arena, stopping in front of a set of double doors where a young man in a suit was waiting. Freddie and I got out of the car, Ralph holding the door open for Wolfie as she slid off the seat.

"Hi Joey, how are you." Freddie greeted him. "This is Emerson, Drew Crawley's girlfriend. Emerson, this is Joey, he works in the PR team for the club."

He smiled. "Hi Emerson, good to meet you. Have you got your passes?"

I reached into my bag and pulled them out, putting them around my neck. "Yep, here."

"Great." He turned back to Freddie. "How are you both? We've set up one of the suites for you."

"Oh, thanks Joey. You're a lifesaver." Replied Wolfie when she joined us. "Let's go."

We walked slowly toward the elevator, getting in.

"We don't normally go to the boxes, we sit down in the

team seats near the ice, but it's too much down there being pregnant. I just couldn't face the crowds jostling me around, so Joey kindly sorted this out for us, plus it means we're mostly out of view of the cameras."

Joey smiled and I noticed his cheeks redden slightly at her praise. "You're welcome Wolfie, it was my pleasure."

"Sounds perfect. Out of the cameras is always my preference."

The elevator doors opened and he led us down a corridor to the suite. Walking through an entrance hall and into the main room, we were immediately hit by cold air because the far end was a half wall of glass over-looking the ice. I'd never realized how enormous the arena was, the crowds already filling the space, their chatter competing with the music blasting from the speakers.

Our box was perfectly positioned at the halfway line, right where the puck would drop. Above it the score box flashed with the players faces and stats, I rolled my lips when Drew's appeared, actively trying to stop myself from bursting out with a giant grin and looking like a lunatic, but my heart was dancing around with more than a little pride.

My first game.

I was watching my boyfriend.

My boyfriend who played ice hockey.

My boyfriend.

Boyfriend.

"It's cool, isn't it?" Freddie joined me against the railings, leaning over. "Do you want a drink?"

"Yes and yes."

We turned back into the room, where a table of food and drinks was set up along one side. Shrugging out of my jacket, I flung it on an empty seat and reached for a bottle of beer.

"You look perfect, Drew's jersey suits you." Wolfie smiled up at me from the confines of the sofa she'd positioned herself on, her hand never leaving her belly. "I'm so excited for you to experience your first live game. I remember watching Jasper when we first met, it was amazing. That was the night I properly started to realize I had feelings for him."

"You weren't dating already?"

Freddie snorted. "God, she made him wait forever. Poor Jas."

"Don't feel too sorry for him. He got me in the end, didn't he?" She pointed to her belly. "And now look. I'm the size of a small elephant, I haven't seen my feet in months and I can't stop peeing."

Freddie passed her a glass of champagne. "Here, this will help you feel better. Molly said you can have a small one."

"Thank you." Wolfie took it, sipping on it slowly, savoring every bubble. "God this is good. I miss enjoying a proper drink."

"Who's Molly?"

"She's my sister-in-law, Coop's sister. She's a doctor." Freddie replied.

Wolfie nodded. "Yes, and hopefully it'll push this baby into deciding it wants to come early and not when Jas is away."

"This stretch is eight days, right? It's so long."

"Yes, they're due back the day after this baby is supposed to come. Thankfully our parents are arriving tomorrow, and I look forward to being waited on hand and foot. Not that Jasper doesn't do it when he's home." Her expression turned soft and sentimental. "I'm not sure I've ever seen him so excited."

"I bet." I smiled. I hadn't spent much time with Jasper, but I could imagine him doting on her, running around for whatever she wanted.

"Anyway, enough about us. How are things with Drew?"

Now it was my turn to become soft and sentimental and I

couldn't hold back the cheesy grin this time. "Good, really good. Perfect."

They both looked at me, their faces telling me they knew exactly what I was feeling. A massive cheer went up from the crowds, I glanced over, the players had started their pre-game skate.

"Em, please can you help me up so I can pee before the game starts?"

I laughed at Wolfie's outstretched arms and pulled her to standing, walking back to join Freddie at the railings, as she waddled off.

All the players from both teams were on the ice, sprinting up and down, knocking the pucks back and forth. I scoured the rink, looking for Drew and when I spotted him I don't know how I missed him. He was with Felix, the pair of them equally enormous, throwing and catching pucks with their sticks. They had such good dexterity and hand/eye coordination, they could probably make it as pro tennis players if they ever quit hockey.

Time was called and the ice was cleared, both teams skating off to their benches just as Wolfie returned.

"Oh good, I didn't miss anything. Let's hope I can hang on until the end of the period before I need to go again." She sat down on one of the chairs overlooking the arena.

The crowds were going crazy, chants and Mexican waves between eighteen thousand people made a lot of noise. The buzzers sounded and the starting line ups from both sides made their way out onto the ice, Jasper and the opposing Captain talking to the one of the referees before they took their positions.

But my gaze was fixed on only one player, Number 77, on the right of Cooper in the middle, Felix on the left. His shoulder was already dropped against the guy he was marking and I almost felt sorry for him because Drew really was absolutely enormous. The puck dropped and I nearly fell off my chair at Freddie screaming. Cooper swept it away, up the ice, passing it over to Felix.

But I couldn't take my eyes off Drew, watching him knock a guy on his ass with what looked like barely a nudge before skating up the ice, keeping close to Cooper and intercepting anyone who got in the way of the puck and the goal. He was so fast, shooting across the rink, taking control of the puck and passing it to any one of his teammates, that if I blinked for longer than a split second, I lost him.

Another guy hit the boards; Drew the human bowling ball and they his feeble, wobbly pins. The girls had been correct, this was nothing like TV and nothing could have prepared me for seeing it live. The aggression was another level. And fucking sexy. I had not expected it to be so sexy.

But, holy shit was it sexy.

I'd never been one to brag, but that was my boyfriend down there.

My boyfriend.

Seeing him take that guy out should definitely not have turned me on as much as it did, but I could say with absolute certainty my panties were no longer dry. And I don't think it had anything to do with the fact that we hadn't had sex today.

My entire body was tingling, his promise of fucking me once we were home at the forefront of my mind while I watched him sprint along the ice, flicking the puck over to Cooper.

"FUCKING GET IT. YES BABY." Screamed Freddie as he shot it to the back of the net, while she jumped up and down.

All the guys landed on Cooper, slapping his back, knocking his head. He looked up to our box and the camera showed him winking at Freddie. She blew kisses back to him, her eyes filling with tears.

The boys took their places on center ice again, ready for

the drop. This time Drew took control, sweeping it away, his massive legs powering him forward. He flicked the puck over to Felix before skimming around the boards, taking control once more and slamming it into the goal. The Rangers had a two nil lead all within a matter of minutes.

It was a wonder the other team even bothered showing up, they'd barely had contact.

Wolfie, Freddie and I started screaming again. The crowds were going wild, those near the boards smacking their hands against the plexiglass. My eyes were glued to him and just as Cooper had, he turned to our box, pointing his stick at me with the biggest grin I'd ever seen. As big as the one I was currently sporting.

The buzzer went, claiming both the end of the first period and my voice, now hoarse from screaming so loudly. I watched all the players make their way off the ice, waiting until Drew was completely out of sight before I turned back to the room.

"It's fucking hot, right." Freddie nudged me.

I puffed out my cheeks. "I gotta say, I was not expecting that. It's so different to watching at home."

"Told you." She grinned. "I hope you'll come to more home games with us."

"Try and keep me away." I laughed, picking up some food from the table.

The second and third periods carried on in much the same way, the game ending in a shutout. Or what I wanted to call total and complete annihilation.

Seriously, the other team should have stayed home.

We waited for Wolfie to pee for the seventy fifth time then left the suite, making our way through the corridors of the arena, the walls covered with pictures of the teams that had played there from Rangers to Knicks, along with bands through the years from Rolling Stones to Madonna.

It was definitely very cool.

153

The further we walked the busier it got, even though we were effectively backstage and none of the crowds had access here. Management staff, arena assistants, physicians and sports journalists were all working hard in their post-game roles. I was so busy looking around that I didn't notice Freddie had stopped and nearly walked into her.

We'd reached the locker room.

"We wait here." She said. "They'll be out soon."

I tried to act cool, but I couldn't. Butterflies were somersaulting in my belly, excitement lacing my veins, and every time the doors opened the smell of sweat and boys hit me in a brutal onslaught evoking forgotten memories of high school, when I used to wait for Pete Walton, my first boyfriend, star quarterback of the football team.

And then there he was, first through the doors.

And like every single time before, he stole the air around me.

He stalked over, looking every inch the hockey player who'd scored half the total goals and taken out nearly all the players on the opposing team. Every inch the hockey player in the suit made for his body, a body that looked even bigger than it did when he'd left me five hours ago. His hair was still wet from the shower, the smell of sandlewood and leather and musk making my knees weak and assaulting my senses.

"Hey Luck. Did you enjoy your first game?"

He didn't wait for my answer before bending down to kiss me, brushing my lips, then taking my mouth in a big, wet open kiss, his eyes still fixed on mine. I could feel his smile, his lips never leaving mine as he dropped his bag on the floor then cupped my face. Sealing me in a full-blown embrace, unabashedly claiming me in the hallway, his tongue stroked against mine with a groan that hit me straight between the thighs.

The pent-up lust from the last few hours almost hit breaking point.

Holy shit.

My entire body was on fire.

Panties incinerated.

Clit throbbing.

I wondered if there was a locker, cupboard, bathroom stall, anywhere he could take me. Any flat surface he could fuck me against would do fine. I wasn't fussy. Wouldn't need long. That kiss bringing me very close to the brink.

There was a loud cough from behind and he chuckled, pulling back from me but not letting me get very far. Felix and Huck were standing behind him, grinning.

Huck raised his eyebrow. "Is it pointless us asking if you're coming for drinks?"

Drew looked down at me, his hand curled around mine and he started tracing little patterns on my palm with the tips of his fingers, which only served as a stark reminder to my body that he hadn't touched me enough today. "Yes. I'd say so."

I glanced around, Cooper and Freddie were also glued together.

It was official.

Hockey was the sexiest sport. No question.

And I don't think it made a difference whether you had pregnancy hormones. You just needed eyes.

I turned to Wolfie, who was leaning against the wall. "Where's Jasper?"

"He'll probably be doing some interviews. But I hope he hurries up, he's going to be pissed if they keep him too long."

As if on cue, Jasper walked out of the locker room, pushing both the doors open together, heading straight for Wolfie, her face lighting up with so much love. He pressed his hands on either side of her stomach, before kissing her gently and whispering quietly in her ear.

"Okay, we're going home. Wolfie's tired." He flung his arm

around her shoulder. "Hey Emerson, did you enjoy your first visit to the Garden?"

I grinned. "I did, thanks. It was awesome."

By awesome, I meant fucking phenomenal.

Best ever.

"Yeah, Drew practically wet himself in excitement at you being here. He's never scored so much, maybe you should come more often." Sniggered Felix.

Drew smirked, flipping him the bird with both hands.

"We all know the only true part of that sentence is I was excited that Lucky was here. And I don't give a fuck who knows it." He rubbed his hands together. "And on that note, we are getting out of here."

He took my hand again. "Ready?"

I nodded. Wolfie, Freddie and I only managed to give each other a small one-armed hug, mainly because the giant hockey players we were attached to wouldn't let us go.

Drew led me away down the ramp to his car.

He pressed the fob to unlock it and gave me a quick kiss as he opened the door before pushing me against the frame. Deepening, he pressed his heavy thigh between my legs, right where I needed it to be. Right where the pressure had slowly been building up over the last few hours. My breathing labored.

I was practically panting when his lips moved to my neck.

"So where does my little horn dog want to stay tonight?" He murmured into my skin.

I pulled away, my eyebrow raised in question.

His face flashed in amusement, his voice gruff and pebbly. "Don't pretend that you aren't dripping wet for me."

Yeah, I couldn't.

"Loft is closest."

"Get in the car."

He threw his bag in the trunk and hopped into the driver's seat, turning to me before he started the engine.

His hazel eyes blazed as they locked into mine. "Do you know how fucking sexy you are in that jersey, how much I loved seeing you in it when I looked up at the box, knowing I was going to take you home with me tonight? That's what I was playing for Emerson, I was playing for you."

His hand was moving up my thigh while he was speaking and I subconsciously shifted, my legs parting of their own accord, allowing him access to where I desperately needed the pressure. His fingers ran along the seam of my jeans, sitting at the apex of my thighs, slowly rubbing hard, but not hard enough.

My lungs were fighting for oxygen, because there was none in this car.

"Did you enjoy watching me?"

I nodded, biting down on my lip as the pressure increased between my legs, his eyes tracking the movement.

"How badly do you need it?"

"So badly." The words came out as a whimper.

He unbuttoned my jeans, helping me wriggle out of them, pushing them down just enough along with my panties.

"Spread your legs."

I moved them as far apart as I could.

He ran his fingers along my slit. "Fuck, you're so wet for me. Did it turn you on watching me?"

I jumped as his thumb brushed over my hyper-sensitive clit, sending tiny seizures through my pussy.

"Did you enjoy seeing me knock all those fucking pansies on their asses?"

I nodded again. I was teetering on the edge.

I groaned loudly, watching his thick fingers disappear inside me, his wrists and forearms flexing as he added another, curling them up, rubbing against my G-spot, his thumb circling my hardened little nub.

"You're so perfect and beautiful. I can't wait to get inside you." He leaned over and flicked his tongue against my top

157

lip. "Look at me, I want to see your face when you come all over my hand."

His eyes were glazed, his pupils dilated. I could see how hard he was, his dick straining against the zipper in his pants. He was as turned on as me. Pressure was shooting down my spine, pooling deep and heavy between my thighs. He flicked my clit one last time and my entire body tensed before I fell apart, unable to hold it, throbbing around his fingers, my walls clamping down.

He stroked me until I could take no more, until I cried out from his touch on my raw, hyper-sensitive skin, removing his fingers and sucking on them.

"Mmmmm. Magically delicious."

His lips crashed onto mine before I could take another breath, tasting myself as his tongue ran round my mouth.

He moved away and started the engine. "Right. We're going home or I'll be fucking you in this car."

We tumbled into the loft twenty minutes later, our lips glued together, his hands on my ass, my legs wrapped firmly around his waist. Kicking the door shut with his heel, I littered my stuff on the floor as he marched across the open space to his bedroom, throwing me onto the bed.

"Clothes off."

He watched me strip as he shed his own clothes. He was so worked up and still so full of adrenaline from his game, every muscle in his body was straining and the sight of him standing in front of me stroking his rock-hard cock sent my heartbeat into orbit.

This was not going to be gentle. A flood of arousal poured out of me.

"Lean back on the pillows and push your tits together. I'm fucking them first. Then I'm fucking your pussy." His voice had reached the deep, low sticky pitch it got when he was finding it hard to concentrate on anything but fucking.

He crawled over the bed, over my body, until he straddled

me, his abs clenching above me. He reached into the drawers by the bed, pulling out a bottle of lube, flipping the lid and squeezing it into his hands. Taking hold of his cock again, he rubbed the length of it. His pupils dilated, his hazel eyes melting into dark toffee, hooded and glazed.

It was the most erotic sight of my life.

With his huge, god like body, he hovered over me, gliding himself straight between my boobs, gripping onto the headboard for support.

His jaw slackened. "Oh fuck. This feels fucking amazing. Oh Jesus, your tits. Fuck Emerson."

His pink tongue curled along his lower lip as he slowly pumped his hips back and forth. His hands pushed mine away, taking over from where I was holding my boobs, squeezing them together, running his thumbs over my nipples, every brush the catalyst for explosions of ecstasy bursting across my body.

My fingers traced around the curves of his abs one at a time, moving up the thick wedge of muscle on his hips and down to his incredible, peachy firm ass.

The ass that I'd stare at all day if I could.

I'd never done this before Drew, never met any guy who loved boobs as much as Drew and never thought about how incredibly sexy it was. But it was so fucking sexy, this giant mountain of muscle above me, struggling to control himself, his breathing heavy and labored and ready to burst.

His eyes were trained on his cock, watching it slide in between my boobs, the soft round head dripping pre cum all over my chest. I stuck my tongue out flat to lick it up the next time he thrust forward, wrapping my lips around the end before he moved back.

His head dropped back with an animalistic groan that hit me straight in my swollen clit, dialing up the deep throb desperate for release.

"Touch yourself. Tell me how wet you are."

I didn't need to touch myself to know I was dripping wet. Seeing him above me, his eyes glazed over as he thrust harder and harder, I don't think I'd ever been so turned on in my life.

This man owned me.

"Fuck, I'm going to come. Emerson, open your mouth."

He took my chin and fed his giant cock through my lips, my tongue flicking the underside as I pulled on his balls. He exploded in a roar, just as he hit the back of my throat, and I swallowed everything, salty and sweet and him.

He dropped his body taking my mouth in his, sweeping his tongue against mine, tasting himself, before moving down my body. Laving along my chest, he bit my tight nipples one at a time, then continued his journey, not leaving an inch of my body untouched until he reached his destination.

Holding my legs apart with his massive shoulders, his fingers spread me further and he breathed deeply. "You fucking beauty."

My groan rolled through me like thunder. His tongue lapped long and flat up my slit, sucking hard on my clit as he reached it. I couldn't move from his vise like grip on my hips and he showed me no mercy. *Lick, stab, suck, lick, stab, suck* went his tongue like his life depended on it.

"Fuck, yes. Do not. Stop. Doing that."

My legs were violently quivering within a matter of seconds, the pressure too much for me to contain and I exploded onto his face, every rippling muscle in my body turning to jelly.

He crawled up slowly, kissing along my hip bones, my belly, my chest before he reached my face, sweeping away the stray hairs stuck to my forehead. He peered down at me, his eyes still filled with lust and silently telling me he was nowhere near finished.

"Shower time." He pushed up on one hand, rising above me. He rolled me to one side, smacking my ass hard, making me squeal. "Let's clean up so I can get you all dirty again."

I wasn't about to argue.

11

EMERSON

I desperately needed to pee.
Desperately.

But also, I was very comfortable in bed and didn't want to move.

However, having a two hundred and thirty pound hockey player stretched across me and pressing into my bladder wasn't helping my cause for not moving.

It was a conundrum.

I turned gently, so as not to disturb Drew, whose face was pushed as close into the side of my body as he could possibly get it. It was a wonder he could even breathe, but I'd learned he liked to hold me tight all through the night.

Christ, I sounded like a Boys II Men throw back. I'd turned us into a cheesy make out song. The need to pee making me delirious.

It was becoming urgent.

I peeled myself out from underneath him and he barely stirred, still exhausted from the night before, from his game and keeping good on his promise of fucking me all night. I stretched out all my aches as I padded quietly through to the bathroom on my tip toes. Catching sight of myself in the mirror, my hair all over the place with a thoroughly fucked look. Because that's what it was.

That's what I was.

I quickly peed and washed my hands, taking the opportunity to brush my teeth and run my fingers through my hair. When I walked back into the bedroom, Drew was still in the same position almost face first in the pillow, one hand above his head, sleeping like the dead.

I leaned against the door frame watching him, his massive traps and lats gently lifting with each breath he took, the sinews of his muscles rippling, the top of the duvet resting in the lower curve of his back just above his incredible ass.

He really was a work of art.

I ran a hand over my stomach as it gurgled, what time was it? He made me lose all track and I realized I had no idea where my phone was, not sure I'd even looked at it since before the game.

I went in search of it, following a trail of discarded shoes and jackets from when we'd come in last night. The October morning sun shone through Drew's giant, floor to ceiling windows which stretched the length of the huge open space. I should probably have put some clothes on because anyone looking through the windows right now was getting a little naked show.

I found my bag, rummaging around until my hand closed round smooth metal and glass, and pulled it out, the screen lighting up at the movement.

MISSED CALL: JUPITER x 3

Jupiter: Why have I just seen you on my television screen at the Rangers game?

I groaned. Guess it was time for us to have a conversation.

I wasn't lying to Drew the other day when I said I just hadn't had a chance to talk to Jupe, but I was also pretty sure I wasn't going to enjoy this conversation. He had always hated Richard, for good reason, but Jupiter's manwhorish ways only made him more overly protective of me.

It was a trait that all manwhore brothers shared.

Fact.

I looked forward to the day he was brought down by a woman, because it was going to happen sooner or later.

I checked the time, nine am here which meant it was still early in California. Not expecting a reply, I shot him a vague text back which hopefully he wouldn't read into until we could talk in person.

Emerson: *Because I was watching the game*

I crept back into bed, Drew still dead to the world and I slunk under the warmth of the covers and his arms as best I could. My phone buzzed on the side table where I'd placed it.

Jupiter: *But why were you in the Players' box?*

Emerson: *Because that's where my seat was*

Jupiter: *Emerson?*

Emerson: *Jupiter?*

Jupiter: *Please tell me you're not dating a player.*

Emerson: *I can't do that*

Jupiter: *Which one?*

Emerson: *Drew Crawley*

Jupiter: *Emerson, have you lost...*

"Who are you texting at this hour?" Drew's gruff voice broke the silence.

I turned to him, his eyes still closed. "My brother, he saw me at the game last night."

"Good, now you can tell him you have a boyfriend. Me. And once you do that you can snuggle back down into this bed because it's too early to wake up."

His soft stubble grazed the crook of my neck as he left a trail of kisses, causing me to let out a loud giggle.

"It's gone nine."

"Yes, exactly. Too fucking early."

I dropped my phone off the bed and let him pull the

covers over us, his arms wrapped around me as he drifted back off to sleep.

Jupiter could wait.

I stuck my headphones in as I walked out of my apartment dialing Jupiter's number, slipping my phone into my pocket as the ringing started up in my ears. Drew had left for a physio session and massage, and I'd come back to mine to pick up some clean clothes ahead of the class I was teaching later this afternoon. I figured my walk to the studio was as good a time as any to call my brother back and get this conversation over with.

"Emerson."

"Jupiter." I mimicked.

Didn't matter how old we were, we would always revert back to the bratty teenagers we'd been.

"Why aren't you calling me on video?"

"I'm walking."

"I'm videoing you. I'd like to see your face."

My phone started beeping, telling me he'd switched us to video and I reached into my pocket to accept it.

"Fuck's sake you're annoying. If my phone gets stolen then you're buying me a new one."

His tanned face grinned out at me through the screen, sweat dripping off his brow which he was wiping with the shirt he'd clearly removed. Always the exhibitionist.

My mouth curled up in revulsion.

"Gross. I didn't need to see that."

"Just good old fashion hard work, Em." He winked, walking through from his gym, past his pool and into his house. In the background I could see the Pacific Ocean glistening in the California sun, from the cliff tops in Malibu where he lived.

The weather was starting to get properly cold in New York and I missed the warmth of the west coast.

"Yeah, yeah."

I crossed the road, paying attention to my surroundings instead of his face, because otherwise it was likely I'd get hit by a bus. Or a passer-by. Several of them already tutting at me for not looking where I was going.

"So...?"

I glanced back down at the screen. Jupiter's phone had been propped up in his kitchen and he was wandering around making a protein shake.

"So?"

"Look Em, you're my sister and I love you. But have you lost your mind? Drew Crawley is..."

"I'll stop you right there." I interrupted. "Because I know you're not about to lecture me on Drew's reputation. Because you're not a hypocrite, are you Jupe?"

He stared straight into the phone. "Emerson, you know nothing about him."

"I know everything about him. And this is really fucking rich coming from someone who can't keep their dick in their pants."

He rolled his eyes. "Emerson. We aren't talking about me. And even if we were, I'm not trying to date anyone and I'm one hundred percent upfront with everyone I have sex with. They know what they're getting into."

I dodged out of the way just as I almost collided with a streetlamp. I really could not walk and video chat at the same time. "Jupe, what are you actually talking about?"

"I'm talking about you and Drew Crawley. How long has this been going on?"

"Fifteen months."

He spat out the protein shake, which turned into a severe cough, his eyes watering as he tried to get his breath back. I took the opportunity to keep walking without needing to see his face. Crossing the giant sidewalk in the Meatpacking District and up toward Midtown.

"What the fuck? Emerson, fifteen months? Are you serious? Is this a joke?"

I rolled my eyes again, such a drama queen.

"We met last summer and then lost contact. We reconnected a few months ago."

He wiped protein shake off his face. "Emerson, seriously. You've just got rid of one sleazebag dickhead, why have you gone straight into another?"

"Oh fuck off, Jupe. Drew isn't a sleazebag, in fact, have you even seen him in the press in the last year. Have you?"

"No, you know I don't read that shit."

"Well if you did, then you'd be able to tell me that no, you haven't. Because since we met there hasn't been anyone else. And yes I know all about Drew's reputation because he told me. In fact, he's been nothing but honest with me about everything."

I looked at my screen. He was still staring. Or maybe he'd frozen.

Either way, I didn't care.

"Look, I appreciate you watching out for me, but you really don't need to. Drew treats me with nothing but kindness and respect, he's sweet and funny and..."

His mouth dropped open in horror. "Oh fuck no. Emerson, are you going to tell me you're in love with him? Please say no."

I checked myself, thinking. Rolled the thought around my tongue a little to see how it felt.

Good. It felt good. And right.

I was in love with Drew Crawley.

"Yes. I am actually."

I used Jupiter's silence to carry on walking without getting myself killed.

"And what about that dick nugget Richard?"

"What about him?"

"Is he still bothering you?"

"No, I haven't seen him in a while and Drew blocked him on my phone."

"Well, least he's made himself useful for something." He grumbled. "But I swear to god Emerson, if he fucks you about or hurts you in any way, I will break him."

I snorted.

"I dunno Jupe. I think his muscles are bigger than yours. I'm not sure you'd get very far."

Winding my brother up was one of my favorite hobbies. His head was big enough already from all the people who stroked his ego on a daily basis, and I felt it was my sisterly duty to bring him back down to earth.

"Fuck off. Look at this." He flexed his massive bicep at me. It would have been impressive if I hadn't seen him do it a million times before. "He is not bigger than me."

He definitely was.

I put on my best patronizing smug face. "Yeah, yeah. Look, Jupe, I'm at work now, I'm going to have to go."

He sighed. "Okay, call me again please. I miss you. You're coming home soon for the holidays, right? In fact, do you want to come for the Series? I'll fly you out."

"No, I can't, but I'll be watching and yes, I'll be home at Christmas. Thanks for being a pain in my ass. I know you're looking out for me, but Drew's here to stay, so you need to play nice if you ever bump into him. I love you, Jupe."

"I love you too. Have fun at work. Maybe I'll come out to see you when the season's done."

"Yeah, I'd like that."

"Good. Okay, I'm hanging up now. I'll call you soon."

He cut me off and I pushed open the doors to the studio to find Ashley, Mikey, Rose and Jessie standing around the desk, all looking up at me as I walked over.

Mikey raised his eyebrow and sized me up. "There's the little dark horse."

"What?"

He pursed his lips. "Where were you last night?"

I laughed at them, after Jupiter's text I figured this would be the next conversation. I looked at Ashley, her palms held up defensively.

"I swear I didn't say anything."

"I know, it's fine." I looked at them all. "Guys, just ask what you want to ask."

I waited for the twenty questions to commence. Mikey went in first, his chin propped on his fist.

"Have you got something going on with a New York Ranger? And if so, which one?"

I looked around at their eager faces, all waiting to be supplied with their next piece of juicy gossip. I rolled my eyes with a chuckle.

"Yes. And Drew Crawley."

Jessie paled, remembering her comments.

I smiled at her. "Jess, don't worry about it."

"But how did this happen? Just from when they've come in?" Rose piped up.

I shook my head. "No, we met last summer and lost touch. Then reconnected a couple of months ago.

Mikey held his hands up. "Wait, you're not fooling around, you're actually dating?"

I nodded. "Yep."

"Like, in a relationship with a New York Ranger?"

I nodded again.

"And that's why they've been in?"

And again. "He knew I worked here and came looking for me."

"At least that explains why they only came to your classes. And why you've been looking particularly glowy lately."

I couldn't argue with that last point. I did feel glowy.

"Why didn't you say anything before now?" Asked Jessie, nervously.

I shrugged slightly. "Because I wanted to keep it to myself for a bit, I wanted to see where it was going. I didn't want to look like an idiot."

"Understandable." Mikey pulled me in for a hug, kissing my head. "Don't worry doll, we'll keep your secret safe. Just be sure those muscles make some regular appearances. And now Drew Crawley's off the market, maybe I'll try my luck with Felix Cleverley. I've heard he's just as big of a demon."

My lip twitched as I tried not to laugh. "Thanks. I don't know how much they'll come back now the season's started, but I'll see what I can do."

"That's all we're asking for."

The reception area had started filling up with riders who'd arrived for the next sessions, including mine.

"Okay, I need to get the class ready. I'll see you guys later."

I threw my hand back in a wave as I walked off chuckling, letting them continue with their gossiping about me. I stuffed my jacket and hoodie in my locker along with my sneakers and took out my cleats, checking my appearance in the mirror before I walked out.

My outfit for today was all white pants and sports bra, which criss-crossed over my back, and were covered in a bright flowers and leaves print. To top it off I'd plaited my hair into a braid crown.

Gotta say, I looked pretty cute. I'd have definitely rocked the sixties.

I made my way down to the studio to set up the music and had it booming from the speakers before the first lot of people entered. Soon the room was filled with sweaty riders powering away, pumping their legs hard to the beat as I pushed them to climb higher and faster over and over again. Happiness surged through me and I couldn't tell whether the endorphins were coming from exercise or Drew.

But I knew I hadn't felt like this in a long, long time and every day was better than the last.

The cleaning crew entered after the final riders left, thanking me on their way out. I reset the sound system and collected my things, heading up the stairs. There was a lot of noise coming from the reception area, still full with everyone who'd been in my class and more. Ashley was handing out shoes to new riders coming for the next session. Then I saw who was standing next to her and my heart started beating hard again, barely having recovered from the class. The way my body reacted to him was like my own personal HIIT session or the strongest caffeine buzz.

Drew was behind the reception desk, leaning over the counter, signing autographs.

He looked up as I got closer, the corners of his mouth turned up into a smile just for me. He signed one more sweaty t-shirt, then put the lid on the Sharpie he was holding.

"Thanks guys. I need to head off now."

The space started to clear as people milled out onto the street and soon it was just new riders and Ashley, plus Mikey and Rose who'd appeared from nowhere. Their Drew homing beacon clearly turned up to max.

"What are you doing here?"

He put his arm around me, giving me a quick kiss. "Came to pick my girl up from work and take her home."

It was a good job he was holding onto me, because this guy made my knees weak.

I cocked my head, with a grin. "Oh yeah?"

"Yeah. Jas used to do it all the time for Wolf and I wanted to do it too." He started laughing. "Plus, I heard you spoke to Jupiter."

My brows knotted together. I'd literally put the phone down on him as I arrived in work. "What? How?"

His smirk was as mischievous as it was infectious. "He texted me and threatened to kick my ass."

My mouth set in a hard line. Fucking Jupiter.

He cupped my cheeks. "Nah, it's all good, Sweetheart. He's just protecting you. Come on, introduce me to your work friends."

We turned to the desk to find everyone staring at us, tracking every movement Drew was making. Mikey had his chin in his hands, his elbows on the desk, like he was watching a movie. He just needed a bucket of popcorn.

And was he drooling?

I huffed, still annoyed at my idiot brother.

"Guys, this is Drew." He nudged me. "My boyfriend." Mikey clutched his chest dramatically and I rolled my eyes. "Babe, this is Mikey and Rose. And Ashley, who you've met before."

"Hey guys, good to meet you. Em talks about you a lot, so I needed to put faces to names."

They all stared. Actually, they were gawping.

In quite an embarrassing way.

We'd had sports players in here before, as well as celebrities, and no one ever seemed to care that much, so I'm not sure what the big deal was here.

Although Drew didn't seem to be phased at all.

"Luck, do you want to get your things?" He turned to me, nudging my ribs again when I didn't move.

"Okay, sure."

As I walked off to the lockers, I heard Mikey ask what Luck meant. Grabbing everything as quickly as possible, not wanting to leave Drew with the pack of hyenas for longer than necessary, I walked out pulling my hoodie over my head to find them all laughing together.

Mikey's hand was still clutched to his chest. "Oh god, that is the cutest story I've ever heard. It's like a fairytale."

Drew took my backpack slinging it over his shoulder and

tugged the last bit of my hoodie down, kissing the side of my head. "Hear that, we're like a fairytale. That must make me Prince Charming."

I looked between the lot of them and couldn't help laughing.

"Oh Jesus."

And then it hit me like the sunrise on my early mornings, this is what a proper relationship must be like with a boyfriend that your friends liked, a boyfriend who made an effort with people who were important to you.

"Come on then Prince Charming, say goodbye to your new friends and let's go home."

He waved. "Bye guys, see you soon. It was great meeting you all, I'll bring the boys back in for a class soon."

"Please do." Called Mikey as I dragged Drew out.

He flung his arm around my neck the second we stepped onto the street, pulling me into him, his open mouth surrounding mine in a hot, wet kiss, slipping his tongue for a brief stroke against mine before moving back.

"That was fun. I've never been introduced as a boyfriend before."

I laughed, his face so full of cheekiness and excitement that I wanted to do it all over again.

"I liked that too. And I loved that my boyfriend came to pick me up from work. That's a new one for me too. And a lovely surprise."

"Yeah?"

"Yeah."

"Well, I'll be doing it more often then." He linked our fingers together in what had become our habit, mine crossed over my chest to find his draped around my shoulder, because it was the closest we could get while we still walked side by side. "Come on, let's get to the car."

We turned the corner and he unlocked it, opening the

door for me to get in. He shut it as I sat down, then jumped in his side.

"Do you need anything from yours before we go to the country?"

I shook my head. "No, I think I have stuff there already."

I'd been storing a few things at his place in the country and the loft, although he had been complaining there wasn't nearly enough. He'd designated me a drawer and an area in the closet and he'd made it very clear he wanted it full.

Yeah, my boyfriend was pretty effing cute.

He started the engine. "Oh, I have news."

I looked at him with expectant eyes.

"Wolfie went into labor."

"What!? How have you made me wait for that information?" I started bouncing on my seat, my hands clasped. "Oh my god that's so exciting. Does that mean Jasper isn't going tomorrow?"

"Yeah, he was having a couple of weeks out when the baby came. Thank fuck it started today and not while we were away."

"Where is she? Is she in hospital? Has it arrived yet? What's happening?"

He stared at me.

"Um Luck, I don't know the answers to any of those questions. I just know on the group text that Wolf went into labor."

I stopped bouncing. "Oh okay. Why are you looking so happy with yourself then?"

"Because Felix and I have a bet on who'll be godfather. Obviously me."

I rolled my eyes.

"Right, time to go home. I'm leaving for nine days and we're having an early night."

And with one hand on my lap, he put the car into drive and turned out of the road.

12

DREW

"**B**abe, are you sure you haven't gone a bit overboard?"

Emerson was staring at the trunk of my SUV. The trunk which was currently filled with two giant cuddly bears, a lion and a dozen pink helium balloons as well as several bags full of pink baby clothes. I'd had to put the back seats down for it all to fit.

Overboard was a matter of opinion.

But yes, I'd definitely gone overboard and definitely got carried away because baby clothes were so tiny and cute. Especially pink ones. And as the self-named godfather, it was my duty to spoil her. And by her I meant Florence Mae Jacobs.

Or Flossie, as I was planning on calling her.

Jasper and Wolfie's new baby daughter.

"Also, what are you wearing? Have you passed a mirror?"

I looked down at the sweater I'd ordered. Orange with a big 3D pumpkin on the front and fucking funny. It was Halloween and in lieu of the usual team party which had been moved to New Year's, Jasper was having a few of us over to smoke some metaphorical cigars, wet the baby's head and officially name me as godfather.

At least he'd better.

And Felix and I had worn our usual matching outfits, just on a smaller scale.

"That'll be less of your lip, Sunshine. Get in the car."

She laughed, opening up her side door.

I looked over at her as she buckled up, pulling her long, dark auburn waves away from her shoulders so they didn't get caught in the belt. I watched her tongue dart out, wetting her bottom lip as she tipped her chin down, her coal-black lashes almost resting on her high cheekbones. She ran her hands over her jumper smoothing it, an orange jumper I'd bought her covered in tiny, little pumpkins. Too fucking cute for words. Fucking cute and smoking hot, the perfect combination. If I was still in college, I'd have put her poster up in my dorm room.

She turned, rubbing her palm on her nose, and caught me staring. "What?"

I pulled her into me, her mouth still open mid-sentence, and took the opportunity to sweep my tongue around. She tasted like cherries from the Chapstick she always kept in her bag and spearmint from when she'd brushed her teeth before we'd left. I couldn't imagine a day when I'd ever get enough of tasting her, every time was like getting your hands on the ripest peach at the height of summer, juicy and perfect.

Nine days away travelling was too fucking long for me not to see her, not to touch her, not to breathe her in. I struggled to keep my hands to myself at the best of times, but when we'd just come home from an away stretch it was fucking impossible.

"Nothing, you're just the most beautiful woman I've ever seen in my entire life, is all."

On cue the rosy blush I loved so much crept through her cheeks, Emerson Pink I called it. And it was my new favorite color in the world.

Her cheeks rounded as she tried to hold back her smile. "Start the engine Romeo, there's a baby I want to see."

"Yes boss." I winked.

We pulled into Jasper's driveway, following Felix. Cooper must have arrived just before us because he had Jasper in a bear hug, standing at the front door. We'd missed him on the ice while we'd been away, while his life had been changing in the best possible way. And Coop's was soon to be the same.

All our lives were changing.

My throat started to get all tight and tingly, and I coughed it away, turning off the engine. Felix was already out of his car and was banging his hands against my window, leaving fucking palm prints on the freshly detailed glass.

Dick.

Emerson squeezed my leg. "You go and say hi, I'll bring the bags in."

"Okay, but just the bags, I'll come back and get the rest."

"Yes, you will, I can't carry that giant bear."

I grinned and kissed her again, opening the door to join Felix.

"As always, we look fucking awesome." He slapped me on the back and we walked over to join Jasper and Coop.

"You know it."

Jasper, however, looked knackered but also happier than I'd ever seen him before. I pulled him into a massive hug, squeezing him hard.

"A fucking dad, man. Congratulations buddy. Fucking awesome." I sniffed as my throat thickened again.

Felix punched me in the arm. "Jesus, Dude. Are you crying already?"

Yes.

"What? It's an emotional reunion for all of us." I pinned him with my best Cheshire Cat grin. "Not every day you get to see your first goddaughter for the first time."

Jasper had been keeping us updated on the group chat the

four of us had, sending pictures, and she was a little beauty. But we hadn't yet seen her in person.

"You take that back." Felix pointed at my chest. "It's not official."

Cooper crossed his arms over his chest, letting out a low chuckle. "Fuck's sake, put them out of their misery."

Felix and I stepped back, Jasper coughing into his hand, clearing his throat. "Coop, Freddie, Wolf and I have made a decision."

They eyed each other in amusement and something that told me I wasn't about to get the news I was expecting.

We both stared at them, our heads moving from one to the other. "And?"

Jasper was just about to speak when he took in the awesomeness of our attire and barked out a laugh.

"Oh my god, you're dressed the same."

Pointing out the obvious, but okay. He was clearly sleep deprived. Felix was less inclined to be patient to his lack of awareness.

"Dude, it's Halloween. Of course we fucking are. Now hurry up with this announcement."

In my peripheral I could see Cooper shaking his head.

"Anyway...?"

"Yes anyway, seeing as you dumdums come as a pair, we don't feel like we can split you up. And as our kids will be cousins, we think it's only right you take them on together."

Woah, what now?

Felix's eyes popped wide. "What? Both of them?"

"Yep."

I stared hard, trying to find a flicker of a joke. Nothing. Their poker faces definitely weren't that good.

Holy shit.

"To clarify, you're both asking both of us to be godfather to both of your kids?"

Cooper rolled his eyes. "Yes, so don't fuck it up."

I punched the air. "Fucking yes."

Felix grabbed me in an embrace, jumping up and down. "Oh we're gonna be the best fucking godfathers."

Too fucking right. Flash-fowards of Felix teaching them the best swearwords and me sneaking them candy.

"Yeah, we're gonna fucking Brando this shit."

I reached out to grab them. "Group hug."

"Fuck off." Cooper pushed us both away, far too easily for my liking. Must have been adding in an extra workout.

"So, when do we get to see her for real, show her who the best godfather is? And how fucking awesome we are?"

Jasper's face suddenly softened, taking on a distinctly gooey look. "She's sleeping right now, but in a bit."

"Where's Wolf?"

"Sleeping too."

"What about Freddie? She sleeping?"

Cooper scrubbed his hand down his face. "Honestly dude, there's a lot of sleeping. You wouldn't even believe it. But Freddie went inside to see her mom."

Shit, I forgot both their families were here too. "Oh dude, have you had a houseful?"

"Yeah, you could say that, between Wolf's parents and mine we haven't had much time alone. But they'll be going to Coop's soon, his turn is coming up." He grinned, punching his shoulder.

"Have Murray and Tate been around much?" Felix asked.

"Yeah, they're inside." He rubbed his hands together. "Where we should be before they eat all the food."

"Lead the way." Felix patted his stomach. "Wait, where's Emerson?"

Actually, where was she? I turned and saw her sitting on the rear bumper of the car, holding her phone.

"Luck?" I called over to her.

She looked up. "Coming, sorry. I was just texting Jupiter."

"Shit, I forgot it's game five today, right?" Felix whispered.

"Yeah, Tate already has the pre-game on."

I turned around. "Actually, you can help bring some stuff in."

We all walked over to the car and Emerson moved away from the trunk, opening it, Felix did the same with his and we all stood there staring at the contents.

Jasper was the first one to speak.

"When did you even have the chance to buy all this?"

I shrugged. "I ordered it while we were away."

"Me too." Replied Felix, whose trunk looked almost the same, expect if you replaced the lion and bears with a giraffe and a monkey.

"Between the two of you, you must have bought an entire store."

"Or a zoo." Drawled Cooper.

"Told you, best godfathers."

Jasper put an arm around each of our shoulders. "Seriously, thank you. Wolf will love this."

Emerson grabbed some bags from inside the car. "While you boys are all standing there, I'm going to take these in."

Cooper pulled his phone out and dialed. "Get your asses outside would you, please?"

Less than two minutes later Murray and Tate sauntered through the front door, Murray finishing off a sub which he shoved into his mouth.

"You summoned us?"

"Yeah, can you help carry this in?"

"Bloody hell, is this you two?" Murray pointed between Felix and me. "Leave some stuff for the uncles will you?"

"Don't be bitter, we can't help being amazing." I laughed, pulling him into a hug. "Good to see you buddy, been a few months."

Returning my hug, he slapped me on the back. "You too, how're you doing?"

"Really good."

He looked at me, his bottom lip rolling as his eyes narrowed, questioning my own assessment.

"Can you two stop yapping and start carrying, I want to watch the game."

We all turned to Tate.

"It doesn't start for five hours."

"But at this rate we'll still be standing here."

Man had a point.

I grabbed one of the bears, it was so cuddly and soft I could probably fall asleep on it myself. Flossie would definitely be loving this.

Win one for the godfather already.

We managed to get everything inside with three trips, taking it all through to the new playroom Jasper had added to his house.

Murray clapped his hands together. "Right, beer time."

"I'll catch you up." I wanted to find Emerson.

I searched through a couple of rooms before I hit the jackpot. She was sitting with Freddie and Wolf, and their moms. And she was holding Flossie. Staring down at the bundle in her arms, she was whispering quietly to her, or just keeping her voice low while talking to the others, didn't matter. A bent finger was in Flossie's mouth, letting her suckle on it.

If I was a girl, I'd be talking about ovary overload or some shit. What was the boy equivalent? Ballsac bursting?

Shudder.

No, that sounded terrible.

Maybe there wasn't a word for what I felt.

I'd always known I wanted kids, vaguely known it would happen at some point in my life, but I'd never given much thought before to who their mother would be.

Until now.

I leant against the door frame, quietly, not wanting to

disturb this picture of perfection in front of me. But I had zero fucking doubt she'd be having my babies one day.

I walked away to find that beer.

A couple more of the guys had turned up when I wandered into the TV snug off the kitchen, everyone gathered to watch the pre-game, including Jasper and Wolfie's dads and I hugged them hello. Dodgers were hosting the Nationals for Game Five of the World Series. Emerson's brother had been having a great season, the commentators predicting him for MVP. He was a phenomenal player, even if he was a dick.

Huck handed me a beer as I sat down on the sofa next to him.

"Thanks Dude."

He looked at me, frowning. "Can you knock that weird grin off your face please? It's freaking me out and you look like you've escaped from somewhere."

"What weird grin?"

But I knew and it probably wasn't going anywhere anytime soon. If I didn't think it would earn me a punch in the face, I'd been shouting from the rooftops I'd met the mother of my children.

I stared at him, my grin getting wider.

His eyebrow raised. "Bet it'll be weird watching baseball in bed now."

Well, that got rid of it.

"What?"

"Well, when you're in bed with Emerson naked. You don't really want her brother on the TV do you?"

I narrowed my eyes at him. "First off. Don't ever fucking talk about Emerson being naked. And second. Yes, you have a point."

Felix sat down on the other side of me, placing a bowl of chips in his lap. "Why are you talking about Emerson being naked."

"We're fucking not. Stop saying that."

Huck threw his head back, laughing. "Chill out, just needed to get rid of that stupid grin. And it worked."

"What stupid grin?" Felix sipped on his beer.

Huck grabbed a handful of chips and stuffed them in his mouth. "He looked like he'd swallowed that dude who plays the Joker."

Jesus.

I rolled my eyes. "You could have just said The Joker."

Huck stared at me, waiting. "So, are you going to tell us why you were looking like that?"

The smile crept up my lips again, I could feel it getting bigger. I had no hope of playing it cool.

Fuck it.

"I just saw Emerson holding Flossie."

Felix looked at me, his eyes smiling knowingly, nodding subtly. He knew how deep I was in it. That I was so fucking in love with her. That she was my future. That my heart was spilling over with her, because every time I was sure it couldn't get any bigger, she'd do or say something, and it swelled all over again.

And the thought that I might have never experienced this, because I'd lost her, made my ears ring.

"You're still asking her to move in with you?"

"Yeah. Bet your fucking ass. I want everything with her."

Huck reached for more chips, but Felix moved the bowl away, not allowing him to have it. He kept it out of arms reach with a snigger until Huck nearly punched him in the nuts.

"Stop being a dick." He stuffed more in his mouth. "So when are you going to ask her?"

"Soon, we spend all our time together anyway, but I've only just got her to introduce me as her boyfriend."

"And how's the bromance going?" Felix leaned back into the sofa, nodding to the screen where the commentators were still talking about Jupiter. "Sent you any more love letters?"

"No, don't worry you're still in the top spot."

"Yeah I am." He put his arm around my shoulder, trying to kiss me.

I pushed him away.

"But it's all good with Luck?"

"Yeah, really good."

"Let's hope you don't fuck it up then."

I forced a loud laugh at his joke, hopefully hiding the anxiety I felt about the very same thing.

Because I couldn't fuck this up. I couldn't lose her again.

I stood up. "I'm going to find pizza."

"Bring some back for us." Huck called after me.

Lazy fuckers.

Walking into the kitchen, Jasper's mom, Patti, was slicing up a dozen large pizzas on the counter. She'd fed our group enough times to know that it was always better to over cater, especially if Felix was involved. Emerson was at the table, smiling at something Freddie was saying as she sat on Cooper's lap, Wolfie laughing too. I loved how easily she'd fit into this group and our lives.

Like she belonged.

Flossie was lying asleep on Jasper's chest. I walked over, taking her in. She'd been dressed in a miniature pumpkin costume, like mine and Felix's, too adorable for words. She was so tiny and pink, her little face scrunched up, squashed button nose snuffling as she breathed in and out, her pouty lips quivering. The tightness in my chest was swiftly making its way up my throat.

"Oh Dude, she's fucking perfect." My voice broke.

He smiled up at me. "Yeah, she is. Takes after her mom."

I dropped a kiss on Wolfie's head. "Congratulations Mama. You guys did good."

"Thanks Drew. And thank you for all those presents. She's going to be so spoiled."

I had no doubt.

I moved Emerson out of her seat and sat on it, pulling her back into my lap, wrapping my arms around her.

"So, how's being a parent?"

"Scariest fucking thing I've ever done. Man, I've cried more than you in the last two weeks and I can't fucking stop."

I snorted. "You'll get used to it."

Jasper looked back down at Flossie, his hand rubbing her back, so big against her tiny body. It was almost incomprehensible how little she was.

And that they'd made Felix and me godfathers, even if it was under duress.

We were definitely going to fuck it up.

Or Felix would.

I pulled Emerson in tighter, burying my head in her hair, inhaling her, running my nose behind the back of her ear.

"You want one of these?" I whispered, nodding over to Flossie.

She shifted in my lap slightly so she could see me better, a smile tugging at her lips, her expression soft. "Yeah, one day."

I brushed my lips against her. "Me too."

Patti placed a couple of the pizzas on the table, taking more into the others still watching the pre-game. Wolfie grabbed some slices off the board and placed them on a plate, handing it to Jasper. She could have just taken Flossie, but I had the feeling removing his daughter from his arms was not an easy task.

Everyone was digging in.

"Fredster, how are you doing? You feeling okay?"

I hadn't seen her for a while and she looked like she'd swallowed a basketball. She was so short with a massive belly, I was surprised she didn't topple over all the time.

"I'm good, just a couple more months left. I just hope it comes during Bye Week."

I reached for another slice, handing Emerson one at the same time.

"Yeah, that would be good for you. Jas got lucky just before we went away." I turned to him. "We missed you a lot though Buddy."

He grinned, looking over to Wolfie. "Thanks, I can't say the same."

Patti joined us at the table. "What do you think of my new granddaughter?"

"You mean my new goddaughter?" I winked. "I think she's perfect."

"Correct answer." She laughed. "She definitely looks like Wolfie, but I think she has Jasper's mouth. And she certainly has his appetite I've noticed. Let's hope she doesn't make Wolfie's nipples as sore as Jasper made mine though."

I coughed on the pizza I'd just tried to swallow, almost all of it lodging in my windpipe, inhibiting my ability to breathe.

Emerson started smacking my back, hard.

Would this be how I died?

Talking about Jasper's mom's nipples.

I fucking hoped not.

My eyes started watering as I managed a breath, Wolfie handing me a glass of water with a smirk.

"Are you okay?"

I nodded, sucking in more air.

"Jeez Patti." I croaked. "You need to warn a guy before you start talking about nipples like that."

Jasper stood up with Flossie. "Okay, I think that's my cue to leave, I am not discussing nipples with my mom. We're going to watch the game."

I gently tipped Emerson off my lap, kissing her, as Cooper did the same with Freddie. "Wait for me."

Freddie started chuckling. "Stupid boys."

"Christ, Jas." I muttered to him. "I hope that's not scarred me from nipples for life."

He shook his head. "Don't."

We all walked into the snug, Cooper parking himself on a giant beanbag while everyone else made way for Jasper to sit down with Flossie, the chatter dropping to a whisper as soon as they saw her sleeping. Felix was chowing down on what was probably his hundredth slice of pizza. I took another beer from the ice bucket on the table and sat back in the corner of the sofa, the cold liquid soothing my still rasping throat.

The pre-game had moved onto interviews with players from both teams, although Jupiter was yet to make an appearance.

"Hey, who's that girl over there with Wolfie and Franks?" Murray walked in, thumbing back over to where the girls were all still sitting at the table, no doubt still talking about nipples. "She looks familiar."

Brogan tipped off the edge of the sofa and around the doorframe to check. "That's Emerson, Drew's girlfriend."

"No shit, really?"

"Yeah."

He spun round, his hand reaching to my shoulder, squeezing it. "Hey buddy, that's brilliant. You've finally moved on from that Lucky chick, thought you were going to be a miserable bastard forever. Good for you. She looks great."

Huck was trying to peer around him as he blocked the screen. "Muz, that is Lucky and can you move out of the way."

He stepped to one side looking at us all, his mouth slightly open.

"Fuck off, seriously? You found her?"

"Yeah." I grinned. "Wolf and Fred did at least."

"How?"

"She was their spinning instructor a few months ago."

"No way. Mate, that's fucking awesome. I'm so happy for you." He laughed loud. "Phew, no wonder she looked familiar. I was worried I'd slept with her for a second and my past was coming back to haunt me."

Huck burst out laughing, giving him a high five. "Fuck, that would have been funny."

My teeth crunched together. I'd learned I had zero sense of humor when it came to Emerson and any list of topics, starting with her and other guys.

"No, it fucking wouldn't." I growled. "You're both dicks."

He moved to sit next to me, nudging me. "Seriously, how it's going?"

I side-eyed him.

"Mate, seriously."

I sighed because I could never hold out from talking about her. "Amazing. I'm going to ask her to move in with me."

"Woah dude, that's great, congratulations. When?"

"Soon, definitely." I grinned. "Anyway, how are you? How long are you back for?"

"I'm here for good. That's why I've not been here the last few months, just finalizing everything back in London with Jamie and the office there."

"No shit, really? That's awesome. We need to go out, you wanna come to the next game?"

"Yeah definitely. Always good to see where my investments come from." He laughed.

Murray ran a successful hedge fund in London with his brother and he'd spent the last year setting up an office in New York for his US clients. A couple of us, me included, had been investing money with him and he was fucking good at delivering a very healthy return.

I smirked. "Next two games are at home. I'll set you up with tickets."

He reached for another beer.

"Cool, thanks man. Although I guess you're not going to be 'out out' anymore." He airquoted with a grin.

Felix smirked, knocking the tip of his beer bottle against Murray's. "Dude, I'm so glad you're back. This one's not gone 'out out' in months. I need a new partner in crime and you'll slot in nicely."

It was true. I couldn't deny it.

But still, I could go out, I wasn't totally whipped.

Although was it even whipped if you didn't want to be anywhere else anyway?

"Hey, I'll still come out. I just have something much better waiting for me at the end of the night." I gave them my best smug face.

Felix shoved me with a smirk.

Wolfie walked in, straight to Jasper, leaning down to kiss him. "Babe, I need to take her."

"Okay." He kissed Flossie's head before handing her over.

"Wolf, where are you taking her?" Felix called to her as she left.

"It's bath time."

"Can I come and help?"

She smiled in surprise. "Of course Felix, if you'd like to."

I'd never seen him get up so quickly, running after her, fist pumping the air. "Godfather for the win."

Emerson passed them on their way out. I patted my lap and she settled into it.

"Has Jupiter been on?"

"No, but they're saying he's going to get MVP." Replied Tate, managing to tear his eyes away from the screen to look at her.

"Huh." She pulled a face.

You could almost see the lightbulb going off in his head.

"Wait, is Jupiter Reeves your brother?"

She nodded.

His eyes widened. "Wow. He's an incredible third base-man, he's done so well for the Dodgers. And he's had a great season. That's pretty cool he's your brother."

Jasper threw a cushion at him. "Hey, jellohead, you have a brother who's captain of an NHL team."

He shrugged, grinning. "Meh."

Emerson chuckled. "I'll let you know when he comes to visit, we can all go out."

He's what now?

"He's coming to visit?"

"Man, you should see your face, don't shit yourself too much." Huck started pissing himself laughing, nudging Tate who was looking clueless at this exchange. "He told Drew he was gonna kick his ass for dating Emerson."

Tate snorted and I heard Emerson groan.

"Shut the fuck up, dickhead. I'm not shitting myself. Because as far as kicking my ass goes, I'd like to see him try."

And as if the broadcasting gods heard us, Jupiter Reeves face filled the screen, his fully tatted arms crossed over his chest in a foreboding way, staring down at us in the room as his stats flashed on the screen.

"Sure about that?" Huck smirked.

"Fuck off."

Emerson leant back into me, stroking my leg in a soothing motion. "Nothing's going to happen."

I kissed her head. "I know sweetheart, they like winding me up is all, because they're dicks. Jupiter and I are going to be best buds, just you wait."

If I said it enough times that would make it true, right?

"Okay."

Her hands were still stroking, the movement of her palms up and down my thigh like a calming salve blocking out the dipshits surrounding us. I wished we were alone. I held her tighter.

"I hope you've had a good day." I nuzzled into her neck as she tilted her head slightly giving me more access. "I liked seeing you holding Flossie."

"Did you?"

"Yeah, I did. A lot." I pushed a hand into her hair, running the ends of her silky strands though my fingers. "In fact, give me the word and we can leave right now to practice the fuck out of making one."

She threw her head back, laughing her laugh. The one I would never get tired of hearing.

Murray nudged me.

"Mate, you know I'm sitting right next to you and you're not speaking very quietly?"

I didn't.

Did I give a fuck?

Nope.

13

EMERSON

I opened the drawers which Drew had given me and were currently mostly empty.

"Shit."

I had an early class in the morning and liked to lay my clothes out the night before so I didn't have to think too much before I was fully awake, but turned out I didn't have anything to lay out.

I could have sworn I had more here, maybe I'd left it in the country.

He walked through from the bathroom, pajama bottoms slung low on his hips, showing off stacked abs and corded obliques. He planted a kiss on my head before throwing the covers back and getting into bed.

"What's wrong."

I pulled my hair up, tying it with a band. "Nothing, I just thought I had more clothes here. It's fine I'll go via mine first thing."

He didn't look up from the book he was reading. "Ralph can take you."

"No, babe it's fine, I don't need him to. I'll just leave a bit earlier."

"No Emerson. It's still dark when you leave, Ralph will take you." He put his book down, picking his phone up and typing out a text. "And I'm driving tomorrow anyway."

I didn't argue because I knew it was pointless.

"Okay, thank you."

"Now get into bed please, it's cold without you. And it's spoon o'clock."

I slipped in under the duvet, Drew pulling me close against his hard body, his arms wrapping around me.

"Have you set the alarm?"

He turned to the clock, double checking, switching the side lamp off at the same time.

"I have." His mouth found mine, sealing it with a kiss before he pulled back and turned me around to our usual sleeping positions.

"Sleep tight Luck. Have sweet dreams for me."

It wasn't the first time I'd fallen asleep wondering how I'd captured this Adonis holding onto me like he never wanted to let go.

Ralph was waiting in the cold morning air, holding the car door open for me.

"Thanks Ralphie, I'm sorry it's so early. I've told Drew you don't need to do this."

He smiled. "It's not a problem at all, I'm happy to."

I jumped in and he closed the door behind me, five minutes later pulling up outside my building.

I really could have walked this, but I didn't begrudge Drew wanting to spend longer in bed. I never used to care that much about being up and out early in the morning, but I was finding it harder and harder to leave when Drew's heavy, warm body was wrapped around me.

"Thanks, I'll be ten minutes."

"I'll be here, take your time."

I sprinted inside, determined to be quick, running around my apartment stripping off as I went. I flicked on the coffee machine to make one for Ralph, the least I could do considering he'd got up at the ass crack of dawn to drive me around. While it was dripping into the takeaway cup, I ran back into my bedroom rummaging around my drawers for a new pair of pants and a bra, pulling them on. Throwing a hoodie over me, I pulled the hair tie off my wrist and scraped it back in a messy twist at the top of my head. I'd sort it out properly when I got to work. Quickly scanning around the room to check I hadn't forgotten anything I picked up my bag, grabbed the coffee and jogged back outside.

Pushing the building door open, I walked down the steps toward the car. But as I reached the bottom a hand grabbed me spinning me round, squeezing my arm so hard I screamed in pain, dropping my bag and the coffee. The scalding liquid splashed my legs, making me jerk hard, but he held firm. His fingers were digging into the flesh at the top of my arm and my blood ran cold at the hatred in his eyes.

"Where've you been?" Richard snarled, his grip tightening, I could smell alcohol on his breath. "I saw you walk in ten minutes ago, where did you come from? Where did you stay last night?"

How drunk was he? Did he not see me get out of the car? I tried to look around him to find Ralph but couldn't move, suddenly terrified he'd driven off.

"None of your fucking business." I winced as he squeezed harder. "Ouch, Richard you're hurting me."

"It's nothing compared to what you've done to me, you fucking bitch." He lifted his hand as though to slap me, I flinched at the impending impact.

"What's going on?" Ralph bellowed, causing Richard to jump back dropping me. "Who the fuck are you? Get your fucking hands off her."

"Who the fuck am I? Who the fuck are you?" Richard spun around, looking to see where the voice had come from.

Considering Ralph was almost as big as Drew and Richard definitely was not, it was unsurprising he backed down when Ralph towered over him.

Spineless fucktard.

I picked up my bag I'd dropped and ran to the car, getting in and out of the way as quickly as I could.

What had just happened?

I rubbed my arm where he'd squeezed me, it was sore and throbbing where the blood had started to flow back into it properly again. My pants were wet where the coffee had spilled and I tried to rub them dry but my hands were shaking. I shoved them between my legs, making them still.

"This isn't over, Emerson." He yelled as he stormed off.

Ralph waited until he was out of sight then got back in the car, turning around. "Are you okay? Who was that?"

I dropped my head, not wanting him to see my tears of shock. "My ex-boyfriend."

"Has he done that before?"

"No, not like that." I shook my head.

He frowned at me. "I don't like that, Emerson."

"Yeah, me either."

He eyed me, his expression soft and worry filled. "Do you still want to go to work?"

I nodded. "Yes, I have to."

His forehead creased in a frown. "Okay."

He started the engine and drove off, dropping me at the studio ten minutes later.

"Thank you. Thank you for driving me and for saving me. I made you a coffee but I dropped it when…"

He looked me over. "Emerson, you're welcome, are you sure you're okay?"

I nodded, clenching my still shaking hands.

"And I'll be driving you every morning from now on."

I gave him a weak smile, opening the door to get out. He waited for me until I walked inside. The reception desk was empty and I headed straight into the locker room, stripping off my hoodie. Big purple fingerprints were wrapped around the top of my arm where he'd gripped me, even through the thick material welts had formed, raised and tender to my touch.

What a fucking fucker.

What was his fucking problem? I'd never seen him like that before. Maybe Drew was right, Richard was crazy.

He'd definitely looked it this morning.

I gulped down some water, pushing away the hot, thick tightening sensation creeping up my throat that I knew would erupt in tears if I let it, and I didn't have time for a meltdown. I shook off the numbness creeping over me and gathered up my things, heading into the studio, desperately needing to focus on my class.

An hour later I trudged up the stairs, exhausted. I'd worked everyone extra hard but had been unable to push the thoughts of Richard from my mind. I'd realized I hadn't thought about him since that day Drew blocked him weeks ago, all that time had been so blissfully quiet without his missed calls and texts, and I didn't want any of that back.

That would be a hard no.

When I opened the door to the changing room, Drew was leaning against the wall. I'd been expecting this. The second he saw me enter he pushed off, striding toward me, wrapping his arms around me in a hug, holding me against his massive chest.

He really should win an award for his hugs. There was nothing better.

He kissed my head. "Are you okay, Sweetheart?"

The high from the class vanished and the tears I'd been holding back burst forth, the dam I'd built no longer strong enough. He wrapped his arms tighter, cupping my head,

196

stroking my sweaty hair. I could hear his heart beating strong in his chest as I cried against him, sobbing uncontrollably until his steady breathing soothed me enough to stop.

"Let me see."

He picked up my arms and examined the dark bruises which had developed.

My breath was still catching. "It's nothing."

He ran his hands so gently over the bruising that fresh tears filled my eyes, his thumb tenderly brushing the welts, but I could feel anger radiating off him. "It's not nothing, Emerson. This isn't okay."

My chin started to tremble again, because I knew he was right.

He brushed away a tear that fell and softly kissed my lips. "I have to go to practice, but can you just get in the car with me now and Ralph can drop you back in the country. Please?"

I couldn't think of anywhere I wanted to be more. Except with him.

"Okay."

He grabbed my bag from my locker, throwing it over his shoulder and watched me as I silently pulled my hoodie on. Holding his hand out for me to take, he led me out of the room, his hoodie up high over his neck, baseball cap low, his head down with a single focus on getting us through the busy reception to the car without being noticed. I waved to Ashley as we passed, her face telling me she knew what had happened.

He held the door open and climbed in the back with me, Ralph driving off as soon as the door was shut. Drew wrapped his hands around me and I snuggled into his chest, letting his strength and warmth radiate through me.

I must have fallen asleep because when I next looked out of the window we'd arrived at the entrance of the Rangers' impressive training facility, driving up to the main arena.

Drew gently lifted me off his shoulder as the car stopped, cupping my face, pulling me in for a kiss. "Are you okay?"

I nodded. "Yes, I am."

"Okay Baby, go home and I'll be there in a few hours." He jumped out, taking his sticks and bag from the trunk and tapped on the roof when he was done. I watched him walk into the building, the car moving slowly off.

Twenty minutes later Ralph turned around as he waited for Drew's big gates to open up. "Emerson, do you need me to get anything for you? I can drop you and then bring it back."

I smiled. "No, thank you, that's really kind but I don't need anything."

"Okay, call me if you change your mind and I can bring it back when I drop Drew."

"Thank you."

"Are you sure you're okay?"

I nodded, stepping out of the car. "Thank you, Ralph. And thank you for being there this morning."

Because if you hadn't...

I shook those thoughts away immediately.

"Anytime. Get some rest okay?"

I pushed open the big front doors and dumped my stuff on the floor of the entrance hall.

How was it only eight thirty am and I'd already had a day of it?

I just wanted to start all over again.

I rubbed my thumbs over my brows trying to ease the tension of an impending headache.

My stomach growled, reminding me I hadn't eaten so went in search of food, coming up trumps when I opened the fridge.

Drew's food delivery had arrived.

I found a jar of overnight oats, poached fruit and coconut yoghurt, dumping it all into a big bowl, then flicked on the coffee machine. I perched on a stool at the island, eating while looking out into the garden. It had started raining and I watched the raindrops bounce on the patio.

Lifting my coffee cup, my arm started throbbing again. I rubbed it, another wave of anger crashing through me, I was fucking pissed.

What the fuck was I going to do?

I'd lost count of the amount of times I was grateful for Drew, grateful for his kindness, strength, warmth and general anti-Richardness.

Fucking Richard.

Every day was better than the day before and this morning made me realize how blissfully happy I'd been the past few months, a level I'm not sure I'd ever had, at least not since I was a kid.

It also wasn't the first time that in the five years we'd been together I'd wondered if maybe I never actually knew Richard at all, although I'd never been genuinely scared of him before. But, I did know Drew and I knew he was going to be really angry. He'd tried to hide it this morning, but I could feel it radiating from him like radioactive energy.

I scrolled through my contacts, everyone I wanted to speak to right now was west coast based. It was still the middle of the night for Mallory and I knew my brother wouldn't be awake either. After the Dodgers had won the World Series he'd escaped on holiday and I wasn't entirely sure where he was. I could try Piper, but she'd either be asleep or up with the kids.

Fuck it, Jupiter was my best bet.

I tried calling but it rang out.

My arm throbbed again, so I went in search of painkillers, finding what I needed in the laundry room.

Now what?

I wasn't entirely sure what to do with myself and Drew wouldn't be back for a while. The thought of having a nap seemed immensely appealing but then realized I was still pretty sweaty from this morning and getting into bed without having a shower was gross.

Bath it was.

Maybe I could nap there.

I walked up the stairs to Drew's bedroom and through to the bathroom. His giant copper tub sat at the end of the room, overlooking the garden. I turned on the taps, pouring a bag of scented Epsom salts and lavender foaming oil into the flowing water, watching the suds rise up.

I stepped into the hot, soapy water, the warmth easing my aching muscles. I'd filled it so much that when I leant my head back against the edge, the water came up to my neck. My eyelids started getting heavy and I didn't fight to keep them open, although it wasn't for long.

"You look so fucking beautiful in there."

I turned, my heartbeat kicking up, filling up with him, with his power and strength and beauty. His dimple got deeper as he made his way over to me, dropping to his knees in front of the tub, his smile salving me in a way the water couldn't.

He cupped my head, his lips brushing mine. "Hi Sweetheart. How are you?"

"Better now you're here."

And that was the god's honest truth. Everything was always better when he was around.

"Good. Want company?"

"Always."

He stood up, shucking his clothes in record speed, with the least graceful striptease I'd ever seen. His arms crossed over his chest removing his hoodie at the same time he wriggled out of his sweatpants and boxers, kicking them free and off to the side somewhere before stepping in behind me. Water sloshed all over the floor, draining away underneath.

"Fuck, this is hot." He hissed, shifting around trying to get used to the temperature, which wasn't that hot considering I'd already been in here a while.

It was very warm at best.

I waited until he finally relaxed, his massive legs barely taking up any more space in the enormous bath as they wrapped around mine.

My head dropped back onto his chest. "How was practice?"

"It was okay." He picked up my arm, examining it. The purple bruises had started to morph into one, making it look much worse than it was. "But I wasn't very focused."

His fingertips stroked along the length of my arm, up and down, running through mine, entwining them together. I watched as he silently sandwiched my palm between his before folding his arms around me, squeezing tightly.

His lips rested against my temple. "Luck, I want you to move in with me."

Come again?

I spun around in the bath, water splashing in my face and I needed to blink several times in order to clear my vision. He chuckled, wiping my eyes.

"What did you say?"

His kissed my nose. "Move in with me."

I stared at him, unable to tell if he was being serious, although if he wasn't it was kind of a weird joke and one I didn't understand.

"Emerson, I want you to move in with me."

"Why? Because of this morning?"

"Well…"

Okay, well that wasn't a reason to move in together. Not to mention four on the romance scale.

"No."

His whole face widened, his eyebrows shooting into his hairline in shock. "No?"

I sighed. "I mean, no I'm not letting Richard scare us into doing this too early. We do it when it's right."

He brushed a few wet strands of hair away from my forehead, tucking them behind my ear. "Sweetheart, it's right now. I'm not asking you to move in with me because of that dick, which we are going to talk about by the way, but in regard to this, no, it's not totally because of him. He's maybe three percent of the reason. I've been waiting to do this since the first time I walked you to yours, after I found you in the club."

"What's the other ninety seven percent?"

His lips touched mine. "Because you're my girlfriend and I love you."

"What?"

He took a deep breath and started speaking slowly, over enunciating every word, just in case I didn't understand what he was saying. "You are my girlfriend and I love you."

He was looking at me closely, waiting for a reaction.

The romance scale started sliding upwards, like the fairground game with the bell on the top, and he was the muscle man wielding his hammer.

"We've never said that before."

"Well, I'm saying it now." He tipped my chin up to meet his lips. "Emerson, I love you and I want you to move in with me."

I tilted my head. "And you're definitely not just asking me because of what happened this morning?"

"No, I told you. This morning scared the shit out of me because I wasn't there to protect you, it makes me rage that you didn't feel safe, that you were hurt, that this." He lifted my arm up to me. "happened, and that piece of shit was even within your vicinity, let alone close enough to lay his hands on you. And I swear to god, if I ever see him, he won't make it out in one piece. But no, I'm asking you because I love you and I've loved you since I first laid eyes on you. We spend every night together anyway so really it's just a case of you doing all your laundry here instead of some of it, packing up all your stuff and bringing it here, so it's here all at the same time. You can even do it a box at a time if scares you. But make no mistake, I love you and I want you to live here or anywhere you want. I don't care. You're my person, Emerson. My future."

Drew smashed that hammer down, the bell at the top ringing loudly.

I mentally checked myself, scanning my body for reaction, an internal inventory for how I was feeling.

Was I scared? Nope.

Did I love Drew? Yes, without a doubt.

I sat up, straddling him, his eyes automatically dropping to my boobs, his cock hardening against me as I came to its attention.

"Eyes up here, Baby."

They slowly moved upwards, each inch they travelled heated my body better than any hot bath did and when they finally arrived at mine, the hazel was warm like honey and filled with so much emotion butterflies flipped in my belly. I could see the love he had for me, the depth of his truth, and it mirrored mine.

"Okay, yes."

"Say again."

"I love you too and yes I'll move in with you. But..."

He wrapped his hands around my head, smashing his lips to mine, sloppy and happy.

"But what?"

"But my lease is up after Christmas, so I'll do it officially then. And it'll be a proper start to the year."

The dimple got so big it seemed to take up half his cheek, his hands running back up my body, cupping the nape of my neck, pulling me onto his lips, his mouth wanting and desperate. With a groan, my body subconsciously rocked against him, goosebumps breaking out across my flesh.

I needed him as much as he needed me and he knew it, reading me like an expert cartographer.

He sat up straight, exuding strength and power and protection, gripping my hips, lifting me up and impaling me on his rock-hard cock in one swift movement. His own loud cry drowning out the volume of mine.

He stilled us, the water continuing to sway over the sides of the bath and I could feel him growing harder, swelling thick inside me as my thighs gripped him. His chest heaving, he held us there for a minute while he ran his hands across my body with precision movement, watching his fingertips trail along my arm and over my collarbone, dipping between my breasts cupping each one, squeezing tenderly.

He looked up at me as they ran around my nipples and underneath. His pupils were shot, dilated so big I could only see a ring of fire around an inky black moon, like a solar eclipse I shouldn't stare directly at.

His cock thickened and throbbed as his hands moved lower under the water where his thumb found my clit, brushing against it back and forth, driving me crazy with desire. The sensation of the hot water against my skin, as his fingers worked their magic, sent tiny flickers to the orgasm swelling deep inside me. Heat curled my spine, burning me through to the marrow.

Running his tongue along my jaw, his mouth once again claimed mine. But where earlier he kissed me with happiness and fun and joy, this was raw and sensual and passionate. Slowly, like he had all the time in the world, his tongue stroked mine, roaming around my mouth, intimate and owning.

And then his hips started circling, unhurried and excruciating, his dick caressing my g-spot sending sparks across my body with each torturous rotation. His jaw slackened as I moaned deep and low, his eyes still fixated on mine, watching my every reaction.

"You like that, baby?" His teeth gritted as he continued his measured rhythm, never picking up the pace. "You'd better, because you're mine Emerson, and this is the only cock you'll ever have for the rest of your life."

I tried to speak but nothing appeared, he'd stolen my speech.

"My mouth will be the only mouth you'll ever feel, on your perfect nipples, on your clit, in your pussy. Mine."

Fuck me. My entire body throbbed at his words.

My fists gripped his shoulders, desperate for more leverage against him, desperate for him to pound hard into me, but I knew I wouldn't get it. I'd never seen him like this before, so controlled and savoring, and I wanted him to take what he needed.

I wanted to give him everything.

He owned me.

His lips found my neck. "I'm going to worship you for the rest of my life."

Blood was coursing through my veins, I could hear the pump of my heart getting faster, my breath shallowing and my chest heaving. My hands moved up into his hair, drenched from the sweat of his control and the heat of the bath. My hips were fighting against the grip he had on them, needing so badly to move against him, but helpless to his power.

"Fuck. I love you so fucking much, Emerson."

Like lightning hitting the ocean, his words were an incendiary device for the orgasm barreling down my spine, gaining power with every second I tried to hold it in.

My head flew back, my hands still clinging to his shoulders, arching my chest into his mouth and he finally unleashed me. I rode him, the waves of water crashing against the sides of the bath as I came and came, clenching his dick until I took him with me, pulling him under. He exploded inside me with a boom, his cock swelling and throbbing through his own orgasm, as he wrapped his arms around me, taking my mouth once more, stealing my breath, consuming me with so much love I thought I might burst.

This is how it's supposed to be.

This is how it's going to be.

14

DREW

"Thanks Bud." I caught the tape mid air, as Huck threw it to me, and sat down to wrap my stick.

When I was done, I looked up to find several beady pairs of eyes staring as I handed the tape to Felix.

"I know I'm pretty but I gotta say, I find it weird when you all stare at me."

"Not that pretty. Just fucking whistling like you're one of the seven dwarfs." Growled Brogan.

My face screwed up in confusion. "What?"

"You're whistling."

"Was I?"

"Yes, stop it. It's annoying as shit and it's piercing my brain."

Moody bastard. I got up and put my arm around him to try and cheer him up.

He shrugged me off. "Dude, what the fuck are you doing?"

Okay, rude. Also, surely it was obvious.

"Hugging you."

"Don't."

I sat back down.

Felix put his arm around me. "Hey, don't be a dick to Drew, he's happy, leave him alone."

I leant into his embrace.

Ah, this is nice. Yeah, this is proper friendship.

"Jesus you two need to get a room." He stormed off.

I turned to Felix who'd gone back to taping his stick. "What's up his ass?"

He shrugged. "Nervous about the game I guess."

Tonight was the first game against Philly since the season opener a few months ago, which had ended in an all-out brawl. Most of us were feeling slightly apprehensive.

I say most, because not Felix.

Obviously.

"Seriously though dude the whistling is annoying as fuck. Want to share why you're even more Disney than usual?"

Gladly.

I grinned. "Emerson agreed to move in with me."

His eyes widened with genuine happiness. "Oh yeah? That's amazing news. Congrats buddy. Is she coming tonight?"

"Nah she has a late class tonight, so she'll catch the end on TV."

"Oh hey, Murray's coming tonight and drinks after. Get Emerson to meet us here, we can celebrate kicking some Philly ass for the second time."

"Oh yeah, good plan. I'll ask her." I grabbed my phone and shot her a text before lifting my pads down and putting them over my head.

Coach walked in while we were throwing our jerseys on, silence descending on the room. The assistant coaches stayed on the periphery as he walked into the middle, standing over the sacred Rangers logo on the floor.

His arms crossed over his chest. "Right team, listen up. Big game tonight and I don't need to remind you of what happened last time. You are the New York Rangers. You are better than them in every single way. Don't fuck it up by getting hot headed. Understood?"

"Yes, Coach." Shouted every single one of us in response.

"Good." He looked around. "Cleverly, Crawley, Marks, Jacobs and Sands. You're up. Bartlett's in charge of not letting any goals in. You've got five minutes to get out there."

He walked off.

Coach Campbell would definitely not be in the history books for giving the most inspirational pep talks of all time.

"Walls is going the fuck down." Huck muttered as Coach left. "He needs to watch his fucking back."

"Yeah." Cooper fist bumped him. "Just don't be stupid because he's also a sly fuck."

I finished lacing my skates and stood up, stick in hand. "You got that right."

The crowds were going crazy, a sea of blue foam fingers filling the arena. The first period had been hard fought, a few of our guys taking some solid hits but we played well and clung on to a two-one lead.

We took the ice for the second, lining up either side of the red line, the ref in place with the puck in hand as we got in position opposite Philly. Jack Howards was next to me and already nudging my shoulder hard as we bent down in preparation of catching the puck off the first pass.

"Back off, Howards." I shoved him back, but not enough that the ref would notice.

Such a fucking tool.

I could see Devon Walls creeping in.

The whistle blew and the puck dropped, I shoved Howards away hard as we won the face off, Cooper taking control and backhanding it to Jasper, who promptly knocked it back over to Coop who'd been left free on the ice before the Philly dumbasses realized what he'd done. He swept it around and over to Felix who pounded up the wing, the disc on the tip of his stick then knocked it along the boards to

Huck, who passed it across the ice to me. I spun round, shooting it back over to Felix, not even needing to look to know he was positioned ready to slam it into the goal.

A flash of black and orange caught my eye, but Felix never saw it coming. Walls cleared air, taking him out from behind, hooking his skate, kneeing him in the back of the thigh as he tripped and went flying into the boards, crumpling to the ice.

All in less than a second.

Walls didn't even turn around as he raced forward, paying no attention to the whistles blowing like crazy over the cacophony of booing Rangers fans.

"You fucking cunt." I bellowed, powering after him up the ice, throwing myself against him, knocking him over.

I jumped on him, my fist smashing into his face, knocking his helmet off and it skidded away.

My fists didn't stop.

Couldn't stop.

Gloves went flying as he punched me back, connecting with my cheek.

His nose crunched under my fist, blood started pouring.

The ice around splattered red.

I was suddenly hauled backwards. "Drew, dude, you have to stop. You're breaking his face."

I looked up, nausea quickly replacing my rage at the scene in front of me. I hadn't noticed the silence which had descended over the crowds.

"Get the fuck off me." Yanking myself free I sprinted over to Felix, the medical team already assessing him, the stretcher getting ready to take him off.

I dropped to his side. His leg was sticking out at an unnatural angle, his arms thrown over his face contorted in pain and I gave silent thanks that he was awake, which meant it was unlikely to be a head injury or at least no serious concussion.

"Felix. Buddy, fuck, I'm so sorry. I'm with you."

I got pushed to the side by one of the physicians as they continued checking him over, preparing him to be lifted.

"Crawley, move out of the way."

I slid back, bumping against Jasper and we watched our teammate lie there on the ice as half a dozen officials tended to him. I picked up his helmet which was lying by my skates and held onto it.

"Okay, on my count, lift him." Doctor Beaumont, the team's head physician, ordered his crew. "One, two, three."

The backboard was slipped underneath Felix and he was strapped in, before they once again lifted him, placing him on the stretcher. The crowds clapped and the players on the benches banged their sticks against the boards as he was wheeled off.

I turned to the boys who were standing right next to me, their faces etched with the worry I felt deep in my belly. "This is bad. This is so fucking bad."

Jasper dropped his head. "Yeah."

We slowly started skating back to the bench. I looked around. "Where the fuck is Walls?"

"He was sent off, he's in the lockers. Match penalty." Replied Cooper.

"Good."

"But you did too." Someone mumbled behind me.

My head whipped round. "What?"

Before he could answer Coach grabbed me, holding the back of my neck, checking my face and staring at me. "Crawley, you okay? You hurt?"

I shook my head. "I'm good, Coach."

"Good, go back to the locker room and cool off."

Fuck the locker room.

"I'm fine. Where's Clevs?"

Coach narrowed his eyes at me in assessment. "He's being loaded into the ambulance."

"Can I go with him?"

"No." He said in a tone that didn't want messing with. "Go back to the locker room and get changed."

"What about Walls."

"He's with the doctors, looks like you broke his nose."

At least that was something. I took perverse joy in knowing I'd provided some form of payback. *Bitch.*

"Good. I'll do it again."

"Drew. Locker room. Now. I'm not going to repeat myself."

The buzzer went off, indicating the end of injury stoppage. Coach left me to sort the new lines for the remainder of the second and I stormed off down the tunnel, ripping my jersey over my head, throwing it on floor somewhere. My shoulder pads followed, launched across the locker room as I kicked the doors open and threw myself down on the bench.

"FUCK. FUUCCCKKK." I smashed my stick against the floor, smashing and smashing until it snapped, then smashed what was left in my hand.

"FUCK."

I slumped against the lockers, my chest heaving from the rage hurtling through my body, tightening with every breath I took.

My veins were flowing molten lava.

Felix's face flashed before me. His leg was broken, of that much I was certain.

This was bad.

Like real fucking bad.

Career ending bad.

At the very least he would be out for months, probably the rest of the season. And we'd only just started.

My nose stuffed up and I realized I was crying, wiping my tears with the heel of my palm before succumbing to full blown, wracking sobs.

I picked up a discarded shirt and blew my nose.

Dave, one of our longstanding locker room attendants walked in and surveyed the destruction I'd left in my wake, collecting the broken remnants of my stick.

He was used to tantrums, but still it was fucking embarrassing being caught in the middle of one.

"I'm sorry, Dave." I mumbled.

He took one look at me, at my face.

"Don't worry, I got this. You get in the shower."

I didn't want to have a shower but I didn't argue, stripping off what was left of my clothes and grabbing a towel.

Five minutes later I pulled on my sweatpants and a hoodie, grabbing the rest of my stuff including my phone.

Emerson: *Hi baby, I'll call you when I get out of the class. Have a great game. I love you xxx*

My throat constricted again, in desperation to see her, to hold her, to feel her warmth and comfort. I dialed her number, but it rang through to voicemail.

Fuck.

"Hi baby," My voice broke. "Felix had an accident and I need to go find him. I'll call you when I do, but go home. Don't come to the Garden. I love you, I'll see you later."

The game would be ending soon and I wanted to get out of here before it did. I needed to find out which hospital they'd taken Felix to. I pushed open the locker room doors and walked down the empty corridor, looking for information.

The entrance to the visitor's room swung out as I passed.

"Off to find your boyfriend? Probably ought to try the nearest hospital." Drawled a voice.

I stopped in my tracks, my blood boiling, and slowly turned around. "The fuck you say?"

Devon leaned against the wall, way too cocky for someone whose face was already bruised and swollen. "You heard."

Oh, you are fucking dead, Sunshine.

"No, what I heard was you asking for me to finish what I started."

His lip turned up in a sneer. "Go fuck yourself, Crawley."

Now here's the thing. I might fight on the ice, but I'm generally a pretty easy guy, takes a lot to get me angry. Just keep me fed and watered and I'm good, add Emerson into the mix and I'm golden. So I've never really given much thought to the term 'seeing red' because why would you. But fuck me. You really do.

Snap.

And that would be the final shred of composure I'd been holding onto before my fist connected with his face.

Again.

He grabbed hold of my collar, punching me in the ribs with a hard upper cut, trying to wind me, but I only stumbled for a second before smashing him with a left hook to his jaw, knocking him back against the wall.

"You're a fucking bully. You have no business being in this game."

He groaned as I returned the hit to the ribs.

"You might have ended Felix's career and you don't even give a shit."

He grunted, spitting out blood to the floor. "No, not really."

Rage flooded my brain. I could only see red.

In the distance, I heard the buzzers go off. The second period had finished and everyone would start making their way back.

Smash went my fist, again, already pulled back for another swing, but I was grabbed from behind before it could make contact and hauled across the corridor. Huck and Dante were holding me in a firm grip.

"Stop. Dude. He's baiting you."

I tried to pull away, but they were holding me firm.

Jasper had Devon Walls pinned, until several of the

Philly's guys turned up, the corridors filling up with sweaty hockey players each taking a side.

"What's going on here?"

Jasper shoved Walls over to the Philly captain. "Someone needs to fucking babysit your teammate before he causes any more damage."

Billy McKenzie glared at me, taking in my bloody fists. "Looks like he's not the only one causing damage."

"Damn right." I mumbled.

Jasper grabbed my shoulder, pulling and shoving me at the same time, back toward our locker room. "Let's get out of here before Coach arrives and this turns into gang warfare."

"Too late." Muttered Dante.

We spun to find Coach walking toward us, flanked by his crew.

"I don't know what's going on here and I don't care. None of you is supposed to be out here, so move."

Everyone dispersed.

"Crawley, not so fast."

Jasper stopped with me. "Coach…"

Coach held his hand up, silencing him. "Drew, I told you to get changed and cool off. And now I find you fighting in the corridors like some fucking high-schooler."

"Coach, he started it…" Jesus. I sounded like a high-schooler.

He silenced me with a raised eyebrow, showing zero patience for my excuses. "I've no doubt, he's a piece of shit and had it coming. But I was on my way to tell you that you've been suspended for six games and I don't want any fucking more. You're one of my best players and I can't lose you now."

I hung my head. "Yes sir. I just wanted to find out where Clevs went so I can go."

He looked at me intently, then pulled his phone out and

dialed a number. "Where are you? Yeah, okay. How is he? Okay thanks. I'm sending Crawley over."

He looked at me as he hung up. "He's at Columbia Presbyterian. He's being prepped for surgery."

Even though I knew he'd need surgery it still felt like another blow to the ribs.

"Fuck."

"They're on the third floor. You can go, we'll talk about this tomorrow."

"Yes Coach, thank you."

"Crawley, get your hand sorted while you're there."

I shoved my hand inside my pocket, wincing but hoping he hadn't noticed how bad it was.

"Yes sir. Thank you."

Jasper turned to me as Coach walked off toward the dressing room. "He'll be okay, man."

"I hope so." I ran my hand down my face. "Can you do me a favor, I've left a message for Emerson but her phone is ringing out and she was supposed to be coming here. Can you make sure Murray takes her home? He's here and I don't know if I'll be able to call from the hospital."

"Yeah, don't worry about it. We'll sort it." He pulled me into a hug. "You go, we'll be there as soon as this game ends."

"Thanks Jas. I'll text you." I picked my bag up from where I'd dropped it and ran down toward the car park where I knew Ralph was expecting me.

Thirty minutes later I stormed into a private waiting room on the surgical floor where Felix was. A couple of the team assistant physicians, Ford and Erica, were sitting on the sofas, their faces greyer than normal.

"What's the deal?"

Erica took a breath. "Open femur break, but his knee was also fractured. His leg crushed behind him as he went into the boards."

I slumped down onto a chair, my face in my hands. "Fuck. What does that mean for him?"

"We need to see what the surgeon says but it's going to be the rest of the season. Six months rehab minimum, I'd say."

"But he'll play again?"

Ford nodded. "Yes, he should do."

My shoulders dropped and I pressed my finger and thumb into my eye sockets, squeezing away the moisture, overwhelmed with relief. I pulled my phone out, checking again to see if Emerson had messaged but she hadn't. I'd tried her a dozen times on the way over but it hadn't connected and now I had no cell reception.

Fucking technology.

"Drew, has anyone looked at your hand?"

I'd almost forgotten about it as I glanced down. The knuckles were bruised and swollen, a gash across my left one from where it had collided with his teeth. I squeezed my fist open and shut a couple of times.

"Nah. It's fine."

He rolled his eyes, got up and walked out, returning a few minutes later with an ice pack and a suture kit, sitting down next to me.

"Where'd you get that from?"

"We're in a hospital." He deadpanned, pulling on some gloves and a mask, laying out a sterile cloth on the table. "Give me your hand."

I groaned but placed it in his reach for him to examine.

"I don't think you've broken anything." He wiped it with anti-sceptic and numbing gel. I winced as the needle pierced my skin, but two stiches later and he was done, covering it with medical grade Band-Aid.

"Hold this for a bit." He placed the ice pack on it. "You're not playing for a few games, so this should be good. Come and see me in a couple of days to check in, but I'll probably be able to take it out in a week."

"Okay, thanks Doc." I grumbled.

The door suddenly flew open and in walked Cooper, Jasper, Huck and Brogan, followed by Dante.

I stood up, Jasper hugging me again, his hand cupping the back of my head. "You okay?"

I nodded.

"How's Clevs?"

"He's in surgery, he's broken his leg and knee."

His eyes bulged. "Fuck, his knee?"

I turned around to the Docs. "What was it?"

"His leg was crushed against the boards, his femur has snapped and he's fractured his knee but we need to see what the surgeon says once they're out." Erica repeated what she told me earlier.

The guys all winced, knowing full well how much recovery time this would take. Knowing how damaging this could be for his career.

"How much longer will he be in?"

Ford looked at his watch. "Maybe another hour, I'm not sure. It depends on the damage."

Jasper turned to me. "Murray took Emerson home. Her phone died so she hadn't got your message. She's gone to the loft."

I sighed in relief. "Oh thank fuck. I've been trying to get hold of her. Thanks buddy."

I was desperate to get home to her, then guilt flooded me at the thought of Felix in surgery, because he wouldn't be going anywhere for a while.

What a shit day. There had to be something to take our mind off this while we waited.

"How's Flossie?"

I don't think I'd ever seen Jasper smile so widely. Even on his wedding day. "She's fucking amazing, man. I swear she smiled at me this morning, although Wolf said it was a burp, but she's so fucking beautiful."

He pulled out his phone and started flicking through photos of her. She was so fucking cute.

"Most beautiful baby I've ever seen."

The fact that I hadn't actually seen many was irrelevant.

"Yeah. I can't even explain it, my heart feels like it's going to give out every time I look at her."

"You should go home, everyone would understand. Clevs wouldn't want you away from his favorite goddaughter."

He laughed. "It's all good, she's in bed. I'll wait to see what the verdict is from the surgeon first."

The door to our room opened and in walked two, pulling off their caps.

I blinked hard.

"Mol?" Jasper and I asked in unison.

Cooper was faster with his reaction, crossing the room and pulling his sister into a hug.

"Molly? What are you doing here?"

"What d'you mean?"

He looked at her, surprise written all over his face, matching ours. "I mean, how did you know?"

She stepped back with a frown. "I work here. This is my hospital."

"Is it? I thought you were..."

She stared, waiting for him to finish his sentence, although it was clear he didn't know how to. "Yes..?"

"I don't know, sorry. I didn't realize." He rubbed the back of his neck.

She narrowed her eyes in disbelief. "This has only ever been my hospital since med school, for almost as long as you've been at the Rangers. You've visited me here. I'm an orthopedic surgeon on the Sports Surgery program. Do you ever listen to anything I say?"

"Yes, yes. Of course I do, sorry. We all just jumped in the car and I didn't pay attention to where we were. Hospitals all look the same and I wasn't expecting to see you. Why are you here?" He snapped.

She turned to the doctor next to her. "Please excuse my brother, he gets hit in the head a lot."

The doctor chuckled. "No problem, you catch up, I need to update the nurse."

He walked out.

Molly shook her head, hands on her hips.

Cooper rubbed his face in frustration. "Fuck Molly, gimme a break. Look, Felix had an accident, a bad one. Can you find out what happened to him and how he is?"

"Give you a break?" She looked at him, her head tilting. "Why exactly do you think I'm here Coop?"

Cooper stood there clueless, until he wasn't, and his eyes widened along with the rest of us.

Fuck.

Little Molly.

Guess she wasn't that little anymore.

I crossed the room and hugged her tight. "Molly did you operate on him? Oh my god, how is he? Sorry, we're just all in shock."

She pushed me away as the door opened and another doctor walked in.

"Hi guys, how are you all? Great to have you here. Big fan. Sorry about the circumstances."

No one answered, ignoring him and the fake smile plastered on his face. We were all trained on Molly.

"It's fine, I know this has been a lot tonight." She rolled her eyes, clearly pissed at Cooper. "Tu es parfois un imbécile. Je ne suis pas un enfant que tu connais?"

Cooper stepped back once she'd finished swearing at him in French, his head shaking. She turned back to the rest of the room.

"Yes, I operated on him. And he's good, it was a good surgery. Went well."

Ford and Erica moved to stand with the rest of us gathered around Molly.

Ford held out his hand. "Hi Doctor Marks, I'm Doctor Burroughs and this is Doctor Brooker."

It was so weird that doctors always introduced themselves as doctors to each other.

"We're the Rangers' assistant physicians. Can you tell us how he is?"

"His patella was fractured from the impact and he has an anterior cruciate ligament tear. His femur was easier to fix as it snapped clean, so it wasn't hard to stabilize, and we've inserted a rod through it to keep the alignment in place. For his knee we needed to pin it, but he will require another surgery to repair the ligament."

Fuck.

Ford nodded. "Best case scenario?"

"Nine months of rehab, minimum."

"So he's out for the rest of the season?"

She nodded.

"Mol, what's the worst case?"

She looked down before she answered, her eyes returning to mine, red and watery. "He's done. He won't play again."

Cooper and I stared at her. Her face showed more than tiredness from a late surgery, I suddenly realized how hard this must have been for her too, Felix was her friend as much as ours.

"Fuck. Fuck. Fucking Walls." Jasper started pacing, his hands on his head.

Brogan let out a long sigh, Huck and Dante sat back down, their faces gray with worry.

"Can we see him?"

She shook her head. "He's still in recovery and he's heavily sedated. He needs sleep but come back tomorrow. I'll let him know you came when he wakes up."

"Are you here all night?"

"Yes, I'll stay with him."

"Jesus." Huck startled as the doctor near the door coughed. Molly turned and frowned at him, we'd all forgotten he was standing there, his weird smile still plastered on his face as he looked back at her.

Okay, you're a fucking super creeper.

"Did you need something Doctor Jessop?"

"No, no. Just observing."

Cooper moved closer to me, his voice low. "Is that fucking doctor staring at Molly's ass?"

I watched him as Molly continued talking to Ford and Erica. His eyes were definitely trained south, but not low enough they were looking at the floor.

"Yeah, I think so. He looks like a fucking weirdo. And I don't think his face moves."

Molly opened the door. "Let me just go and find out what room he'll be in, so you can go straight there tomorrow."

She walked out and this time the look from Super Creep was definitely not a quick glance. He was full on checking her out as she walked down the hallway.

"Hey Doc?"

Super Creep spun around straight into Cooper's hard, intimidating glare.

"Coop…" I warned, my voice low.

"Do me a favor, keep your eyes north of the border and off my sister's ass."

He tried to hide his shock at being caught. Not sure why, seeing as he was as subtle as an ambulance siren. Then his eyes widened with interest.

"Doctor Marks is your sister?"

"Yep." Cooper let the p pop for emphasis.

He spluttered slightly before regaining his composure. "Well I can assure you, I was doing nothing of the sort."

Everyone was staring, momentarily lifted out of their shock to watch what was happening.

Cooper grinned but it didn't reach his eyes. "Great, so we have an understanding that in future you're keeping away from Molly and her ass?"

Molly returned, taking in the stand-off between Coop and Super Creep.

"What's going on?"

Cooper rolled his bottom lip, not taking his eyes off the guy in front of him. "Nothing, we're all just getting acquainted, aren't we Doc?"

"Qu'est-ce que tu as fait?" She hissed at her brother.

Cooper shrugged, turning away.

She rolled her eyes before focusing on the rest of us in the room. "He's going to be in Room 306. But go home, it's late and there's nothing you can do right now. You had a hard game tonight. You need to rest too."

I looked at the clock, it was twelve twenty am.

I pulled her into a hug, my throat tightening again. "Thanks Mol. Thank you."

She rubbed my back, returning my hug. "Do you want me to look at your hand?"

"No it's good, it's been sorted."

Huck stood back up. "What does everyone want to do?"

Jasper turned to everyone. "We go home. Molly's right, we aren't going to do any good here and we need to rest. We still have to play in two days, everyone go and we'll be back here tomorrow."

"Thank you, Doctor Marks. We'll be in touch tomorrow to discuss next steps. Thank you for your work this evening." Ford held his hand out and Molly shook it, followed by Erica's.

"You're welcome."

We all collected our things and started for the door. Cooper flung his arm over Molly's shoulder, kissing her head as we walked out, holding onto her until Super Creep had disappeared down the corridor.

"Sorry Mol. I did know this was your hospital and I do listen to you. It's just been a lot tonight. And I wasn't expecting to see my little sister in Doctor fancy dress or operating on one of my best friends."

"It's not fancy dress Coop, this is what I wear every day and I'm excellent at my job. Top of my class, in case that was something else you'd forgotten." She shoved his shoulder.

"I know, I'm joking. And I'm proud of you, he couldn't have been in better hands."

"Thanks. Anyway, I need to go and check on him. I'll see you tomorrow. Give Freddie and the bump a kiss for me."

"Yeah, I will. I'll see you tomorrow. Love you."

We all hugged her goodbye, all of us so grateful for what she'd done. Grateful she was one of us and with us, that a stranger hadn't been working on Felix.

She knew the stakes.

I turned before she left. "Hey Mol, who was that pervy doctor?"

"Who?"

"That weirdo in the room with us?"

"Oh, I don't know him really. He's a resident covering this week from Mercy."

"We didn't like him."

She laughed, knowing exactly what I meant. "I'll see you tomorrow. Go home."

She walked off toward Felix.

"Okay guys, let's get out of here." I clapped Huck on the back before I realized I'd completely forgotten I'd left before the end of the game. "Oh hey, what was the final score? Did we win?"

"Yeah, four – two."

At least that was something.

I let myself into the loft, closing the door behind me as quietly as possible so I didn't disturb Emerson, who I hoped was asleep. I dumped my bags by the door, walking into the kitchen. There was a bottle of whiskey on the counter and, picking it up, I poured myself a glass downing it in one, the liquid burning my throat.

Exhaustion and anxiety hit me like a Mach truck.

Fuck me.

But knowing I wasn't coming home to an empty apartment? That fucking floored me.

Tears started prickling in my throat at the profound gratitude I had for Emerson. The thanks I gave every day that I'd found her again. That my loneliness had been replaced by indescribable happiness.

I sniffed. I really needed to get my shit together.

No one likes a cry baby.

The bedroom door was open and I could see a light flickering, the soft hum of the television in the background. I walked in, my heart pounding in my chest, wiping away the tears which spilled over as I took in the sight, sniffing.

Fuck's sake.

She'd fallen asleep in one of my jerseys, curled up in the duvet, tv remote in her hand. Her thick auburn hair fanned out across the pillow, her lips parted slightly, quivering as she slowly breathed in and out. Some of her freckles had faded since the summer but there were still plenty scattered across her face. Still plenty for me to kiss one at a time.

ESPN was playing a repeat of Felix's accident and I gently took the remote from her, switching it off.

I padded into the bathroom, quickly brushing my teeth and taking a piss before stripping out of my clothes and getting into bed, switching off the bedside lights. I pulled her body into me, breathing in her warmth, soaking her in, taking comfort in her presence.

I was so fucking lucky.

Her hand snaked up my neck, rubbing through my beard as she let out a soft moan.

"You're back. Thank god." She whispered, still sleep drunk. "Baby, I'm so sorry. How is he? How are you? How's your hand?"

"Shhhh, it's all good. Go back to sleep, I didn't mean to wake you. We can talk about it in the morning."

"Tell me."

I wrapped my arms around her more, holding her tighter. "It's bad. His leg is broken, torn his ACL and fractured his knee. He'll be out nine months minimum."

She let out a deep breath. "Shit, baby, I'm so sorry."

"Thank you." I kissed her head, my body starting to come alive. It didn't matter how tired I was, I never not wanted her.

Her face moved up toward mine. "I love you so much. I'm so happy you've come home to me. I'm so happy you're okay."

I held her chin, my lips capturing her smile. "Me too, Luck. I can't even explain it."

There was no moon tonight and our bedroom was almost pitch black, which only served to heighten every other sense before our eyes adjusted to the darkness. Her lips slowly trailed across my jaw and I could feel the softness of her lashes flickering fast against my cheek, like hummingbird wings.

She was electricity and magic.

Her tongue ran down my neck and my dick punched her hard in approval.

"Baby, what do you need?"

I ran my hands down her body, rolling on top of her. "You. I need you."

Her legs fell open. "You have me."

I groaned at how hot and wet she was against me, and as

with every time before my dick swelled even more. Because it couldn't get enough of her either.

I slid my hands under the jersey, removing it, before my mouth descended on hers, our tongues softly stroking together. With her fingertips she began tracing the divots in my spine until they reach my ass, her smooth soft palms running over my butt cheeks, cupping them, pressing me further into her.

I lifted my hips, rocking against her swollen clit, then slipped straight into her tight, drenched pussy as she trembled against me. Even after all this time I still needed a second to compose myself. To hold myself up against the wonder of how perfect she was, how perfect we were together, to stop the onslaught of pressure building up in the base of my spine, squeezing my balls like a vise.

Her breathing labored as I started circling my hips, grinding against her clit, slowly but forcefully as my tongue left a trail of saliva down the column of her throat. Marking her.

Mine.

"Oh fuck, babe." Her eyelids started fluttering, her voice raspy and low from her sleep, and so fucking sexy it shot thunderbolts down my spine. "That is soooo good."

"I know. You feel so fucking incredible."

I dropped down, my heavy body enveloping hers, my hands cupping her chin, holding her still so my mouth could devour her while I slid in and out of her perfect, velvety soft pussy with excruciating slowness, losing ourselves in each other.

I wanted to stay here forever.

"I love you so fucking much, Emerson."

Her soft mewing became more pronounced as she got closer, her muscles griping me tighter trying to stave off her impeding orgasm. She was so close to tumbling over the edge and I wanted to follow.

I'd follow her to the ends of the earth.

I bit along her neck, growling into her. "You want to come, Baby? You want to make me come with you?"

She sucked in her bottom lip, nodding.

I took her hands in one of mine, holding them above her head, holding myself up above her. The other ran down her side, gripping onto her ass, lifting it up as I started moving inside her with more force, but still measured and precise, wanting to feel every single molecule of her against me. She lasted seconds before her thighs tightened, squeezing me hard as they tried to close but I wouldn't let her as her pulsating took hold of me, pulling me along with her.

My orgasm barreled down my spine, falling into her slip-stream, until I couldn't do anything else but let go and I exploded inside her with potent force. With my mouth surrounding hers I breathed her in, filling my lungs with her essence. Her love.

She was mine. I was hers.

It was visceral.

We didn't move, sleep overcoming us both and we fell asleep still fused together.

15

EMERSON

Drew's thickly muscled forearm curled around me, pulling me into him, waking me from a heavy sleep.

He kissed my shoulder. "What time is it?"

I groaned, lifting my head to look at the clock on the bedside table before turning back toward him.

"Ten thirty."

His eyes were still closed, his brows pinching together. "Was last night a bad dream?"

I ran my fingers over the crease, smoothing out his forehead. "No baby, I'm sorry. It wasn't."

He moved forward, brushing his nose to mine, running it along my jaw before he rested his head on my shoulder.

He let out a deep sigh. "Fuck. Poor Felix. I need to go and see him."

I rubbed my thumb along his stubble. "I know, let's get showered and go."

"Don't you have classes today?"

I shook my head on the pillow. "No, I switched them with Mikey. I wanted to be with you so we could go to the hospital together."

Emotion flashed over his face, his eyes flooding with

gratitude and tenderness. His lips pressed against mine. "Thank you."

I caught a tear from his cheek before it fell.

"You're welcome. I wouldn't have been anywhere else." I slid out from under the duvet, holding my hand out. "Come on, I got you today."

He took it and followed me into the shower.

An hour and a half later we walked into the hospital, where we would have been sooner if Drew hadn't insisted we go via several stores. Our arms were laden with bags full of Felix's favorite junk food, an Xbox with every game he could find and a giant stuffed bear like the one he'd bought Flossie because *'he might be laid up, but he still needs reminding I'm the best godfather and the t-shirts I've had printed haven't come yet.'*

Cooper and Freddie were already in his room when we arrived. Felix was sitting up in bed, grinning, his leg secured in a full brace and eating what looked to be a massive bowl of green jello.

"Dude, you're such a child. Jello for breakfast? Really?" Drew put the bear down and strode over, hugging him hard and holding him close for several beats before releasing him. "How are you doing?" His voice broke slightly.

He shook his arm around, the one which was attached to a drip. "I'm morphined up to the max and I'm eating jello. Life is good."

I dropped the bags on the floor and hugged Cooper and Freddie, who were on the sofa, before turning to Felix, hugging him too. Drew moved off the bed and sat on the only spare chair, pulling me into his lap.

"Awww, you guys." Felix looked at us then Freddie and Cooper. "And you guys."

Yeah, he was definitely high.

He sat up excitedly, waving his spoon. "Oh hey, guess who operated on me?"

Cooper glanced over at Drew with a low chuckle.

"It was Molly. I didn't even know she'd finished med school, but she did a pretty good job." He banged his leg. "Ouch."

Freddie rolled her lips also trying to hide her amusement at a stoned Felix. "You did know she'd finished med school. Exactly how long did you think med school lasted?"

Felix shrugged. "I dunno, it's ages right?"

He went back to the jello.

I looked at Drew. "Who's Molly again?"

I vaguely remembered someone mentioning her before but couldn't remember the connection.

"Cooper's sister. She's a surgeon and in Clevs' defense, Coop also didn't know Molly was here."

Cooper let out an exasperated breath. "I did fucking know, I just didn't realize which hospital we were in."

"Oh come on, we were all shocked."

"What happened?" Freddie shifted forward moving cushions around to get more comfortable, looking to Cooper who was rubbing her large belly. "You didn't know she was a surgeon here? How? We've been here and visited her."

"Fuck's sake. I just wasn't expecting to see her as the surgeon who operated on Felix. I didn't realize this was her hospital. They all look the fucking same." He grumbled.

Freddie frowned at him before tilting her head toward me. "Molly's an orthopedic surgeon here, she studied at Columbia Med and finished her residency at the beginning of the summer, then stayed on as an Attending as part of the sports surgery program. She's a lot of fun, we'll go out with her when she gets some time off."

"Sounds good, can't wait to meet her."

"Can I come?" Asked Felix, his eyes wide with excitement.

"Sure, we'll all go out once your leg is better."

"Great."

Drew started rummaging around in one of the food bags

we'd brought, pulling out a protein bar and opening it. "How long have you guys been here?"

Freddie held her hand out for one of her own, catching it as Drew threw her his, followed by another one to Cooper.

"About thirty minutes, not long before you guys got here."

"Has anyone else been in?"

She shook her head. "No, not since we arrived. Coop said Coach and the doctors were here earlier for an assessment though. Jas and Wolf will come as soon as they figure out how to leave Florence with the grandparents, and I guess the rest of the guys will turn up at some point."

Drew looked at Felix. "Clevs, how was the assessment? What did they say?"

Felix's glazed eyes lifted to where the question came from. "Who?"

"Coach and the team docs?"

His face dropped in confusion. "Coach was here?"

Drew turned back to Cooper, his eyebrows raised in question.

"Dude, he's pretty out of it. You won't get much from him."

"Have you seen Molly? Super Creep not sniffing around?"

Freddie shuffled her pillows around again as Cooper shook his head. "Who?"

"Some fucking perv doctor who kept staring at Molly's ass while she was talking to us last night. He was so weird. You should have seen his face when Coop called him out. So fucking funny." Drew snorted.

She scrunched her nose up. "Sounds gross."

"Yeah, he was."

"Did I have some pervy doctor operate on me?" Asked Felix indignantly.

Drew turned back to him. "No, I got the impression he was just a cling on. Molly didn't seem to know why he was in the room."

He threw his head back laughing. "Cling on, that's funny."

"Someone needs to record this for prosperity." Muttered Cooper under his breath.

The door opened and in walked a doctor wearing a white coat with a stethoscope around her neck, tight curls bouncing on her shoulders. Even if her name hadn't been embroidered on her left breast pocket, I would have known who she was. With the same amber colored eyes and dark hair, she was a much smaller female version of Cooper. Although where Cooper always seemed to be scowling, her face exuded cheerfulness.

"Molly! Molly's here, everyone. I mean, Doctor Marks." Felix giggled, waving his spoon around as though conducting an imaginary orchestra.

Cooper lifted Freddie's legs off him and stood up to hug her, followed by Drew who'd moved me from his lap but kept hold of my hand.

"Hey Mol. I want you to meet Emerson."

She pulled me into a big embrace. "Oh god, I'm so excited to meet you. Freddie told me they'd found you. I'm so happy you guys managed to work it out. It's brilliant, brilliant."

She clapped her hands together in unadulterated glee. If she wasn't in orthopedics, she'd have made a great pediatrician. And she might have looked like Cooper, but that was where it stopped. I could never imagine him being so excitable.

"We have to go out soon or go around to Freddie and Coop's for drinks, because I want to hear all about it."

I liked her immediately. Hugging her back.

"I'd love to."

Molly moved away to kiss Freddie and pat her stomach. "Hi bump. How're you doing?"

"It's good, kicking a lot today though." She rubbed her hands across it, back and forth.

Molly put her stethoscope to it, listening. "Yep, loads of wriggling."

Drew laughed. "That your medical assessment, is it?"

"Sure is. Wriggling is an official term." She grinned, putting her stethoscope back around her neck.

"And what about this one?" He thumbed to Felix, who'd fallen asleep. "How long can you keep him on morphine? Because he's fucking funny."

Molly sighed, becoming serious, her hands pushed into her coat pockets. "He's on a pretty strong dose right now, but we'll reduce it tomorrow then he'll have it to use if he needs it. He's going to be in a lot of pain for a while, but I want to see how he moves without it."

"When do you need to operate again?"

"We need to let his leg start healing first, it'll be in about six weeks or so."

"How's he been?"

I watched Molly's eyes flicker with something I couldn't decipher, and she didn't look at anyone as she replied. In fact, she was studying the floor very closely.

"As expected. Same Felix he always is."

Cooper rubbed through his beard. "Does he know the extent of the damage?"

"I've told him but he'll need reminding, he won't remember." She looked at her watch, then walked over to Felix, checking his charts and his vitals. "The nurse will be in soon to take his bloods, how long are you guys planning to stick around?"

Drew shrugged. "We've got nothing else to do."

"Okay but he needs to rest too. Don't be here all day on Xbox. And can you message the others to stagger when they're going to visit?"

"Yes, sure. We can go for lunch while he's asleep and come back? Can you come too? Do you get a lunchbreak?"

"I'm not sure today, I'm pretty busy. But if we go down to

the cafeteria, I can squeeze you in for thirty minutes." She laughed.

"Wow, my sister. Big shot surgeon squeezing me in for lunch." He poked her in the ribs, making her squeal, and she nudged him back.

"Yeah and don't fucking forget it this time."

Drew wrapped his arms around me, my back to his chest, his chin on my shoulder as we laughed at the two of them messing around. They were making so much noise I was amazed Felix was sleeping through it.

"Are you good with lunch here?" Drew kissed me, his nose rubbing along my cheek.

"Yes, I'm happy anywhere."

"What a coincidence, because I'm happy wherever you are." He kissed me again as the door to the room opened and another doctor walked in.

No. No. No. This can't be happening.

Drew groaned but my blood ran cold. This was not his hospital. I'd double checked last night when I knew where they'd taken Felix.

"Fucking Super Creep." He whispered into my ear, not noticing my body had gone stiff in his arms.

And as Drew was also not looking at him, he didn't see the fury descend over Richard's face as he took in the scene.

"Emerson?" He practically spat, pointing aggressively at us. "This guy, this is the guy?"

Everyone stopped what they were doing.

Drew's head shot up, flicking between the two of us. I could almost feel the second he made the connection to who this man was, his body clenching tight with unconcealed wrath.

He spun me round to face him, pointing at Richard. "This guy? This is him?"

He didn't wait for me to confirm before crossing the room in a split second, like a viper ready to strike. Cooper moved between them in breakneck speed, his hand on Drew's chest. Richard backed himself toward the door as Drew got right up in his face, towering over him.

"You're lucky I'm not pummeling you into the wall for what you've done to her." He snarled.

Richard smoothed down his coat as he tried to regain the composure he'd lost. But Drew and Cooper were paid a lot of money to be intimidating, and it was working.

"How unsophisticated and typical you sports players are, just like her loser brother, always resorting to your fists." He looked down at Drew's taped up hand. "Although doesn't look like yours is working very well."

Drew inched another step forward, his voice threateningly low. "You come anywhere near her again and you'll find out exactly how well my fists work. I will fucking end you."

Even from across the room I could see Drew shaking with anger. I walked over and placed my hand on his chest, moving Cooper's away, hoping to soothe him before turning around.

What had Jupiter called Richard? A dick weasel.

I swallowed the sudden urge to laugh in his face as I looked at him, he did kind of look like a dick weasel.

"Richard, I don't know how to make this any clearer. Leave us alone, leave me alone."

He looked at me, his eyes beady and cold. "Oh Emerson, you'll come running back when he dumps you on your ass. Just wait and see."

I rolled my eyes, tugging on Drew's hand to come back over and sit with me, but it was like trying to move a stubborn bull.

"Baby, come. He's not worth it. Come."

Molly snapped out of the wide-eyed shock she'd held as the scene unfolded, rolling her shoulders, shifting back into professional mode.

"Doctor Jessop, I'm not sure why you felt the need to

come into here in the first place, you are not on this case, so I suggest you leave."

Richard startled, as though he'd not even realized she was in the room. "Yes, Doctor Marks, my apologies. I just came in to check on his vitals."

She crossed her arms over her chest, glaring at him. "That's not your job."

"Right, right." He flustered. "I'll be going back to rounds."

His jaw clenched, looking between Drew and me, before he walked away. Cooper closed the door behind him.

"What just happened?"

I turned to Drew, cupping his face in my hands, making him look at me. "Baby, are you okay?"

"Yes, fuck." His eyes snapped away from where they'd been focused on the door and he pulled me against his strong chest, his heart pounding with adrenaline. "Are you?"

I nodded, moving to look at him again. "Yes, I'm fine. Thank you."

He took a deep breath, visibly calming. "I was so close to beating the shit out of him, Luck. I fucking knew there was something dodgy about him yesterday."

He dropped his mouth to mine, kissing me softly, both of us the elixir for the other. As we turned to walk back to our chair everyone was staring, except Felix who was still asleep. It was so easy to forget anyone else was around when he kissed me.

"Are you both okay? What was that? What's Super Creep got to do with Emerson?" Freddie got the questions in before anyone else could.

I sighed. "That was my ex-boyfriend."

Cooper frowned. "The one who won't leave you alone?"

I nodded. "Did Drew tell you?"

Drew sat down, pulling me back into his lap. "Only that he was bothering you. I haven't told them about the other day."

"What happened the other day?"

"He hurt me."

Their eyes all opened wide, eyebrows shooting into their hairlines.

"What?" Growled Cooper.

Drew nudged me gently. "Tell them what's been going on."

"We were together for a few years and broke up last summer, which is when I met Drew. But we ended up getting back together and moved here, although it wasn't long before I realized I'd made a massive mistake and found him having sex with a nurse at his hospital."

Molly pulled a face. "God, so cliché."

"I know. But we've been broken up nearly a year now and he won't let go. I don't understand it at all. He would turn up where I was, or I'd have dozens of missed calls and messages. Then on Monday I had to swing by mine early because I had a class and didn't have any spare clothes at Drew's, and he was waiting outside my apartment when I came out. He grabbed me really hard and hurt my arm. He was so angry and I'm sure he was drunk. I actually don't know what would have happened if Ralph hadn't been there."

Molly looked horrified. "Shit, Emerson. I'm so sorry. Did anyone look at your arm? I can now?"

"Thanks, but it's okay, it was just badly bruised. And I think I've been so wrapped up and happy," Drew kissed my head, "that I hadn't noticed how fucked up it was. I just thought he was being annoying and it would stop when he found a new girlfriend. I'm not sure what I can do though."

"Restraining order." Drew mumbled and I turned to him. "What? Give me the word and I'll sort it."

My eyebrow raised. "Really? You don't think that's a bit extreme?"

"No, I fucking don't. The guy is a tool. And I don't like

knowing that he's out there, turning up where you are when I'm not with you. I nearly lost my mind the other day."

We'd talked about Richard a couple of times and what to do about him, but beyond Ralphie taking me to the studio I hadn't got very far. However, looking at Drew, I could see the worry on his face and for the first time I realized the depths of how much this was affecting him too and my chest started aching.

I held my hand against his cheek. "Okay, thank you."

His relief was palpable.

Freddie shifted around again. "I think it's a good idea too, for what it's worth. Even for peace of mind for when the boys are at away games. You don't want him rocking up anywhere again."

"Yes, I guess so." My shoulders dropped heavily, I hadn't even thought of that. A lump lodged in my throat and my eyes started burning with tears of frustration. "Fuck's sake, I haven't done anything wrong, why's this so messy?"

Drew kissed my head. "It's not, Sweetheart. We'll sort it and he'll go away, he won't be able to bother us again."

"Okay." I gave a weak smile. "What about here? Does he work here now?"

"I'll deal with that." Molly got out her phone and started typing away. "He was only covering for a week from Mercy. And that week should be up. I'll email HR to let them know we shouldn't get him back. To be honest, I hadn't seen him before yesterday, when Felix was brought in."

I sneered. "Sounds about right. He's always been a star fucker. Used to drop my brother's name at any opportunity."

Cooper made a noise to show his disgust.

Drew stroked my head. "Actually, Sweetheart, you know you mentioned Jupiter was coming to visit?"

I nodded.

"You remember we have the away games over Thanksgiving? Why don't you see if he'll come here and be with you, you guys can stay at the loft or in the country and hang out."

I hadn't even thought about Thanksgiving. Because I'd known Drew wouldn't be around, we'd already discussed me taking longer at Christmas and travelling with him for some away games, which included California and meeting my family. So I'd agreed to cover a few shifts at the studio to give the others some time off, hosting a schedule of Turkey Burn rides for those staying in the city.

Maybe Jupe coming wasn't the worst idea. And I hadn't seen him properly in months, it would be fun to hang out. "Yes, I guess I can ask him."

"Please, Emerson. I really don't want you to be alone." He pleaded.

"Alright, I will." I smiled at him.

We all turned at the sound of a jug being knocked over, water splashing to the floor. Felix was groggily trying to sit up. He looked around at all of us staring, Molly righting the jug and mopping the water with some towels.

"Hey guys, how long have you been here?"

"Oh Jesus." Cooper groaned.

16

EMERSON

I slowed the speed on the treadmill until I reached a steady walking pace, allowing my breath and heart rate to settle. Ten miles. Pretty happy with that.

Even with the cool air in the gym I was dripping with sweat, the towel I was wiping myself with didn't seem to be able to absorb it fast enough. I stepped off as the tracks ground to a halt, grabbing my water bottle in the process and glugging what was left.

The rain was pelting down outside as I walked through to the house. Freezing and disgusting.

I hated the cold. Although not as much as Jupiter.

I laughed at the thought of him coping without blazing sunshine for the next ten days. I'd told him to pack warm and knowing him he'll have sent his personal shopper out to order cashmere jumpers in every color. I wouldn't be surprised if he turned up in a woolly hat and scarf.

According to the clock in the kitchen he'd be here in an hour and I was so excited to see him, although it was at odds with the gnawing in my stomach at the thought of Drew being gone. He was only going to be away five days, but it already felt too long and he hadn't even left yet.

Who had I become?

But after a few weeks ago at the hospital, except for work, we'd barely left each other's side and my love, appreciation and gratitude for him had deepened more every day, as well as my understanding of him.

Understanding that as long as I was happy then he was.

And I was happy when he was happy.

It was that simple.

Love math, if you will.

He'd organized his lawyers to file a restraining order, Richard now couldn't legally contact me or come within five hundred feet. And in the end, he'd called Jupiter inviting him to come and stay, although he also had to point out that he'd be gone for the majority of the time to actually seal the deal, because Jupe was still being a grumpy fuck about us being together.

Because, boys.

I found Drew packing in his dressing room.

"Hi Baby. I'm just going to jump in the shower." I kissed him on the cheek as I walked past, stripping off and turning on the taps, stepping underneath the giant shower head.

I leant back against the wall as the hot water pounded my muscles. When I opened my eyes my breath hitched at the sight greeting me. Drew was standing naked, lazily stroking his perfect dick, a knowing smile slowly forming. His hazel eyes leisurely trailed up my body in a way that made my clit throb hard and my pussy drip with longing.

My heart began pounding heavily in anticipation, because from the look he had blazing through his hooded eyes, I knew I was going to feel him until he returned to me.

"Thought you were getting ready to leave."

He stepped into the shower, his thumbs brushing against my tight, aching nipples. "I am. This is part of getting ready because I can't go without being inside you, feeling you clench against me as you milk my cock, so I have one more memory I can jerk off to while I'm gone, while I'm without you. I need it to carry me through the next five days, Emerson."

Pressure started building low in my belly.

Fuck, this man could get me off with words alone.

His hands trailed along my rib cage, leisurely down my waist, following the droplets of water flowing over my body. They travelled at a torturously slow pace across my sensitive hips, causing my stomach to convulse, a fresh flood of arousal pouring out of me, until his fingers found what he was looking for. I winced as he thrust three inside me before pulling them out and sucking on them.

"You're so fucking sweet." He groaned loudly. "But this isn't going to be. Turn around."

I did as I was told and he spread my legs with his, holding on to my hips. His dick was nudging the base of my spine as he ran his fingers over my ass, probing and squeezing, before slowly, teasingly rubbed them in a wet trail between my cheeks from my clit and up through my crack.

My legs started shaking as his dick replaced his fingers, hard and swollen and thick, nudging its way toward my quivering pussy, notching at my entrance. He dipped down behind me slightly, hooking my thigh under his arm, lifting it as he plunged into me in one long, hard thrust, burying himself deep inside me with the full length of his dick. The sensation of him, so full inside me, stretching me out, set a deep pulsing in motion that I couldn't stave off.

My body a slave to his bidding.

"Christ, your pussy Emerson." He growled. "It was fucking made for me."

I cried out as he bit down on my shoulder, creating an epicenter of tremors shooting across my body, my clit throbbing, my nipples so tight the pain fought against the desperate release I needed from him.

He lifted his leg up on the shower bench, taking my thigh

with it. His arms encircled me, holding me in place, and my head fell back against his shoulder wanting his lips and he obliged with a sweep of his tongue round my mouth. He started to rock inside me in long savoring strokes, making sure we could both feel every delicious inch as he pulled almost all the way out, before thrusting back in.

It was fucking incredible, incredible fucking.

A deep moan rumbled up my throat. "Baby please, I need more."

"Hold on tight, Luck." His hand wrapped around my throat, pulling me back and claiming my mouth once more, harder and bruising, a silent warning for what was coming.

His breath labored as his hips began pistoning into me, passionate and brutal and owning, fucking me in symphony, one hand between my legs thrumming my clit, the other twisting my nipple, fucking me harder than he'd ever done before.

My moans turned to groans, then to whimpers, desperate to escape from this incredible torture.

"Nearly Sweetheart. Christ you feel so good." Drew grunted.

I could barely stand, my legs shaking violently as my orgasm hurtled down my spine, ready to suck the life out of me and take him with us. I let out a cry, feral and unrecognizable. My breath trapped in my throat, unable to move, Drew holding me tight as his steady rhythm became frenzied and wild.

"Oh fuck. Shit, I can't hold it. EM. ER. SON. Yes. I'm fucking coming."

As though my body had been holding on for him, waiting until we could cross over the finish line together, I let go, collapsing in his arms and our bodies shuddered in sync over and over, his hot cum hitting me right in the cervix, his fingers still bringing me down until I was so sensitive I pushed them away, unable to take any more.

He pulled me onto the bench, neither of us able to stand longer, sitting me in his lap, holding me against his chest as our breathing slowed down. His mouth found mine, his soft, warm tongue gently brushed against my lips before sweeping inside, kissing me long and hard. The languid way he sweetly roamed around was the antithesis of the raw, animalistic claiming he'd just exhibited. I returned him stroke for stroke, allowing the motion to convey the words neither of us wanted to say, but both of us felt.

Don't go.

I miss you already.

Mine.

He pulled back, my bottom lip caught between his teeth, his eyes staring deep into mine.

"I love you so much, I can feel it right here, every damn day." He placed my hand on his heart. "I'm so fucking lucky, I don't even know how it happened."

I cupped his beautiful face. "I'm the lucky one."

And I meant it, almost like my eyes had been opened to the shitty relationships I'd had, and Drew was my prize.

He grinned at me before smacking his open lips to mine, wet and sloppy.

"Right Sweetheart, as much as I'd love to stay in here with you, we need to get showered properly and dressed. If you promise to keep your hands to yourself, I'll let you share the showerhead with me instead of making you get under the other one." He winked.

"Hey, this was my shower you hijacked. I'm the one sharing with you."

He stood us both up, laughing, his arms still wrapped round me, and positioned us underneath the water as he reached for the soap.

Twenty minutes later after pushing me under the other shower and insisting we wash separately, I took one of Drew's old hoodies from the drawer, pulling it over my head.

It swamped me and I loved it. It was the perfect rainy-day cure.

I inhaled against the fabric.

It smelt like him and warmth and comfort.

I glanced up to find him buttoning his shirt, his tie hanging around his neck, watching me with a smirk. He was dressed in his game day suit. I mean, men always look good in a properly fitting suit, but Drew in a suit? Out of this world.

He walked over, bringing the edges of my hood up and tugged me to his lips, humming softly against them. His kisses always stayed so chaste when he knew he couldn't take them any further.

"You good? Looking forward to hanging with Jupiter?"

I nodded. "Yes, but I wish you were going to be here with us too. I'm going to miss you."

He brushed his fingers across my forehead, cupping my cheek. "I know, Baby, me too. But it's only for a few days and it'll be good for you to spend time together. Then we can all hang out when I get back. You can warm him up to me a bit more." He grinned. "You have the car to go wherever you want, although keep Jupiter away from the Ferrari. And Ralph is around too."

I nodded. As always, he'd thought of everything. Everything I could need while he was away. Making sure I was taken care of.

I ignored the heaviness sitting in my chest.

The intercom buzzed, alerting us to someone at the gate.

"Go finish getting dressed, I'll bring him in." Drew tapped my ass and rushed out.

By the time I'd pulled on some yoga pants and blasted my hair quickly with the dryer, Jupiter had got out of his car, into the rain and sprinted to the house where I could already hear him complaining about the weather.

I ran down the stairs to the bottom, where they were both

standing, not looking totally dissimilar. Drew was slightly taller but they were about the same width, Jupe had definitely packed some muscle on since I last saw him. Must have taken my comment to heart about being smaller.

I smirked.

"There she is." Jupiter held his arms out and I jumped into them. "Shit, have you put on weight? You're fuck heavy."

"Yeah, right." I shoved him. "If you weren't so puny you'd be able to carry me. Maybe I need to put you on a proper training regime while you're here. You've gone soft in the off season."

He scoffed, eyeing me up and down in assessment as I stepped back into Drew's body. "Nah, you look good Em. Maybe this dipshit does agree with you. Jury's still out though."

"Good job I don't give a shit what you think then isn't it? Tell it to stay out as long as it wants."

Drew chuckled softly into my hair, kissing the top of my head.

"Well, as much as I would love to stay and watch this go down, I need to head off." He held his hand out for Jupiter. "Thanks for coming, Man. I know it was to see Emerson, but I appreciate the timing. Honestly."

Jupiter took it. "No problem, thanks for sorting out that sniveling cock weasel. Fuck, I hated him so much."

Drew rolled his lips, nodding in agreement, but didn't say anything.

"Also should have said I was sorry about Clevs, fucking shit luck."

Drew's hand found mine and squeezed it. "Thanks man, I'll tell him."

"Yeah, maybe Em and I can go and see him while you're gone. He still in hospital?"

"No, he's out and grumpy as fuck. So, you should definitely go and see him."

I listened to the two of them, this was an unexpected turn of events. Weirdly polite, but still, I wasn't complaining.

"Awww, isn't this nice, both my boys getting along?"

"Hmmm." Jupiter scowled at me. "Anyway man, good luck. Kitchen this way?" He slapped him on the shoulder, pointing behind him.

"Yes, help yourself." I called after him as he walked off.

"I'd planned to."

'Course he did.

I turned and wrapped my arms around Drew.

"I'm sorry you won't be playing."

He kissed my nose. "It was worth it."

I brushed my hand along the soft scruff on his cheek. "I love you. Thank you for everything you've done for me."

"I'd do anything for you, Luck." He touched his lips to mine. "Right, you should go and make sure there's still food left before Jupiter eats it all."

I chuckled. "Yeah."

"I'll text you when I'm on the plane." He picked up his bag, throwing it over his shoulder, before taking my chin gently in his fingers, kissing me again. "I love you. And I can't wait to come back to you."

I stood by the door, watching him get into the car and drive off.

I stood there until I heard a crash coming from the direction my brother went.

I rolled my eyes.

Always destruction.

"Are you breaking stuff already?" I walked into the kitchen to find Jupiter rummaging through the cupboards, protecting himself from the pots and pans currently raining down on him.

Just so happened that the one he'd opened was the one I liked to put all the things in, when I didn't know where they actually went.

And it *may* have been a little full.

"Why has this cupboard got so much stuff in it?" He picked up a plastic bowl from the floor. "You did this, didn't you? Does Drew know about your habit of stuffing everything in one place? Used to drive mom crazy."

I chuckled. "No, not been busted yet. Drew mostly cooks and I put the things away."

"So why don't you just rearrange the cupboards, so you know where things are?"

I shrugged.

Wasn't going to tell him it had never occurred to me.

"Anyway, what were you looking for?"

"Something to cook the pasta in." He nodded to the bag of fresh pasta he'd found.

"You sit, I'll do it."

He winked, rounding the kitchen island and slid onto one of the stools as I tidied up the mess he'd made. I took a couple of beers from the fridge and passed him one.

He twisted the cap off, taking a swig. "So, talk to me. What's been going on?"

"What did Drew tell you?"

"More than you did, which I was pissed about. Em, you know you can call me about anything."

I looked up at him. "Yes I know, I just didn't think this was anything until the other week and then I tried to call you, but you were off the grid."

His eye twitched slightly, a tiny amount of guilt crossing his face.

I threw the pasta into the pan of boiling water I'd started. "Good tan by the way. Where did you go?"

"Maldives."

"Nice."

"Yeah, better weather than here, for sure. It's fucking freezing. How long's it gonna rain for?"

249

I raised an eyebrow. "I dunno, want me to call the Meteorological Society?"

He stopped just before the beer bottle touched his lip. "Wise ass."

I grinned. "I missed you, Jupe."

"Yeah, missed you too." He looked around. "Gotta say though, I meant it before, you do look good, you look happy. I like it, I haven't seen you this happy for a long time. And I like this place, have you moved in?"

"Not officially. But I'm either here or at the loft, we don't often stay at mine. I'm moving the boxes after Christmas."

I opened the fridge again, there were a few options for pasta sauce but I knew which one Jupiter would want. Arrabiata with extra parmesan.

I started heating it, then drained the pasta.

"So this is it then, it's real?"

Real. Really fucking real.

I nodded, smiling wide, trying not to look like a lunatic.

"Yup. Real. So can you stop sending him threatening text messages please?"

He grinned, with zero shame. "It was one message."

Both brows went up this time.

"Okay three, maybe four. But I'll give him credit, he didn't back down."

Of course he didn't, because he mostly found it funny but also respected that Jupiter was being protective. If fact, it would have been more of an issue for him if he hadn't.

"He loves me."

"When are you introducing him to mom and dad?"

"They've met him on Facetime, but in person will be Christmas. I have some time off and he's got away games on the west coast, so I'm going to travel with him and we'll come home for a few days. See Piper, Andy and the kids too."

I threw the pasta in the bigger pan with the sauce and started stirring it all together. Grabbing the pasta bowls from the drawer, I filled them, then passed them over to Jupiter along with a giant block of parmesan and two more beers.

He put his nose down to the pasta. "This smells amazing."

He grabbed the cheese grater and I watched in silence as he covered his bowl with an inordinate amount of parmesan. It was almost obscene.

"Home for the holidays. That'll be fun. Good plan starting him early on what he's getting into with you. Dad's already sorting the decorations."

Our father was a Christmas nut. Any decoration, you name it, he'd bought it. Growing up we were one step away from being that weird house on the block that people travelled miles to see. At least now the house was away from the street and the only people subjected to the blinding display of Christmas cheer were those who actually lived there or visited.

And Jupiter would never tell anyone, because it didn't fit with his grumpy, unapproachable public persona, but he secretly loved it too.

He forked up a mouthful. "What have you got planned for me while I'm here?"

"Not much, I just wanted to hang out. We could drive into the city tomorrow, but if you want to stay at the house that's good with me too. I'm just happy spending time together."

"Nah, let's hit the city. I never spend time here, let's go for a walk. Need to test out my new winter woollies, don't I?" He smirked.

I knew it.

"And what about Thanksgiving?"

I twisted the pasta noodles around in my bowl. "I have a class in the morning, which you're going to come to, then I figured football, movies and sofa time. And Thanksgiving tacos."

"Tacos?"

"Yeah, I miss them. And you can make them for me." I grinned.

"You have yourself a deal, young lady. You really want me to come to your class?"

I nodded. "It'll be fun. Then we'll come back here and hibernate, I don't fancy going out much."

"Okay done. Now let's eat and watch a movie. Then I'm going to go for a run, assuming NHL players can afford treadmills on the pittance they earn, because there's no fucking way I'm going out in that weather."

He pointed up to the glass ceiling, where the rain was still hammering down.

I rolled my eyes.

To be fair, he had a point.

The phone rang throughout the car and I grabbed it before Jupiter answered from the steering wheel.

"Hey Sweetheart, where are you?"

"Driving into the city." I turned the phone round so he could see we were on the interstate, Jupiter flipping him the bird as he came into screen.

"Scratch my car, Reeves, and you're buying me a new one."

Jupiter let out a low chuckle.

"Where are you?"

"Just heading to the arena for morning warm up and skate."

"You still have to practice even though you're not playing?"

He nodded. "Yep."

"How's everyone feeling this time?"

The first two games without Drew or Felix didn't go so well. And I know he was warring with himself at the guilt for being off the ice and his satisfaction at beating the shit out of Devon Walls. They were better by the third and fourth, but still shaky.

And I also knew how much he was missing Felix.

He shrugged. "Okay I think, they're going to be fine and it's allowed Carter and Dante to step up to first line, so that's good."

"Hey Crawley, who've you got tonight?"

"Dallas."

"Em and I will be watching. You should do alright, they've been playing like crap this season. So maybe it's good you're not at full strength. Least you're not playing Chicago."

Drew rolled his lip, considering what Jupiter said.

"Yeah, you're right."

"I am, when I got suspended last year for knocking out that dick Travis, it fucking sucked. I know how you feel, but you've only got two games left and it's worth it for Clevs. Devon Walls is literally the worst human being I've ever met. No one will blame you for not playing. And you're already top of the table, it won't affect anything."

Drew sighed. "Thanks man, I appreciate that."

"Don't get used to it, I'm still gonna kick your ass if you hurt Emerson."

I saw him try and hide a smile. "Noted. Anyway, Luck, I need to head off to practice. I'll speak to you later. I love you."

"Okay babe, have fun. I love you." I hung up.

"I love you." Jupiter mimicked in a high-pitched girly voice.

My brother. Such a fucking douche.

But I had zero come back. Especially when he'd actually been really sweet, and surprisingly helpful.

"Thanks for saying those things to Drew, he's found the last two weeks hard without Felix and he's been worrying about him a lot."

"That's understandable, he'll be okay though." He patted my knee. "But it's the name of the game, we all live with the knowledge that one accident could be all it takes. And hockey is brutal as fuck."

I let out a huff, because I knew all this. I knew. And Felix's accident had only cemented the knowledge further, for both of us. I had no doubt it had a lot to do with why we'd been so clingy with one another the two past weeks, even more so than we normally were. That and Richard.

"Emerson, if you're going to seriously date an athlete then you need to know the deal."

I turned in my seat so I could face him. "I know the deal, I grew up with you, remember?"

"Then consider that a reminder."

I swiped away his hand as he tried to ruffle my hair.

"Anyway, where are we parking?"

"At the loft." I put the co-ordinates in the GPS lady and she fired up. "Listen to what she says."

We drove into the underground parking, into Drew's space and hopped out. I watched as Jupiter put on a thick winter parka followed by a woolie beanie, pulling it down low, then flipped his fur lined hood over the top.

I couldn't, even.

"You know you're dressed like you're going to the Arctic, right?"

"Hey, it's fucking cold. It's very nearly freezing. And we're going to be outside, walking. My Californian skin needs to be kept warm."

"You know what, if you ever get a girlfriend you better pray she's less high maintenance than you. Actually, ignore me, there's no way she could be more."

He shoved me in the shoulder. "Whatever. It's freezing cold and you know it. You've just got used to New York. Come back to Cali and you'll soften right up."

"No thanks. I'm here for the long term."

I never thought I'd find anywhere I loved more than California. And if I hadn't met Drew I'd probably be back there. He'd changed everything.

But New York wasn't my home, Drew was.

And I knew that wherever he went, I would follow.

"Brrrrrrr." Shook Jupiter dramatically as we stepped out into the frigid air.

I'd call him a drama queen but he had a point. I zipped up my own thick parka. At least my hood wasn't fur lined, I wasn't a total sap.

"Come on then, let's go."

17

EMERSON

"I'm having a bath and then changing into sweats. And have you got any Epsom salts, because I'm going to need all the help I can get after that class. I'm amazed I can even walk." Jupiter announced as we got out of the car and headed into the house.

He'd joined for my Thanksgiving class, a class that had been full, with a wait list for the wait list – because New Yorkers didn't stop for holidays - and he'd spent the entire ride there scoffing in disbelief that anyone would seriously get up to exercise on Thanksgiving, and the ride back whinging about his hamstrings.

Grumpy ass.

Although I think his mood had more to do with the fact that as soon as we got there he'd been swarmed for autographs and selfies, when he'd wanted to stay under the radar. But with his sleeves of tattoos and his closely shaved head, he was a very recognizable magnet for women. I didn't understand it myself, I thought he looked like a douche, especially when he'd started tattooing his neck.

"Wow Jupe, do you complain this much to the Dodgers trainers? Do they not get you to work hard? Maybe that's why you've still got a fat ass." I dropped my bag at the door and followed him up the stairs.

"You know I didn't actually want to go right? I'm on my season break. It was at nine am on Thanksgiving. We got up at seven when normal people were still asleep. And we both know I do not have a fat ass. It's pure muscle, baby."

"What sort of sister would I be if I let you stay in bed after the amount of popcorn you put away last night?"

"And will put away again very soon. Anyway, salts? Where are they?"

"Go and run your bath, I'll get them."

I walked into my bathroom and picked up the Kilner jar of salts which sat on a little table by the tub, then decided against it and put it back down. Instead, I opened one of the bathroom cupboards and removed a giant bag of salts, because this way he couldn't complain I'd not given him enough. I carried it through to his room and handed it to him, his bath already half full.

"Here you are, go nuts."

"Thanks, I'll see you in a bit." He opened the bag and tipped it into the water.

"Sure, shout if you need anything else."

I walked out, running downstairs quickly to grab my phone before heading back to my bedroom for a long shower, knowing Jupe would be ages. I dialed Drew's number and he picked up immediately, his face filling the screen. It looked like he was in his hotel room.

"Hi baby, you're a sight for sore eyes. How was class?"

"It was good. I made it super hard, mainly because I knew how much Jupiter would hate it." I grinned.

Drew threw his head back, laughing. "Good girl. I would have paid a lot of money to see that."

"Yup. He's in the bath right now, with the giant bag of salts." I rolled my eyes. "Anyway, how are you? Everyone feeling good about the win?"

The Rangers had won against the Stars last night, which gave them a much needed confidence boost after the last week, especially to Dante and Carter who were still a bit green at being part of the starting line-up. But it had also helped Drew as he sat watching from the box, away from the team.

"Yes, everyone seemed pretty happy this morning."

I walked through to the bathroom and sat back on the chaise lounge, which ran along the wall near the bath. "And how are you, baby? Are you feeling okay?"

He shrugged. "Yeah. It's weird travelling without Felix though and I miss you."

"I miss you too. I'm sure, it's weird. How are Jasper and Cooper feeling?" I took my hair out of my tie and ran my fingers through it.

"The same, it's just like something's off a bit. But we need to shake it or it'll get in our heads and we'll tank."

"I understand that. You'll find the focus, baby. Don't worry."

"I know, hopefully last night helped." His eyes turned devilish and a smirk appeared. "The only good thing is that I have the room to myself, which means tonight you're mine. And you're going to show me exactly what I'm missing."

A deep throb hit between my legs. Every time he'd travelled we'd had some element of phone sex, usually while Felix was off with a girl. And it was just enough to see us through the long stretches until we were back with each other.

"Can't wait."

"Good. I want you ready and dripping wet for me." He growled. "Let me see your boobs, I need to know they've missed me too."

"Babe, exactly who are you missing more?"

He winked. "Sweetheart, you know I can't say it out loud, I don't want to hurt their feelings."

I rolled my eyes with a giggle. "You're ridiculous."

I heard banging on his door, followed by shouting.

He groaned. "Fuck, Em, I have to go. Coop is outside and we're heading for food. I'll speak to you later, 'kay. I love you. I love you, boobs."

"We love you too."

He hung up and I stayed where I was, tiredness from the early morning class taking over for a second before I stretched my arms and legs out, easing my muscles and getting back on my feet. I debated having a bath, but decided against it, instead turned the shower up high and stripped off, chucking my workout gear into the laundry basket before stepping under the hot water.

Jupiter was still in his room by the time I'd got out and dressed, so I made some oatmeal and used the time to create the playlist for my next class. I was starting to wonder if he'd got sucked down the plughole when he appeared.

"Feel better, Grumperson?"

He grinned. "Much. Thanks."

He walked into the pantry and came out with his arms full of food, which he put down on the island counter. I watched as he started piling up a bowl of cereal, yoghurt, berries and nuts, which he ate while he stared at the bread he'd put into the toaster, popping it as soon as it was at the right level of done.

This was making me hungry again.

I snatched up one of his slices of peanut butter covered toast and turned on the coffee machine.

"What movies are we watching, because I intend to spend the rest of the weekend in front of the screen?"

"So far we have Avengers and Die Hard. What else do you want to watch? What time does football start?"

He thought for a minute as he gobbled up some cereal. "We'll watch the second game. And nah, not Die Hard. It's not Christmas yet. What about Wolf of Wall Street and something with Ryan Reynolds, because he's funny as fuck?"

"Deadpool?"

"Yes. And where did you put all the snacks?"

Ah, yes. The snacks.

Jupiter was incredibly strict with his diet during the season, but the second it ended his palette reverted to that of a seven year old boy. On the way back from the city yesterday he'd made us stop at the store so he could stock up on junk food for our movie day. Red Vines, popcorn, Mike and Ike's, Goobers, Milk Duds and Reese's Pieces. I hadn't yet decided whether he was legitimately trying to put himself in a diabetic coma or at the very least make himself sick.

"They're in the pantry."

"Good, just checking you hadn't put them in the trash when I wasn't looking."

It would be a lie to say I hadn't been tempted.

"Chill out, they're still there. But let me know ahead of time if I'm going to need to take you to the emergency room to pump your stomach."

"Yes, Mom."

"Whatever. Shall we just go now then?"

"Hell yes. Movie room in five?"

I nodded. "I'll clear up here if you go and set it up."

He ran off downstairs, taking his toast with him, as I loaded the dishwasher, making two more coffees and grabbing the blankets before I joined him, handing them over as I sat down.

"This house is actually pretty cool." Jupiter wriggled into one of the giant velvet beanbags on the floor.

I got comfy on another one. Instead of movie style seating, Drew had wanted what Freddie apparently had at her house in London, which was a cinema room with massive sofa beds on the back wall but giant beanbags at the front, making everything super cosy and snuggly. We'd been spending a lot of time in here under the blankets as the weather had got colder.

"Okay, no talking Emerson."

I rolled my eyes as Jupiter pressed start on Avengers, hunkering down under the blanket, trying to stop myself from falling asleep.

My stomach started rumbling loudly as the credits rolled and the film finished.

"Can we eat now please? I'm hungry."

"Yes, tacos. I'll go and make them, and we can bring them back here. You want to stay or come and talk to me while I cook?"

I was kind of comfy.

He walked off knowing what the look on my face meant, but thirty seconds later he was back, standing in the doorway, frowning at his phone as mine started buzzing on the table next to me. I leaned over to grab it, Drew filling the screen.

He never failed to bring a smile to my face, he smiled back but it looked… different. Weary almost.

"Hi Sweetheart, how are you?"

I frowned. "I'm good, babe. Are you okay?"

"Jupe's with you, right? Can I speak to both of you?"

Jupiter dropped down on the beanbag next to me and I tried to sit up and position the screen so he could see us both.

I glanced between him and Jupe. "What's going on?"

He looked pained, rubbing his thumb back and forth over his forehead.

"Mary called me. I've just been on the phone to her." He looked at Jupiter's puzzled face. "My manager."

Jupiter sat forward, his elbows on his knees getting closer to the screen. "Mary Masters? She's your manager?"

Drew nodded.

"Ballsy."

"Yeah." He took a deep breath. "Anyway, she's told me there's a story coming out tonight on Page Six. It'll be in print tomorrow."

"Okay?"

I wasn't really sure what he was trying to get at, but I felt Jupiter tense next to me. "Crawley, what have you done? I swear to god I will beat you to a pulp when you get back."

Drew's jaw clenched.

"Jupiter, for once just shut the fuck up." He snapped. "It's not about me, not directly anyway." His eyes trained on mine. "Em, it's about you."

I frowned. "What does that mean? I don't understand. How can there be a story about me?"

Drew looked like he was close to tears and for the first time I noticed how pale he was, his face etched with worry.

He gave a deep sigh. "Richard sold a story saying that you and I were having an affair behind his back. And that he caught us."

I started blinking, trying to figure out if I'd heard him correctly. And also, for some reason, trying to wrack my brains for a memory of when he'd caught us. But I couldn't find it because it hadn't happened.

You can't remember something that never happened.

"I don't understand. That's not true."

"I know it's not true, Mary's told them, but they're printing it anyway."

"But it's not true." I repeated.

Panic started whirling around deep in my belly, flip-flopping as though I was on the end of a bungee rope swinging in the air, my heart pounding in my ears. My breath had shallowed, I was finding it hard to get enough oxygen in at once.

Jupiter took the phone from me, I was shaking too much to hold it.

"Drew, have you seen what's being printed?"

He shook his head. "No, but they called Mary for a

comment, so we know the gist. They gave her until three pm today, but she already told them it was categorically untrue. And I don't know if that fucking dickhole is even mentioned. She said they were sketchy with the details except that he's made himself out to be some hot shot surgeon, so he's coming across as credible."

"Course he fucking is. He wouldn't know a scalpel if it cut his tiny dick off." He growled. "I'm going to break every bone in his body."

"Yep. And I'll fucking hold him down."

I tried to remember what I'd just heard. This can't be right. Drew must be mistaken.

"Babe, are you sure? This didn't happen, it's not true. How can they print it?"

Drew looked so pained and upset. "Because they don't care. It's a juicy story for them. I'm working with the lawyers on stopping the print, but Mary's not hopeful, they've given us no time."

Bile started churning in my stomach, my eyes heating up, burning with tears of anger and injustice.

My face dropped in my hands. "How could he do this? What do I do? Oh my god, people are going to read it."

Jupiter started rubbing my back.

"Sweetheart, all the people who know us know that this isn't true."

I looked back up at Drew. "But what about all the people who come to the studio?"

He flinched. "Baby, I know, I'm so sorry, I'm trying to stop it. I'm working with Mary."

My throat thickened until I choked on the unshed tears and they started pouring out in loud sobs. Jupiter put his arm around me, drawing me into his chest as I cried and cried.

"Dude, let me call you back. What time is it going up?"

"Okay. In an hour. Fuck, Jupe, I've tried to stop it."

"Yeah, I know, this isn't on you. When are you back?"

"The day after tomorrow."

"Okay, I'll call you in a bit."

Jupiter dropped the phone and put both his arms around me, holding me as I wept inconsolably.

"Em, it's okay, it'll be okay."

"It's not okay." I croaked, my voice hoarse with anger and tears. "How could he do this? I've done nothing to deserve this. I don't understand. He cheated on me. HE CHEATED ON ME. ME."

Jupiter kept rubbing my back. "I know, Em. I know. He's a total dick weasel. We will sort this out though, he will pay for this. Count on it."

He held me tight as I continued sobbing, telling me over and over they would make him pay, until I'd had enough.

I sat up and stared hard at him. "HOW? HOW WILL YOU? He didn't get the message when I blocked him on my phone, then he turned up outside my apartment and assaulted me. Then I thought it would be over following the restraining order and now he's trying to publicly humiliate me."

"I know Em, but we will fix it. Let's see what Drew's lawyers say and I'll call mine to see what can be done too. And everyone knows Page Six is full of shit."

I stood up unable to stay sitting anymore. It was harder to be angry sitting down.

"Doesn't stop people reading it though, does it? People fucking love gossip and the more salacious, the better. Out of anyone, you should know that."

"No, I know."

I hung my head and sobbed through my words. "This is so unfair, Jupe. It's so unfair. And it's unfair on Drew too. He's done nothing wrong."

"I know." He stood up and hugged me again. "Come on, let's eat. It'll make you feel better."

I wasn't hungry anymore, but I didn't know what else to do with myself.

I was helpless.

I let Jupiter guide me numbly back to the kitchen and sit me down on a bar stool while he started cooking. He took two beers from the fridge, opening them, handing me one. I took a sip.

Maybe I should just get very, very drunk.

I groaned, placing my head down on my forearms. How was this even happening?

Maybe it wouldn't be as bad as Drew thought.

I reached over the counter to where I'd left my laptop and slid it over, opening up Google. I typed in my name and Drew's, nothing coming up except news of his suspension. I started hitting the refresh button every five seconds, until I became faster than a twitchy teen jonesing for Ariana Grande tickets.

And then it appeared.

I clicked on it, my hand flying up to my cover the gasp leaving my mouth.

This was worse than bad.

There was one picture of me watching Drew at a game, but Wolfie was still pregnant, so they must have taken it as a still from the replay.

But another was of him picking me up at the studio last week. Followed by several pictures of him kissing me full on the mouth, through the car windscreen, making us look like a pair of horny teenagers. I zoomed in, gasping again in horror, at my tongue which was visible as it slid toward his.

The pictures were almost worse than the article.

Almost.

EXCLUSIVE: DREW CRAWLEY IN LOVE TRIANGLE WITH FITNESS INSTRUCTOR

Emerson Reeves, a rising star in the fitness world, has been completing some extra-curricular activities in the form of after-hours workouts with New York Rangers star player, Drew Crawley, including big plans to spend the Thanksgiving holidays together.

While Crawley is no stranger to bed hopping with beautiful women, he clearly didn't care that his latest conquest was already taken. And according to sources, this has been going on for a while.

However, the news is very much to her current boyfriend, hero cardiologist, Dr Richard Jessop's, dismay.

One source added, "He's been shocked by this. He saves lives for a living, but it doesn't compare to a professional athlete earning millions a year. When he found out, he had just finished a long heart surgery, went home and discovered them in his bed."

Unfortunately for Dr Jessop, he won't be able to mend his own broken heart.

We contacted Drew Crawley's representatives, but they were unavailable for comment.

I felt Jupiter tense next to me, as he read over my shoulder.

"Oh my god. Oh my god."

I didn't know what else to say.

"I think I'm going to be sick. There's not one shred of truth in this. They've basically called me a gold digging, cheating whore. Jupe, what do I do?"

He rubbed his hands over his face, scratching his beard.

"Jupiter?" I screeched.

"He's a sneaky fuck. He's not directly tied to this. They can deny it came from him and sources are protected. He must have gone to them straight after you saw him at the hospital if those are recent pictures. They've been waiting to catch you together." He started chewing on his lip and he read it again, almost mumbling to himself. "The lawyers won't be able to stop this in time for print. They might be able to get some of it changed as it's easy to find out he's not a cardiologist and just a fucking basic doctor."

My tears started up again, unable to hold them in any longer.

He picked up his phone and dialed, putting it on loud speak. "Hey man, we're reading it now. It's fucking bullshit."

"I know. Is Emerson there?"

"I'm here." I said through wracked sobs.

"Baby, I'm so sorry. I'm trying to get it taken down online. Mary and the lawyers are on it too, on all of it."

"Okay." I sobbed. "Drew, it's so unfair. Nothing is true. I've done none of this."

"I know Sweetheart, I know."

Jupiter leaned onto the counter, nearer the phone. "Crawley, let me know if there's anything I can do too. I can threaten a lawsuit too."

"Yeah, that would probably help."

"Okay, I'll call them."

"Thanks man. Emerson, I love you. It'll be okay and we'll sort this."

I wish they would stop telling me it was going to be okay.

Jupiter took his phone back and dialed another number. The urge to get very drunk hit again. I took a sip of my beer. This wouldn't do it, I needed something stronger.

I walked into the pantry and found a bottle of tequila, swiping it off the shelf. I looked around to see if there was anything else I wanted, before spying the massive carrier bag of candy.

You're coming with me too.

Jupiter was over by the far windows staring out at the garden. I grabbed a glass and poured myself a large drink, knocking it back in one, the liquid burning my throat before it hit my brain. It was amazing how alcohol just made you feel better immediately.

I poured another.

Maybe they were right and it would be okay.

I rummaged in the carrier bag until I found the Red Vines I used to love as a kid, breaking the packet open. I'd forgotten how good they were. And they went perfectly with my tequila.

How did I not know that before?

The screen was still open on the horrible article, the pictures automatically scrolling across the page.

Why the fuck did the camera have to be pointed at that angle?

Had my tongue always been that big?

My mom and dad were going to see these.

I topped up my glass, looking over to Jupiter who was still on his phone.

I didn't know how they were going to fix it. It was already out there. Everyone was reading it. At least the team at the studio knew it wasn't true.

I hoped.

No, they did. They knew. Drew had told them the story of Vegas.

I jumped as the screen snapped shut just when I started flicking through the images from the beginning.

"Stop looking at those." Jupiter sat back on the stool next to me. "Right, turns out Drew and I have the same lawyers, which has made it easier. They're sending an intent to sue from both of us separately. We can't stop the print, but we might be able to get it taken down from the site."

I looked at him, I'd been holding some hope that this was going to go away. That no one would have seen it because they'd be too busy watching the football and eating turkey. But now everyone would.

Instant news.

What was I going to tell my parents?

I reached for my glass, gulping the rest of my drink down to stop the tears starting again, before filling it back up.

"Thanks Jupe. I appreciate it."

He went to pull me into a hug but instead glanced around, picking up some of the trash on the counter. "Emerson, how much candy have you eaten?"

I shrugged.

His eyes widened. "You finished the Red Vines!"

I shrugged again.

He kissed my head. "It's okay, you needed them more than I did."

My throat prickled and my eyes became hot again as the tears returned. "How do you do it, Jupe?"

"Do what?"

"Just live with people reading lies about you all the time."

He got off the stool and took a glass from the cupboard pouring himself a drink. "Well, I don't read it, for one. I pay my lawyers a lot, for another. But it's not usually such a fabricated story like this one is. This isn't the papers though Emerson. This is Richard, and we will make him pay."

My sniffed, wiping my nose with my sleeve. "I don't know how."

"Let Drew and me worry about that for the moment. Now come on, how about we finish the tacos to go with the tequila and then get very, very drunk."

"Okay."

My head banged with each step I took down toward the kitchen. I would have stayed in bed but I'd run out of water and I couldn't find any painkillers. As it was it took me almost thirty minutes to sit up.

Every second spent reliving the horrible day before. The anxiety clawing at my insides, swirling around my alcohol singed stomach.

What time was it? I was supposed to teach a class today

but the thought of facing people who might have read that article was making me want to puke.

The smell of coffee was making me want to puke.

My hangover was making me want to puke.

Maybe I should puke.

The caffeine aroma hit me again as I reached the bottom step. I found it hard to believe Jupiter was even awake, let alone up enough to make coffee.

It wasn't Jupiter.

"Hey Emerson. How are you?" I bent down gingerly as Freddie pulled me into a hug, her massive belly squashing into me. "Sorry I let myself in, I rang but there was no answer and thought you might want some company."

I was hit with a wave of emotion and I couldn't tell whether it was from gratitude or my hangover.

"Thank you." I hugged her back, taking in the state of the kitchen. "Did you clear up? You really didn't have to. It must have looked like a bomb went off."

She laughed. "No, just that you'd raided a sweet shop."

"What time is it?"

"Ten am."

"Come on, come and sit down and I'll make you some breakfast."

I walked over to the island and sat on a stool. "Actually I'm not hungry, but I'd love some cold water."

I put my head down on my arms just as a buzzing started up. I raised my eyes to see my phone vibrating across the worktop and grabbed it before it stopped.

Work. This wasn't going to be good.

"Hi Emerson, it's David."

David was the big boss, owner of the studios and I'd worked for him for six years, both in LA and in New York. But if he was calling then this definitely wasn't going to be good.

"Hi." I croaked.

I looked at the screen, thinking we'd been cut off. But no, just an awkward silence.

He let out a sigh. "Look, I'm sorry to do this. Do you know why I'm calling?"

"I have an idea."

"Are you okay?"

My throat grew thick and scratchy again. "No. I'm not actually."

"Right. I'm sorry to hear that, Emerson. Look, I think it's better if you lay low for a few days, we've had some calls from customers who've complained."

I started fiddling with the corner of my laptop, which was still on the counter. "What does that mean?"

He sighed again. "It means take a little break until this all blows over, we'll cover your classes."

I could feel my anger levels rising again.

"David, none of this is true."

"I know, but people know that the players have been in the studio and they're connecting the dots."

I ground my jaw hard. This was a fucking joke.

"Wow, you can't have it both ways you know. You enjoy the wait lists they've created and the publicity. Something I've had nothing to do with by the way, I never asked them to come."

"I know, Emerson. And we support you, just take a few days off, that's all. It'll calm down. This is best for everyone."

"Fine."

I hung up and slammed the phone back down on the counter, Freddie expectantly waiting for me tell her what just happened.

"I've been told to lay low. They don't want me coming into the studio." My chin started trembling before the tears fell again.

Freddie moved surprisingly quickly, considering the size

of her giant belly, and put her arms around me. "Oh Emerson, that's such bullshit. I'm so sorry."

"He said it was just for a few days, but…" I didn't have the energy to get through the rest of that sentence. "This is so unfair and nothing can be done, I'm helpless. I've worked my ass off and now it's all gone to shit because my ex-boyfriend can't handle that I don't want to be with him anymore and my company is more concerned with its image than standing by me."

I wiped away my tears of rage.

Her eyes started to glisten with her own tears. "I know how awful this must feel. I spoke to Molly and she's going to do some digging at the hospital, see if she can find anything out about him. He was only covering for a week at Pres, but everyone had something to say about him, so there has to be more from Mercy."

I heard some footsteps and we both turned to find Wolfie walking into the kitchen, holding Flossie.

"Hello, Freddie said she was coming over and so we thought we'd come. Thought a cuddle with Florence might help."

I smiled weakly, wiping my face, and sat back on the stool as she handed Florence over. She'd grown but she was still so tiny, her big navy eyes blinked up at me before she gurgled a bit then fell asleep. I watched her breathe, her little chest rising and falling, and felt my own heart rate start to calm.

Wolfie was right, this did help.

"Thank you, Wolf. I really appreciate it, and I really appreciate you both coming over."

Freddie poured me some more water and placed some painkillers in front of me, along with a coffee. "We have to stick together, we know this life isn't easy."

We all turned around to see Jupiter standing in the doorway.

Jesus, why couldn't he find some properly fitting pajama

pants, they looked like they were about to fall down. And if he was always complaining about being cold, why didn't he have a shirt on?

"Jupe, put some clothes on."

"Sorry, I didn't realize we had company." He grumbled at my snapping, walking through to the snug returning with a sweatshirt he pulled over his head.

"Woah. That's your brother? He is very easy on the eyes." Wolfie muttered under her breath.

"Jupiter, these are my friends, Wolfie and Freddie."

"Hello." He responded, then he frowned. "Are you holding a baby?"

"Yes, this is Florence."

"Well, if there's a baby here, I'm going back to bed. Once I've made a coffee."

Freddie thrust a steaming mug at him. "Here, I'm making them."

"Thanks." He took it and sipped. "Not bad."

She raised her eyebrow at him. "I'm going to be making breakfast if you want to stay."

Before he could respond, a phone started ringing. He reached into his pocket, scowling at the screen before he answered.

"Hey Matty. What's up." He looked up at me as he listened, his frown deepening. "Yeah, she is."

The clawing started up in my belly again, like a wild animal desperate to get out, scraping my internal organs. Jupiter walked outside but didn't close the door behind him and we could hear his voice rise in anger.

"What? WHAT? You had better be fucking joking. What the fuck, Matt?"

We all watched him storming up and down the garden, his fist clenching. We listened in silence, knowing I was going to find out soon and it was clear I wouldn't exactly like it.

"No, she's my fucking sister. No I haven't. Of course I haven't, are you crazy? You know me."

He stopped pacing.

"Yeah, call me back." He looked at his phone and typed out a text. "FUCK."

He rubbed his hands through his head in frustration, glancing up to see that we'd witnessed his outburst. His eyes shut and he took a deep breath, before opening them and walked toward me into the kitchen.

He stood in front of us, then looked at me, and with incredible gentleness removed Flossie from my arms and handed her back to Wolf.

"Jupiter?"

He sighed. "I need to talk to you."

"Oh my god, what now?"

18

DREW

I leant my head back on the rest as Ralph drove us out of Teterboro, heading to the house. It was still early enough for the roads to be quiet and his foot was to the floor.

I couldn't get there soon enough.

My eyes were stinging from tiredness. From lack of sleep at being away from Emerson, the forty-eight hours of hell we'd been through and my non-existent ability to protect her from any of it. I clenched my fist again at the memory of her sobbing inconsolably over the phone last night, Jupiter comforting her when I should have been there.

The blood that used to course through my veins had been replaced with pure, unadulterated rage.

Heads were gonna roll for this.

I looked at my phone again, at the photo of Jupiter and Emerson leaving the studio, and the article underneath, reading it for the thousandth time, the words almost taking on new meanings.

SPOTTED: RANGERS STAR FITNESS GAL WITH THIRD BASE BROTHER

Yesterday we broke the news that Ranger's star, Drew Crawley, is currently embroiled in a love triangle between his new fitness instructor, Emerson Reeves, and her heart surgeon boyfriend. Today we can exclusively confirm they met earlier this year through her brother, baseball's bad boy, Jupiter Reeves, third baseman for the LA Dodgers.

Introductions took place at one of Reeves' infamous sex parties, known throughout Hollywood circles for only granting access to the beautiful elite.

Other guests present at the A'list only event included sports stars and models Jackson Foggerty, Felix Cleverly and Justin Blackshaw as well as awards winners Morgan Watson and Henley Crane.

A source at the party said, 'It was clear Emerson was going home with Drew that night. She wouldn't let anyone else near him.'

Seems like the Reeves family is building quite the reputation. No representatives were available for comment.

I ran inside as we pulled up to the house, leaving my bags for Ralph to sort. I found Jupiter in the kitchen on the laptop, looking up at me as I walked in.

"Hey man, how're you doing?"

He scratched his beard. "Yeah, fine. Just trying to figure out this fucking ballache."

"Where's Em?"

He nodded toward the snug. "She's on the sofa. It's not pretty though. She was up pounding the punching bag early this morning, but her work called an hour ago and they've suspended her. Or fired her. I couldn't really tell because she was crying so hard, but she kicked me out."

I let out a long breath. "Fuck. They fired her? What the fuck? This isn't her fault."

"I know, it's mine." His shoulders slumped.

"Fuck that, it's not yours either."

276

He raised his eyebrow at me.

"It's not Jupe. We've both been in this game long enough to know what the deal is, this isn't on you. The fucking studio though, way to stand by their employees."

He sighed. "I know, she's better off out of there anyway. I tried to tell her, but she didn't want to hear it. Anyway, the lawyers have said she can sue for defamation of character and they've sent another letter of intent. We have a call with them in a couple of hours."

"Okay cool, thanks man. I'm glad you were here." I thumbed behind me. "I'm going to find Emerson."

He nodded at me and I walked toward the snug. She was lying on the sofa wrapped up in a blanket, hoodie pulled over her head, staring blankly at cartoons on the television. Her tear-stained face was red and swollen from crying.

Even though my heart was breaking from the sight of her, just being in close proximity again soothed me, making me feel like I could fix this, that it would be okay as long as we were together.

Because we were and it would.

She looked up as I moved toward her, her mouth turned down as her chin started to tremble and the tears flowed again. I sat and pulled her into my chest, trying to absorb her sobs, stroking her hair as she heaved against me so heavily that my own body was shuddering.

"Baby I'm so sorry. I'm so so sorry."

"They fired me."

I kissed her head, pulling her in as tight as I could. "I know, Jupiter told me. I'm so sorry, Sweetheart. It's going to be okay. It'll be okay."

She sat up, pushing away from me, her bloodshot eyes burning with irate fire. "All you two have been telling me is that it's going to be okay. You don't know that."

I stared at her as she jumped up.

"You don't know if it's going to be okay. STOP TELLING ME THAT."

Jupiter appeared in the door, clearly having heard her shouting.

"What's going on?"

"You two. You two are what's going on. You don't know what's going to happen. Stop telling me it's going to be okay."

Jupiter and I both scrubbed our hands down our faces, mirroring the frustration we were both feeling at having contributed to this situation.

"Emerson, I know it seems shit right now and it is. But it will be okay," Jupiter gestured between him and me. "We know, we've been through this before."

"Not like this you haven't."

I looked up at her. "Sweetheart, we're written about all the time."

She pointed at us aggressively. "You work in sports, people are supposed to write about you, it comes with the territory."

Jupiter gave a deep sigh. "Emerson, it'll go away, I promise we're sorting it, but you have to ignore it. I know it's hard, but you can't let it get to you. I thought you didn't care what people think."

"BUT I DO. I DO CARE WHEN IT AFFECTS MY JOB AND I GET FIRED."

"Sometimes it affects our job too." He shrugged. "Sometimes we get traded because of bad press, maybe think of it like that."

I watched her jaw grind in frustration.

"I don't want to think about it as being traded. I've not been traded. I've been fired. Traded means you still have a job, which I don't now. Because of you two."

"Hey." Jupiter growled.

Emerson looked at the floor, I saw her wince slightly at the words she couldn't take back. She didn't mean it, but it wasn't far from the truth, and I knew Jupiter and I felt like shit about it.

"I've worked so fucking hard. So fucking hard and now I have nothing to show for it and what little reputation I had has gone. All I'm ever going to be known for is your sister." She pointed again to Jupiter, then at me. "Or your girlfriend."

"Emerson, these stories have involved us too." He reasoned, although it was clear it wasn't helping.

"Jupiter, there's a story out every week that involves you. It's almost expected. But with me? These optics? I'm at the start of my career, you aren't. I bet the club hasn't even been in contact about this, they barely give a shit because it's the off season. I'VE BEEN FIRED. And you don't seem to understand that. You earn nearly forty million dollars a year. No one's going to hire me for a long time."

Fuck that. I'd be looking after her forever. She didn't have to ever work again if she didn't want to.

"Sweetheart, you don't have to worry about that."

She shot me a death stare, but Jupiter spoke before she had time to retort.

"I can help you with money." He said, kindly.

She threw her arms up in exasperation. "Oh my fucking god, it's not about the money."

This conversation was taking a swift and heated detour, and I stayed where I was not wanting to anger her further. In fact, I'd never seen her so angry, her eyes changing from turquoise to a deep mossy green making the golden flecks burn bright with rage. Although the anger was probably good.

It was also fuck hot.

I knew I shouldn't find this arousing but in my defense I hadn't seen her in five days and…

Oh my god, make-up sex.

We were having our first argument.

Sort of.

Shut up and focus.

I really needed my dick to calm down and stop filling my brain with wildly inappropriately timed thoughts.

But oh my god, the make-up sex.

"Why are you smiling?"

I snapped out of my daydream to find her glaring at me.

Fuck.

I blinked, like a rabbit in headlights, trying to come up with something. Anything. However, my mind was blank except for thoughts of hot, sweaty make up sex.

"No, please, tell me what's so funny right now."

"Nothing Sweetheart, nothing is funny."

I could see Jupiter frowning at me, probably wondering what the fuck was going on in my pea-brained head. I was wondering myself.

"Why are you smiling, Drew? Tell me." She seethed. She was actually quite scary.

I eased my fingers over the tension in my brows.

How to word this.

"Um, well, it's just that this is our first argument, sort of. And you know, I was just thinking about when it was over…" My voice trailed off as her eyes narrowed to slits.

Jupiter's eyes, however, were wide open in shock at what I dared to voice.

She placed her hands on her hips. "Are you actually insane?"

"Sweetheart, I…"

Her lip curled up in a snarl. "Don't you Sweetheart me. That genie is not going back in the bottle."

"Emerson…"

"Tell me one more time that it's going to be okay and see what happens. I dare you." Her voice was ominously low as she glared at both of us. We didn't dare even move. She started pacing up and down, her head in her hands. "Fuck, I need to get out of here."

She looked up at the pair of us both silently waiting for her next instruction.

"And don't either of you fucking follow me!" She stormed out and in the distance we heard the front door slam.

Neither of us spoke for a minute, trying to comprehend the sharp nose-dive which had taken place.

I ran my hands through my hair. "Fuck. I think I fucked up."

"Dude, even I know that was a fucking stupid thing to say."

"Yeah. Fuck."

He let out a long sigh. "Don't worry about it, she needs to be angry."

Panic was rising in my chest. "Should I go after her?"

"Fuck no, give her some space and just let her stew for a bit and calm down. She'll be gone for a while, but she'll come back." He scratched his beard. "We can spend the time figuring out what to do about that fucktard Richard."

This wasn't something we were going to solve by ourselves. The two of us clearly too stupid to know what to do. We needed more heads in the mix.

"Okay." I looked at my watch. "I'm going to go and change, then let's go to see Felix. He can help us come up with a plan."

"Let's do it. After that display we probably need all the help we can get."

I groaned, but at least we were on the same page. "Tell me about it."

Forty-five minutes later, we pulled up in front of Felix's house and jumped out. There a few cars in the driveway already, including Freddie's which I recognized. Thank god, the more the merrier in sorting out this shit show.

Cooper and Jasper were in the kitchen when we walked

in, sitting at the table with Felix, his leg in a brace propped up on another chair.

I bent down to hug him. "How're you doing buddy? I fucking missed you."

Even though we'd text almost throughout the entirety of every day I was away, we'd never spent so much of the season apart. It had been harder than I thought. I wasn't looking forward to playing without him.

"Bored as fuck." He grumbled, hugging me back before greeting Jupiter. "Hey man, good to see you again."

"You too dude, sorry about the leg."

"Thanks." He nodded toward Cooper and Jasper. "Guys, you know Jupiter, right?"

Greetings took place around the table, they'd all met in some capacity but never spent any time together. Just knew who each other was out of mutual appreciation for sport mates at the pinnacle of their game. At that moment, Murray strolled in, walked over and squeezed my shoulder, looking between Jupiter and me.

"Hello chaps. Do stick me on the guest list next time you throw a party. Sounds right up my street."

Felix and Cooper snorted into the beers they were already drinking.

"Fuck off, Murray. Not now."

"Who's this dickhead?" Growled Jupiter, not finding him quite as hilarious as everyone else did.

"Their brother-in-law." I nodded over to where Cooper and Jasper were silently grinning in amusement as Murray sat down at the head of the table.

Felix shifted his leg uncomfortably on the chair. "Anyway, how are you? How's Emerson? Is she with you?"

I shook my head. "No, she stormed off wanting to be on her own."

His eyes widened. "Oh, fuck. That bad?"

"Yeah. Pretty fucking bad. The studio fired her."

Cooper gave a low whistle. "Fuck. That's savage."

I walked to the fridge and took out a couple of beers, handing one to Jupiter who'd taken a seat. "I know. Then she just got sick of the both of us and left."

I found an empty chair near Murray and sat down.

Jasper scratched his beard, thinking. "It'll be okay though."

"That's what we told her, but it just made her more mad." Jupiter brought the bottle to his lips, sipping.

"Why?"

"Because she said that we can't know it's going to be okay."

Cooper scoffed. "Of course, you can. You've both been through shit like this before and ridden the wave."

I shrugged. "I know. But she lost her job and she's upset about that and how they've treated her at the studio. Which I completely understand. She's really hurt and she's fucking angry." I sipped my beer. "I mean I'm fucking angry too. Especially at that fucking dickwad who started all this."

Cooper nodded. "I think the girls have got Molly on the case for some investigating. You know how she loves playing Jessica Fletcher."

"Oh, cool thanks. Where are the girls anyway?"

"Upstairs with Florence and Molly."

Felix sat up straight, his head darting from side to side. "Molly's here? When did she arrive? I didn't see her."

Cooper shrugged, not seeming to notice Felix's strange outburst. "Dunno, just before these two I think."

"Oh." Felix slumped back in his chair. "Hey, you know, this thing with Emerson is kind of like getting traded, isn't it?"

"Yes." Jupiter banged the table with his palm. "Thank you. That's what I told her."

"Yeah, but it's also what pissed her off the most."

He took another long draw of his beer, eyeing me as he

did. "No, Crawley, you're the one who pissed her off the most."

"What did you say to her?"

We all turned to find Wolfie, Freddie and Molly walking into the kitchen.

"Nothing. I didn't say anything." I glared at Jupiter to keep his trap shut.

I'd rather eat a shit sandwich that share that intel with the girls. And I liked my balls, thank you very much.

"Well, what did you say then?" Freddie nodded toward Jupiter as she sat down on Cooper's lap, his arms moving around her giant belly, holding her close.

He shrugged. "I was trying to tell her everything would be okay and said it was like us when we got traded."

Wolfie put some more drinks on the table and sat down, her and Freddie exchanging looks of horrified confusion as Molly scoffed from over on the kitchen counter.

Why was Molly so far away?

"You told her that being fired from her job after she was exposed publicly as a," Wolfie started air quoting, "'cheating, money grabbing slut who loves to go to her brother's sex parties' was like being traded?"

Yeah, that didn't really sound like what we meant.

How did girls always twist words so well?

"Yes?" Jupiter replied, although now he didn't sound so sure of himself.

"How would you even know?" Wolfie shouted, pointing at all of us. "None of you has ever been traded. You have no idea what it's like. And you also expect it to happen, it's par for the course in sports. In twenty-four hours she went from having a career she loves, to being fired because of lies spread by her cunty ex-boyfriend."

Freddie tried to lean forward to make a point, but it was hard with her belly getting in the way. "Guys, we were there yesterday. She was devastated she'd even been told to lay

284

low. This is her job and she's not been supported by the company that she works her fucking ass off for. You hockey boys are so used to the press and the tabloids. You have no idea how it can affect people. She's not protected like you. Another studio isn't just going to snap her up because winning the Cup or the World Series is more important than gossip."

Wolfie leaned across the table with more success. "And people live for gossip. Even before all this happened, we'd hear people gossiping at the studio about you both when she wasn't around, even her own friends. We cancelled our membership because of it."

"Yeah and doesn't help with Hugh Hefner and his Playboy Mansion over here, throwing sex parties or whatever." Freddie thumbed to Jupiter. "It's not just on Page Six now, TMZ has it, so have all the gossip sites. The pair of you are as bad as each other."

Jupiter put his beer down on the table, staring hard at Freddie. "I don't, nor have I ever thrown fucking sex parties. And even if I did, I wouldn't invite my fucking sister."

She rolled her eyes. "Whatever. Point is, you two have fucked up and not taken the time to see it from Emerson's perspective."

I smirked. Freddie wasn't easily intimidated. And Jupiter was nothing compared to Cooper when he was in a mood.

Jupiter pointed to Freddie. "Is she always like this?"

All five of us nodded in silent response.

I ran a hand over my face, scratching my beard. The guilt that had been bubbling away over the last two weeks flared up again. Fuck, I was a shit boyfriend, I hadn't done enough to protect her. Protect her from the press, protect her from that asshole, protect her from me.

I turned to Molly. "Mol, what have you found out? Boys said you were looking?"

She leaned against the counter. "I found out that a few

people complained about him at the hospital for harassment. But it's been hard to pin down."

"Sounds about right, he's a sneaky fuck." Snarled Jupiter.

"I did find out that he's on a contract though."

"What does that mean?"

"That it's not a permanent job, that's why we could get him at Pres for a week. So, they won't want to keep him if he's tarnished."

A flicker of a plan emerged in my head.

"Oh. That's something. Jupe, we need to work on a statement. We can send it to the hospital as well as the press. The lawyers are calling in... when?"

He looked at his watch. "Twenty minutes."

"Okay, we'll get their opinion but I think we need to refute everything that's been printed. Including the fact that he's a surgeon. We should check and see if it's okay to tell the hospital about the restraining order. If not, we definitely should tell them anyway. The fact that they're hiring a doctor who's had a restraining order for harassment taken out against them isn't good, right?"

I looked at Molly.

"No, I don't think they'd be happy with that. Hospitals aren't big on negative publicity and they have a shit ton of lawyers to stop it from happening."

"Okay, let's do that, then we'll speak to Mary too. She can draft what we want to say. In fact, I'll let her know we'll call her."

I pulled out my phone and shot her a text telling her what we wanted to do, asking her to get a head start on a joint statement. I checked my messages when I was done, but nothing from Emerson.

"Have you heard from Em?" I asked Jupiter. He pulled out his phone, shaking his head after checking it.

I shot her a text just in case she decided to she wanted to talk to me again.

Drew: *Baby, I know you're upset and you have every right to be. But I want you to know I love you so much and we're going to fix this XXX*

I turned back to Jupiter. "Who's your manager? They need to be looped in with Mary."

"It's Matty McLeish at TBA."

"Okay. I'll let her know. She can contact him."

I got up and started searching through the kitchen drawers.

"Can you get some more beers while you're up?" Felix called over to me. "Also, what are you looking for?"

"A pen and paper."

"Go into my office."

I walked off and found them where he'd said I would, taking a seat back at the table a few minutes later, handing some to Jupiter.

"Start drafting what you want to say. Two paragraphs, tops."

I began jotting down some ideas. It needed to be irrefutable and unquestionable.

"Oh hey, Mol." Wolfie interrupted my train of thoughts, calling over to her. "What happened to that hot doctor who asked you out?"

"WHAT?"

Everyone startled, turning to stare at Felix, who was looking slightly flushed.

"Sorry, I was talking to Drew, looking at his statement." He mumbled, his head dropping.

I glanced down at my piece of paper where I'd written absolutely nothing, because I'd been typing it into my phone instead. I stared back up at Felix, but he was engrossed in his phone. No one else seemed to have noticed how weird he was being.

"Mol?" Wolfie pressed.

"Oh nothing." She turned to get something from the fridge.

"Well, there are a ton of hot doctors in that hospital." Wolfie continued. "Freddie and I saw loads when we were there the other week. We're going to come and find some more for you."

"Fucking stupid expression." Felix mumbled under his breath, but not quietly enough.

Everyone turned to stare at him again.

"Pardon?" Asked Wolfie.

"I said it's a stupid expression. You can't find someone for another person like they're lost property. Like you'd need to go to Lost and Found for them." He mumbled louder so everyone could hear him.

He was also staring at Molly as he said it and she'd gone bright red.

"Shit, look at the time. I have to go, I have a shift I'm going to be late for." Molly picked her bag up off the floor and started walking out. "See you guys soon. Bye."

We all stared as we watched her leave.

I don't think I'd ever been more confused in my life. Mostly because as I looked around no one seemed to have noticed how weird that was.

"Now look what you did." Felix grumbled again.

"Clevs, are you okay? Is it time for some painkillers?" Asked Jasper.

I stared at Jasper, who was looking at Felix, and seemed genuinely concerned for his comfort levels and not at all questioning why he was being shifty as fuck.

"Yeah, thanks. I am aching actually. But I'll get them, I need to keep moving." Felix reached for his crutches, pulling himself to his feet, hopping about slightly.

Jupiter stood up too. "Okay, I can't fucking concentrate. And we have our call now, so let's go."

I thrust my phone at him where I'd written up what I thought would work. "Here, how's this?"

He read it over, his eyebrows shooting up. "This is really good, man. Really good. We can use this."

He passed it to Jasper, whose hand was outstretched. Cooper reading it over his shoulder, both nodding.

"It's good." He passed it back to me.

"Let's run it past Mary first."

We used Felix's office to call our lawyer, dialing him in on the conference phone. I took a seat at the desk while Jupiter paced back and forth, his hands on his head.

"Hello?"

"Hi David, it's Drew and Jupiter."

"Hi both, how are you holding up? How's Emerson?"

"Not great."

He tutted. "No, I can imagine. Look we have some good news, we've managed to get both stories pulled down from Page Six, but it has gone elsewhere, so we suggest the same approach for all outlets."

"Yes, fine, sounds good. Thank you. Whatever you can do."

"Have to say, it's been nice to work on something completely fabricated. Makes our jobs slightly easier."

Jupiter blew out an exasperated puff of air and rolled his eyes.

"David? The restraining order you drafted, is it confidential? Can we send it to the hospital that Richard Jessop works at?"

He was silent for a moment. "Yes, technically you could. Why? You want to do it?"

"Yes, we're putting out a statement to say everything is false, which Mary will send out, but if we share it with you, can you draft a letter and send it to the hospital with the statement and proof of the restraining order?"

"Yes, I can."

"Great, Mary will share it with you. Thanks David, thanks for your help. We'll chat later."

"Okay, bye."

Well at least that's something. I punched Mary's number into the phone.

"What've you got for me then?" She answered in typical Mary fashion, getting straight to the point, without bothering to say hello.

"I'm sending you what Jupiter and I have drafted." I told her as I forwarded it over to her email.

She was silent as she read it over.

"This is good, let me edit it a bit and I'll send it back. Give me ten minutes."

"Okay thanks."

"Drew, I'm glad you're doing this, that girl deserves it."

I leaned forward in the chair. "Yes, I know."

"Jupiter, are you there?"

He moved closer to the speaker on the desk, leaning over. "Yep."

"Good, I'll send this over to Matt and he can share it. Makes a nice change this does. Also, let me know if you ever want new representation, I do a better job at keeping my clients out of the press than he does. Usually anyway."

Jupiter chuckled.

"Sure, thanks Mary. Speak to you later."

I hung up. We went back into the kitchen and sat down, waiting.

"All sorted?" Asked Jasper.

"Yeah, just need Mary to send the final edit through."

Mine and Jupiter's phones both pinged at the same time. I opened up the email to the statement Mary had sent.

A STATEMENT
We have always been honest with our fans and though we

wouldn't normally comment on our private lives, we don't
believe we've been left with any other options.
The stories reported over the last few days are not only
inaccurate but completely fabricated. While we understand
the interest in our professional lives, it cannot be at the
personal cost of someone we both love.
To straighten some facts; Mr Crawley and Ms Reeves met
socially eighteen months ago, independently of her brother.
Ms Reeves was not in a relationship with anyone else at the
time. Any reports described otherwise are entirely false.
Additionally, Mr Reeves' private social life, while often the
subject of tabloid gossip, has never included the so called
'sex parties', as labelled by salacious media publications.
There will be no further comment on this matter and we
trust you, our loyal fans, to recognize the truth from the lies.

I took a deep breath, I hoped it would help. Wasn't much more we could do and at least the stories were being taken down, slowly.

"Okay, press send on our social media. Mary has issued it to the press and sent it to the hospital. The lawyers have also shared it with the hospital along with proof of the restraining order."

"And now we wait for the fall out."

"Yep." I stood up. "I need to find Emerson before it starts getting dark. I've tried her and she's not picking up her phone."

"Have you looked for her?" Felix asked.

"What do you mean? How am I supposed to have done that?"

"On your tracker."

I frowned at him. "What tracker?"

"Your car tracker. She's in your car. Use the tracker, genius. Or look on Find My Friends."

"Jesus. Stalker 101 over here." Muttered Cooper as he walked over to the fridge.

I pulled up my car tracker app, the little blue dot was flashing and I zoomed out, my heart nearly pounding out of my chest when I realized where she was.

I fucking loved this woman more than I could possibly have ever imagined and I didn't deserve her in any way.

Jupiter handed me his phone. "Find My Friends says she's at home."

"What? No she's not. That's not where the car is."

He shrugged. "Maybe she ran out without it then, she was pretty fucking angry."

"Yeah maybe. Well, I need to go home first anyway before I go to where the car is, so either way I'll find her. Are you staying here or coming?"

"Nah, I'll stay with Clevs for a bit, beat his ass at Xbox."

Felix snorted.

"Okay cool, see you later."

I grabbed Murray as I walked past him and out of the house. "Hey Muz, is everything still good on what we discussed last week? It's all ready?"

He nodded. "Yeah, ready for when you need it."

I slapped him on the arm. "Thanks Buddy. I appreciate it."

I ran outside and jumped in the car.

Off to find her.

My love.

My future.

My soulmate.

19

EMERSON

I picked up a stone and threw it in the water before finding another one, kicking it along the beach. The waves were crashing hard against the shore, sprays of salty mist hitting my face and mixing with my hot, angry tears.

I pulled the hood on my jacket back up, trying to stop the wind from whipping my hair around. It was going to take a bucket load of conditioner to remove the knots as it was.

Stupid wind.

Stupid beach.

I kicked another stone.

I reached into my pocket to grab my phone, momentarily forgetting I didn't have it.

Fuck's sake.

Didn't have my phone, didn't have my job.

I screamed frustration into the air. I was seconds away from jumping up and down like a toddler. I'd been so fucking angry and run out in such a hurry I hadn't noticed it on the kitchen counter, I was lucky Drew had left his coat in the car because I hadn't picked that up either.

But now I couldn't listen to music, couldn't call my mom, couldn't call Mallory, couldn't even buy a hot chocolate.

So yeah, this day was sucking balls.

My chin trembled again and I tried to sniff up the lump that seemed to be permanently stuck in my throat, but it didn't work. Even driving for an hour to get here, sobbing to depressing as fuck emo music hadn't dislodged it.

The only saving grace of rushing out and forgetting my phone, was that I didn't have it to obsess over the horrible things that had been written about me.

See those horrible pictures of me one more time.

I was never kissing with tongue again.

At least in public.

I don't know how the boys did this on a daily basis. Just stood back, defenseless, at the mercy of the press, while they wrote what they wanted and called it entertainment news.

Although in Jupiter's case he usually brought it on himself.

THIS wasn't even true.

That was the worst part. People believed the lies. And now I didn't have a job because of them. Only Ashley and Mikey had checked in on me, asking if I was okay.

I shoved my hands forcefully into my pockets. What the fuck was I going to do?

I wasn't equipped to be a woman who stayed home and waited for her husband to come back. I'd worked too hard.

Would Drew even want me to be?

What would I do with myself while he was traveling?

Another stone was aggressively kicked, sand flying everywhere as it hurtled into the water.

I brushed away another angry tear that fell. I didn't have a job. Everything I'd worked so hard for, the career I'd built, had been snatched away in a matter of hours.

Gone.

I'd have to start from the beginning again.

And no one would want to take me on.

Shame and hurt washed over me again as I remembered David's words. *'Emerson, it's not a good idea for you to continue working here.'*

Six years I'd been with that company, helping them grow it from the small LA studio, and after everything I'd done for them, they'd cut me loose without a second thought.

Fuckers.

I felt weary through to my marrow, the stress and exhaustion from the last forty-eight hours catching up.

And as much as I'd shouted at them, I knew it wasn't the boys' fault. Even if they did say some fucking stupid things sometimes.

I rolled my eyes.

And if anyone was to blame, it was me. They were just collateral damage to the bitterness and resentment of a jealous ex-boyfriend. One that I should have dealt with sooner and better. They didn't ask for this any more than I did.

And they were still trying to fix it.

Is this what our life would be like? Firefighting against a maelstrom of gossip and funding clickbait.

I reached the lighthouse and turned around, tracing my steps back along the beach to where I'd started. I could still see my footprints on the compacted sand. All of them. I'd been walking up and down this stretch for the past three hours.

Just walking.

And kicking.

When I'd stormed out of the house and jumped in the car I didn't even realize where I was going until I got here. Didn't realize I even knew the way.

But I guess this place had cemented itself in my heart as much as Drew had.

I thought back to that day, nearly two months ago, the

day I knew I'd fallen in love with him. When I knew I couldn't picture my life without him.

The day I fully understood the extent of how much he'd been with me since we met in Vegas and not just when he found me again.

Because looking back to the past year, even when I was with Richard, I knew I'd just been going through the motions of day-to-day life, followed by the wash, rinse, repeat of singledom. Dating but never really making the effort to find a connection. I could put it down to not wanting to jump back into a relationship, but it would be a lie. Because really, I'd been waiting for him.

I just hadn't known it at the time.

I watched the clouds rolling in across the water, thick and dark and ominous. A small panic curled around my bones as it dawned on me no one actually knew where I was. Drew would probably be going nuts, if he hadn't sent a search party already. I half expected the Coastguard to appear through the storm.

Because I hadn't been humiliated enough.

A tiny laugh pushed through the tears at the thought of how crazy he'd be making everyone while he tried to find me. Because I knew he wouldn't rest until I came home. I shouldn't find it funny, but I did. And I started laughing loudly, the grip around my heart easing. It was the first time I'd felt happy since this shit had started.

Because of him.

I don't think I'd ever felt so loved by one person, made to feel the way Drew made me feel on a daily basis.

He was my best friend. My person. The one I wanted to see at the beginning and end of every day. And if I had to go through a shit storm, I didn't want to do it with anyone else.

And all I wanted was to be in his arms.

Because that's where I belonged.

I reached the lighthouse for the last time and turned. It was time to go back home.

I stopped, squinting through the mist at the familiar shape walking toward me.

I don't know how, but he'd found me.

My heart could have been auditioning for Dancing with the Stars with the rate it was jumping about.

He grinned as we reached each other, holding the edges of my hood like he always did, bringing me in to kiss him, humming on my lips then stepped back slightly. "I like you in my clothes."

I couldn't hold back my smile. "What are you doing here?"

"You left your phone at home and I thought you might want it."

My face scrunched up. "You drove all the way out here to give me my phone?"

He chuckled softly and pulled me into his arms, wrapping them around my waist. "No Emerson, I drove out here to find you and bring you home. And to tell you I love you and how sorry I am for everything." He brushed some hair away from my eyes, leaving his hands cupping my wet cheeks. "I'm so sorry, I really am. I should have protected you from the beginning, not just the last week. Protected you against Richard, all the gossip and the tabloids. I should have done a better job of everything."

I sighed into his embrace, I could see the responsibility weighing heavy on him and wanted to take it away. "Babe, you have. This isn't your fault. It's mine, I should have dealt with him better, instead of ignored him."

He shook his head, his thumb brushing across my swollen cry face.

"Don't you dare blame yourself. You have done nothing wrong. Nothing." His arms moved back to my waist and wrapped tighter, pulling me closer. "But we've made a start to fixing it, Jupiter and I have managed to get everything taken down from Page Six and the lawyers are working on the rest. And we also put out a statement which has gone everywhere. The lawyers also sent it to the hospital with a letter including information about the restraining order. He's not going to hurt you again, Sweetheart."

"Hurt us." I ran my hands around the back of his neck. "You and Jupiter really wrote a statement?"

He nodded, taking his phone out and handing it to me. "Yes."

It was open on his Instagram page. I read through it, my heart heaving with emotion. It had over one hundred and forty thousand likes already. I checked Jupiter's page and his had nearly two hundred thousand.

I sniffed. "Thank you, seriously. This means a lot to me."

"Emerson, we're in this together. I'm always going to have your back in the same way I know you have mine. Any problem and we fix them together. We're each other's safety net."

He dipped down, his eyes staying open as he smiled against my lips.

"I have something for you."

He pulled out an envelope from his pocket, handing it to me.

"What's this?"

"It's your Christmas present. But I thought you could probably do with it now."

Excitement was radiating off him as I opened it up, pulling out a thick brochure for a warehouse and ownership papers with my name on them. I flipped through it to take a closer look, yes it was definitely a warehouse in Soho.

Cool exposed brick, but still a warehouse.

We hadn't ever properly given each other presents before, so I wasn't quite sure what to make of this.

I looked at him with more than a little confusion. "Babe, thank you. This is very sweet, but why do I want a warehouse?"

He responded with a lopsided smile. "It's not a warehouse, Sweetheart. It's a studio space. Your new studio, if you want it."

Say what now?

I looked at him, his eyes wide and serious, filled with hope and expectation. Filled with love. Because they were always filled with love.

And I knew that this wasn't something he could have sorted out overnight, he'd put thought and effort and time into this. My heart burst open and overspilled with all the tension I'd been carrying around, the crying starting up again.

"You bought me a studio?" I sobbed.

He wiped away my tears before taking my hand, placing it against his heart.

"Luck, I love you and I've always believed in you. Your dream was to open a studio and I want to give you your dreams. You've given me my future, I want to give you yours."

Oh my god. My own studio.

Only one small problem.

"I don't know how to run a studio, I haven't learnt enough."

His eyes glinted. "Sweetheart you know everything you need to know. And Murray will help with the commercial side of things. He's already set things up for me, I'm investing in you and in your business. And we can get Freddie to help renovate it."

His level of faith and trust in me was overwhelming.

"I don't know what to say, this is incredible and kind and sweet and I don't deserve this."

"Emerson, if anyone deserves it, it's you. You're going to be incredible at this. You'll have wait lists for your wait list's wait list."

I laughed, throwing my head back.

"You think?

"I know." He pulled me in against him, his lips surrounding mine.

"Wait." I pushed him back. "No tongue."

He laughed, before pulling the hood of his jacket up then the hood of mine, holding onto it firmly. "There, now no-one can see. Because I'm fucking using my tongue."

His mouth cocooned mine again and I opened for him, his tongue stroking slowly through my mouth, warm and delicious and loving, melting my insides and branding my heart.

Branding my soul.

"What am I going to call it?" I muttered against his lips.

He moved back slightly, although still holding my hood.

"I have an idea." He winked.

"Are you going to share?"

"Yes, but can we finish the rest of this conversation at home? It's fucking freezing and I've lost count of how many days it's been since I was inside you."

I quickly pressed my lips back onto his. "How about we go home via mine and start packing those boxes?"

His face lit up like a kid on Christmas, or like my dad on Christmas. "That's a fucking brilliant idea. Maybe we even stay there in the tiny bed, so we can cuddle all night long."

I giggled, the heaviness in my chest vanishing. He was right, as long as we had each other we would be fine.

Better than fine.

Perfect.

"Yes, we can stay there."

He bent down, running his finger through the wet sand.

He stood back when he'd finished, taking my hands in his and kissing it. I looked at what he'd written.

"Forever, baby. For ever."

EPILOGUE

DREW

E ight months later

I pushed through the big double doors of Body by Luck, Emerson's new fitness studio.

I came up with the name. Obvs.

There were a few people standing at the juice bar as I walked in.

Yeah, that's right. Juice bar.

The Radioactive Green Juice was a surprisingly popular choice. Definitely not mine, I thought it tasted like a puddle, but still, some people's.

It had taken a fuck load of work and, apart from keeping the exposed brick, the warehouse was now unrecognizable, thanks to Freddie and her team. And the space was big enough that it offered more than just spinning. In fact, there were two bike studios, plus one for yoga and Pilates. There were also sports massage and acupuncture rooms, which had been booked out from Day One with injuries and sore muscles needing to be fixed.

My heart burst with pride every single time I was here.

I saw Ashley behind the reception and headed over to her, quietly, not wanting to be noticed. She was standing underneath the studio name, which hung wide across the wall, lit up in blue neon.

"Hey Ash."

She looked up from opening one of several large boxes I could see.

"Hey. She should be finished soon."

"All good, what've you got there?"

"New stock arrived." She started pulling out the contents, placing them on the counter. Bright colors of yoga pants, t-shirts, shorts and hoodies all adorned in some way with the studio logo. They looked fucking awesome.

I took an XL pale blue hoodie from the pile and put it on, taking a selfie and posting to Instagram.

"You're gonna get in trouble." Ashley muttered.

I frowned. "What? I haven't broken the rules."

Her expression told me she knew I was full of shit. Mostly because Emerson had strictly forbidden me from promoting the studio in any way, including and especially across social. I'd admired it, because she wanted to make sure she was doing it by herself. That people came because of the reputation she'd built within her industry and not because they hoped to see me or one of my teammates, or any sports star or celebrities.

She needn't have worried though because in the two months it had been open, the studio had become the new place to be. And not because of famous faces who came. Because of her. Because she was that good.

When she'd been fired from her old job, Mikey and Ashley quit too, in protest. And they'd come to work for her, helping her with the renovations, helping build it up.

Her six am crew had also followed her, along with the wait lists.

I still didn't care for the early mornings, but as long as she came back to me at the end of every day, I made my peace with it.

And Mikey's fan base had come too. His Pop Rides were a firm favorite with the over 40s women and more than a couple of the boys.

"Ah, she'll get over it. I'm protecting my investment." I smirked.

Even Murray had been impressed by how well the place had done since it opened although, because he was the biggest stirrer on the planet, he was mostly crediting himself with his hire of a shit hot business manager.

Dickhead.

The first tired, sweaty faces emerged from her class and made their way into the reception area. While I did sometimes stick around, I wasn't in the mood for the attention I'd get today, I just wanted Emerson.

"Ash, can you tell her I'm in her office?"

"Sure." She nodded as I rounded the reception.

I punched the code in the door behind the counter and walked down the corridor. I sat at her desk, breathing in her scent which always lingered in here from the candles she liked to burn. To the side of her laptop, sitting in a frame, was the photo of us I'd taken in Vegas. It was hard to believe it was two years since that night. And a year since I'd found her again. I could barely remember what my life had been like without her. Except I knew that it had been empty.

She'd given me my life.

She was my life.

I'd never known happiness like it.

And in the eight months since Jupiter and I had put out our joint statement, aside from the excitement of the studio opening, the press had almost left us alone. Richard had also been let go from Mercy hospital. It turned out that the reason he'd left California in the first place was because he'd been rejected from the Sports Surgery Program at LA Gen. He'd taken the temporary position at Mercy while he tried to bribe his way into the Sports Surgery Program at Columbia Pres by using Jupiter's name, and for that he also needed Emerson. And since his medical license had been revoked, he was forced to leave New York state and our lives. What a fucking brilliant day that had been.

Jupiter started his season and we'd been out to watch a few games, visiting Emerson's family whenever we were there. And we'd become friends. Like actual bros, who enjoyed hanging out. And before he'd been back playing, he'd even come to New York and hung out with me and the boys. Watching the games, keeping Felix company while he waited impatiently until he could get back on the ice.

I picked the frame up, my fingers running over her beautiful face. Her freckles were back in abundance since the start of the summer, especially after the vacation I'd insisted we take at the end of the season. She been working so hard to set the studio up she'd barely had a break, and I knew she wouldn't take another one any time in the first few months, so I'd whisked her away for a week to a private villa in Anguilla.

We returned with absolutely no tan lines whatsoever.

My head spun at a noise behind me and I found her leaning against the door frame, watching me, a soft smile creeping up, her eyes dancing as she looked at me. Her tan made them appear bluer than blue, the golden flecks on fire. She was wearing one of her Body by Luck branded pants and bra, in my favorite shade of green. She was fucking breathtaking and she still consumed me with her magic every damn day.

I held my arms out wide and she walked over, flicking the lock behind her. I pulled her to sit in my lap, my fingers running up and down her warm, damp spine.

"I'm all sweaty." She half protested.

"I could give a fuck."

My mouth took hers captive, her soft lips opening up under mine like second nature so I could roam my tongue around her mouth, tasting every inch of her, because each time was different. Each time like the first time. I cupped her boobs through her bra, running my thumbs along the outline of her nipples, trying to contain my excitement at how fucking huge they were about to get.

She pulled back, sensing what I wanted. What I always wanted. What I needed.

"Okay. I have to shower. How long have I got?" She twisted the watch on my wrist. "Twenty-three minutes."

She stood up, my lap immediately missing her weight and her warmth.

"Can I come?"

Her laugh wrapped around my body like a comfort blanket.

"No, we don't have time."

When this place had been built, I'd insisted she had her own space to work, an office big enough where I could just come and hang out sometimes so I could be near her. And that had also included a shower, somewhere I could join her on occasions that I took her classes.

"I'll be quick." I looked at her eagerly.

"We both know that's a lie."

I gave myself three seconds to watch her fine ass walk away from me and into the bathroom before I followed her in and perched on the vanity unit. Because now she'd been in my sight, I couldn't bear to let her out of it if I didn't have to. She stripped off and stepped into the shower under the water, standing there until her thick mane of dark bronze waves was completely saturated.

"How was your class?"

"So good." She grinned as she squeezed shampoo into her

hand, before rubbing it into her head. "They were loving the music today."

I watched, mesmerized as the suds started to flow over her body, trying to imagine how it would change. How her taut muscles would soften and bloom.

"Was it a hard one?"

"Not too hard. I've done harder."

I swallowed the urge to tell her I knew for a fact she'd definitely done harder. "And you felt okay?"

"Yes, baby. I felt good."

Over the past week she'd been complaining of not feeling great, as well as exhausted and she'd been falling asleep almost as soon as she got home. But we'd put it down to the opening of the studio. It was only yesterday when she realized she'd missed her period that we bought some pregnancy tests. When the sticks in the first packet came up positive, I went out and bought another ten boxes. All reading the same.

And now we were an hour away from the doctor confirming what we knew. To say I was an emotional wreck would be the understatement of the year.

She rinsed off and I held a towel out wrapping her in it, rubbing her belly and my baby growing inside her.

My fucking baby.

"And how are you feeling?"

Her smile was soft and happy. "I mean, we probably could've planned it better, but with us, I guess timing is relative. We trust the universe, right?"

"Damn fucking right, we do."

She ran her hands through my hair, resting them on the back of my head. "How are you feeling?"

My throat started to get tight. "Like this is exactly where I'm supposed to be."

She moved between my legs and kissed me. "I love you so much."

My dick thumped hard against my zipper because it had

less control than I did around her. I looked at my watch. "You know we still have eight minutes before we have to leave?"

She stepped back, her eyes rolling. "You can take me home and do whatever you want to me as soon as we're done with the doctor."

I almost shoved her away. "Emerson. Get fucking dressed right now and let's go."

She laughed so hard it set me off, the pair of us giggling together like kids before I stopped dead, my face serious. "I'm not kidding. Don't make promises you can't keep. Clothes, now."

She squealed as I smacked her ass.

Thirty minutes later we were ushered into the OBGYN's office. The nurse handed Emerson a gown and instructed her to put it on and get on the bed. While she was changing I looked around the room, above the desk were several framed certificates from Harvard Medical School, easing my nerves slightly. I turned to the walls then wished I hadn't because they were covered in posters of childbirth, vaginas and diagrams of pregnancy. I sat down and closed my eyes before I started to get queasy.

Because, fuck me.

Emerson appeared from behind the screen and hopped on the bed, which I hadn't noticed until now was not a normal bed. And her feet were in some sort of weird sex club vibe harnesses. What the fuck were they for?

"Babe, can you try not to look so horrified please?"

I blinked up at her. "Sorry, I just... what are those?" I pointed to the sex club holders. "Why do you need your feet in them?"

She looked at me like I was a simpleton. "Because the doctor can't examine my vagina with my legs crossed."

It had better be a woman doctor.

"Oh, okay. Makes sense. Cool. Cool cool. Cool coooool."

Emerson was staring at me as I tried very hard not to

freak out. But thankfully at that moment the door opened and in walked a female doctor of what I'll diplomatically call an experienced age. In fact, she looked as experienced as fuck, which was good because I wasn't about to let some Doogie Howser loose on my baby.

"Emerson Reeves and Drew Crawley?" She glanced down at her chart and back up with not one flicker of recognition, which I gave a silent thanks for because I didn't want some kiss ass doctor examining Emerson. "Hello both of you. I'm Doctor Humphries."

"Hello." Replied Emerson, so soft and sweet that I just wanted to scoop her up and cover her with kisses.

"Right, now what have we got here? Emerson, you're twenty-eight, is that right."

She nodded. "Yes."

"And you had a positive pregnancy test?"

"Twenty-two." I confirmed at the same time as Emerson said yes.

"Sorry?" Doctor Humphries frowned at me and Emerson squeezed my hand tight in a silent warning for me to not be a dick.

I coughed away my awkwardness. "I just meant, we had twenty-two positive pregnancy tests."

I definitely saw the doc try and hide a smile before she turned back to her computer. At least I was amusing someone.

She started typing up notes. "And how have you been feeling overall?"

"Um, okay, tired though."

"And when was your last period?"

"I can't remember, I think six or seven weeks ago maybe."

Dr Humphries stood up and moved over to Emerson, switching on the mini monitor by the bed. "Okay, well let's have a look."

She picked up a large tube of gel from a little tray and

309

covered the bottom half of Emerson's body before she opened her gown, exposing her belly. She winced as the gel hit her skin.

"Sorry, it's a bit cold."

Doctor Humphries took the ultrasound monitor and placed it on Emerson's stomach, watching the screen as she did. Emerson's hand squeezed mine as our faces were both glued to the monitor, not knowing what we were supposed to be expecting until a whoosh of white thumping noise filled the silence.

"Oh yes, there we go." Doctor Humphries turned the screen so we could see it better. "And that's your baby's heartbeat."

I couldn't hold back the strangled choking sob which erupted, followed by hot tears which streamed down my face. Emerson turned to me, her face so filled with love, lifting her hand up to cup my cheek and I leant into it.

"Our fucking baby, Luck."

"I know." Her smile turned into the biggest grin I'd ever seen in my life.

We looked back at the doc only to see her eyes narrowed, staring at the screen, still moving the monitor over Emerson.

"Is something wrong?"

Dr Humphries held her palm up, silencing me while she continued to stare at the screen. I could feel my blood rising, the euphoria I'd felt less than a minute ago crashing and burning. After a fucking lifetime she looked back at us.

"No, nothing is wrong."

Jesus Christ. I'm not sure I liked this doctor and all her experience.

She looked at Emerson. "When did you say you had your last period?"

Emerson nervously bit her lip. "I can't remember."

"That's okay, I suspect you're around eight weeks, but I want to have a better look."

She picked up a weird stick thing and I watched wide eyed as she rolled a condom over it, then covered it in lube. She did it with such speed and precision I irrationally wondered if we should get her into the club and teach the new rookies how to wrap up their dicks.

When I blinked again, she'd wheeled her stool around and was now by Emerson's open legs.

"Okay, open up a bit more, this will be cold."

Emerson's hand gripped mine harder than it had yet.

"Sweetheart, look at me. You okay? Does this hurt?"

She shook her head. "No, but it's uncomfortable."

"I'll make it better later." I mouthed to her, receiving a grin in return.

The doctor's eyes stayed trained on the screen before she pulled back, throwing the rubber in the disposal. "You can close your legs now and sit up."

Emerson did as instructed, swinging her feet over the bed so they were dangling off the side.

"I was right, you're about eight and half weeks. And you have a healthy baby growing in there, alongside another healthy baby."

Emerson's eyes bugged, as did mine.

"Sorry, doc. Say that again please."

"Two babies. You're having twins." Dr Humphries smiled as she reached over to take some paper which the monitor had spat out. "Emerson, you have two babies growing inside your womb. I couldn't quite see it from your belly exam, but from the transvaginal there are definitely two fetuses. And two very strong heartbeats."

She handed us the print outs, pointing to a fuzzy blob. "See, right here."

I think I blinked. But I couldn't be sure.

"Are you sure?" Emerson whispered.

Doctor Humphries nodded. "Yes, absolutely. When you

come back in a couple of weeks it'll be much easier to see them."

Two. Two babies.

My tears started up again. "Twins, Luck." I leant over to kiss her.

She wiped my wet face with her palms, laughing as she did. "Oh my god, I'm going to have three cry babies to deal with now, aren't I?"

"No, I've got seven months to lock this shit down." I sniffed.

She smiled softly. "No, don't you dare. I love it."

She kissed me quickly before jumping off the bed and walking behind the screen to get changed. I looked down at the photo in my hand, my heart beating so heavily I thought it might burst. My eyes watered over again.

"Doc, can you show me again please?" My voice broke.

Her fingers pointed to a big blob in the middle. "This wavy bit here is one baby, and this wavy bit here is another."

"Thanks Doc. Got it."

I definitely didn't have it.

I stood up as Emerson emerged fully dressed again. Doctor Humphries handed us some print outs and leaflets.

"I've booked your next appointment for three weeks' time and here's some literature for you to read before then, tells you what to expect and what you should be doing. My number is on there if you need anything at all."

Emerson took them and put them in her bag. "Thank you."

I opened the door and held my hand out for her to take. We walked out of the office, into the elevator, down to the lobby and back into the sunshine without saying one word. We were half-way down the block before I couldn't take it any longer and spun her around to face me, startling a passer-by.

"Emerson?" I pulled her sunglasses down her nose so I

could look into her eyes, which were wide with shock. "Sweetheart, are you okay?"

"Twins, Drew. Twins. Twins."

I cupped her face in my hands. "I know, babe. But we can do it. We trust the universe, right?"

She smiled at me, her perfect beautiful smile which shot me straight in the heart. "Yes, we do."

"Good and as long as we have each other, everything will be okay. I love you so fucking much." I kissed her nose, pushing her sunglasses back up. "Now let's get the fuck home, because you have a promise to uphold."

She laughed loudly and practically dragged me up the street.

My future, carrying our future.

THE END

ACKNOWLEDGMENTS

Alex, Ben, Cody, Hannah, Jess K, Kendall, Leanne, Olivia, Robin, Tunde and Wilpers. For every single time you unstuck my mental blocks. For telling me to straighten my crown, because you cannot get stronger without getting stronger.

And my Saturday girls, even though you never knew.

EHJ and your merry band of willing medical cohorts, for answering all my questions. Strap in for the next book, because this was just the beginning.

And with absolute and profound gratitude to everyone who's enjoying this ridiculous journey with me, your sweet messages and kindness make my day. I hope I'm doing you justice.

ABOUT THE AUTHOR

Lulu is currently navigating her way around Romance Land one HEA at a time, and trying to figure out the latest social media platform she needs to post to.

She'd love to hear from you, loves hearing your opinions and thoughts, so please message her on any of the below (plus TikTok) - @lulumoorebooks

ALSO BY LULU MOORE

THE NEW YORK PLAYERS

Jasper

Cooper

Felix's book will be out in the Fall.

Printed in Great Britain
by Amazon

63168736R00190